Also by Jean Thompson

Novels
City Boy
Wide Blue Yonder
The Woman Driver
My Wisdom

Collections
Throw Like a Girl
Who Do You Love
Little Face and Other Stories
The Gasoline Wars

Do Not Deny Me

——Stories

Jean Thompson

Simon & Schuster Paperbacks

New York   London   Toronto   Sydney

Simon & Schuster Paperbacks
A Division of Simon & Schuster, Inc.
1230 Avenue of the Americas
New York, NY 10020

First Simon & Schuster trade paperbacks edition June 2009

"Wilderness" first appeared in *One Story*, no. 105 (2008). "Soldiers of Spiritos" first appeared in *Northwest Review*, no. 47.2 (2009).

For information about special discounts for bulk purchases, please contact Simon & Schuster Special Sales at 1-866-506-1949 or business@simonandschuster.com.

The Simon & Schuster Speakers Bureau can bring authors to your live event. For more information or to book an event, contact the Simon & Schuster Speakers Bureau at 1-866-248-3049 or visit our website at www.simonspeakers.com.

Designed by Nancy Singer

Manufactured in the United States of America

10 9 8 7 6 5 4 3 2 1

Library of Congress Cataloging-in-Publication Data
Thompson, Jean.
    Do not deny me : stories / Jean Thompson
        p. cm.
    I. Title.
    PS3570.H625D6 2009
    813'.54—dc22

                                                      2008041316

ISBN 978-1-4165-9563-2
ISBN 978-1-4165-9846-6 (ebook)

*For my family of friends who share their lives
and stories with me, and whose expertise makes
it possible for me to build treehouses, sing in German,
sew quilts, and catch the right trains—
at least, on the printed page.*

Contents

Do Not Deny Me

Soldiers of Spiritos

The heat in Penrose's office had not worked properly all fall. By December his nose and ears were pink with cold, his fingers too thick and numb for typing. He wore a heavy, ugly wool sweater and fortified himself with thermoses of tea. He looked and felt ridiculous. Suffering had made him ineffectual. Outside his window the campus trees went from vivid color to rags of leaves to bare branches filled with ice. Students hurried along the sidewalks, intent on their own urgencies. The air in his lungs felt frosted. "This place will be the death of me," he said aloud, since there was no one there to hear him.

The cheerful young department secretary said she would call Building Maintenance again if he wished, and Penrose said yes, would you please. When nothing had come of that he called them himself, sifting through the confusing listings in the directory. Did he want Operations? Routing? Environmental Hazards? He finally found the right office and called three times and each time they asked him to spell his name. "P as in Peter, E as in Edward, N as in Nancy . . ." Pen plus rose, he wanted to say, how hard is that? How hard is it to send out a repairman?

Then on this morning near the end of the term, he found his office door open and a workman on a ladder with his head and upper body engulfed by a hole in the ceiling tile. Penrose, relieved but annoyed, contemplated saying something snappish about the long delay. He would have been within his rights. But there was always the fear of alienating the man and never getting his heat fixed. Besides, there was never any one person to blame for such things; that was the nature of the behemoth bureaucracy.

The ladder took up most of the small room. Penrose stood in the doorway. "Hello, are you here to fix my heat?"

"Gonna try," said the man, still hidden in the ceiling. His voice was muffled. A bit of a drawl, a countrified voice.

"It's been a problem for months," Penrose said, irritated by *try*.

There was a series of hollow metallic bangings. Words came out in the intervals between them. "Yep . . . hydraulics in . . . these old buildings . . . can't seem to get their systems squared away."

"Ah," said Penrose, as if he knew anything about hydraulics and was agreeing wisely. As usual, it was nobody's fault; it was the system. He reached for the stack of Modern Drama I papers on his desk. "I guess I'll go sit in the coffee room and stay out of your way." He wanted to tell the man to make sure he locked up when he left, but that was pointless, the maintenance people had keys to everything, they came and went as they pleased.

Penrose retraced his steps downstairs and along the main corridor, walking as he always did, with his head canted downward and a half smile tucked into one corner of his mouth. That way if anyone greeted him he would be ready to respond, and if they chose to ignore him, as was often the case, he could pretend to be absorbed in his own ruminations. He imagined that the new generation of faculty, if they thought about him at all, wondered why he had not already died or retired or both. But he couldn't afford to retire yet, and the health benefits being what they were, he could barely afford to die.

The coffee room was empty, he was pleased to see. He pulled one of the plastic chairs over to a side table, draped his coat on its back, and got out the notes for his upcoming class. A piece of paper lay face up on the table.

New Course, Please Announce!

English 405, Indigenous Critical Theory: Oriented toward imagining far-reaching social change through knowledge production as sites of indigenous activism and political thought, the course develops analytical frames at intellectual crossroads where epistemologies that gather under the "indigenous" sign meet democratic inquiry (and its concerns with recognition) and a transhemispheric critical theory.

There was more, but this was enough to unman him. The first time Penrose had encountered this new and hideous jargon, he'd thought it was a joke, a parody of all that was pompous and inflated, purest gobbledygook. He still felt that way, but it was a joke no one seemed to get except him. Scholarly papers, conferences, entire careers were now built on it, this language that was a fraud of a language, meant to obscure, mystify, bully. All the new, bright young hires wrote of hegemony and late-capitalist strategies of empire and protofeminists and psychomorphology and colonialism and elitist reification. It was an evil code he was unable to crack. Although this new generation now in ascendancy seemed to be against many things, racism and sexism and other isms, Penrose had not been able to discern what, if anything, they approved of. No matter; they had the wind in their sails. If any one of them had complained about the heat in their office, a fleet of maintenance trucks would have been dispatched immediately.

He was a dinosaur, a relic. They gave him the Intro to Literature courses to teach, the basic survey usually left to graduate assistants. He'd only held on to his drama courses because no one else wanted them. The knowledge of this beat him down day by day, curdled his disposition. He would have liked to point out to the smart, preening young scholars, so caught up in their third-world literatures and hermeneutics, whatever that was, that someday they too would be dead white men, just the thing they so disparaged. Most of them. There was of course the occasional woman, the occasional minority hire, full of nervous self-importance.

Penrose's wife had long since tired of hearing about all this. "Why are you so obsessed with these people? Who cares what they do? You need to get on with your own work, whatever makes you happy." Of course she was right—there was something cowardly about how eloquent he became in complaint, it shamed him—but the truth was, his own work had ceased to interest him. Even if there had been any demand for the kind of careful, stately reviews or papers he'd once produced, or a sequel to the book on nineteenth-century stagecraft that had won him tenure so long ago, he had no heart for it. It was finished, over, rusted shut. He'd said everything he'd wished to say, then resaid it in as many ways possible. It had been discouraging to realize that great, timeless literature, even that portion of it for which he had professed his special affinity and critical passion, was not an endlessly refilling well. He understood, in spite of himself, the appeal of the new order: at least it was new.

So these days, when he shut himself away in his study at home to do his "research," he had a special project. It was a science fiction novel which recast a number of his departmental colleagues as grotesque and menacing aliens, androids, and intergalactic creeps. The title was *Soldiers of Spiritos,* the Spiritans being a cultured but vigorous and warlike race, menaced by various dark and degraded forces. The meanest and most arrogant of the critical theorists became Commander Gorza, a lizardlike creature deep in treacherous schemes, with a habit of spitting when agitated. The weak and craven Polypis, hereditary ruler of Spiritos, bore a striking resemblance to the department chair. There was also a pop-eyed robot modeled after the department's serial sexual harasser, and Farella, a leather-clad shape-shifting demoness who called to mind the new assistant professor, brought in to head up the Lesbians in the Gothic Paradigm course. It was all great, trashy fun to write. Penrose thought he might someday publish it under a pseudonym—Penrose's pen name!—amaze himself and everybody else by earning some actual money. Meanwhile, it gave him no end of pleasure to write lines like, "Curse the Spiritans and their doomed resistance! Soon their planet will be the latest outpost in the Devorkian Empire!"

One of the graduate students came in and began opening and closing cupboards in an annoying way. Penrose gathered his things. It was almost time for class.

But he wasn't quick enough to avoid Herm Sonegaard,

blocking the door, a heavy figure in a parka and galoshes. "Dick! Long time no see!" Sonegaard wore a striped ski cap with a tassel and exuded rosy winter warmth.

With other colleagues, Penrose could exchange polite greetings in mutual indifference. Herm demanded full engagement. "How've you been, Herm?"

"Never better," said Herm, delighted at his own wit, something wry, precious, and British in his robust American mouth. Herm said it often enough that you imagined him ascending, rung by rung, into beatitude. "Just a sprint to the finish line, then Jessica and I are off to Puerto Vallarta."

Penrose made appropriate envious noises. Herm had the poetry franchise in the department. His poems were widely published in journals Penrose had never heard of, then regularly bundled into collections by the university press. Penrose had not yet found a space for Herm in his novel. It was hard to parody someone who already seemed to be a walking parody.

Now Herm said, "You and Ellen should head south some year, stop in and see us. The place'll get your blood flowing again. Sun on your skin. Sea air in your lungs. We hardly even wear shoes down there."

"That sounds great, Herm." As usual, Penrose had to increase his wattage to match Herm's enthusiasm. "Maybe some year when the kids aren't coming back for Christmas, you know how that is."

"Quickie trip. Get on a plane in a snowstorm, get off and it's eighty degrees. Daiquiris. Hibiscus. Water skiing."

Penrose promised to consider it. He wondered, with some distaste, what going native with Herm and his newest, youngest wife might involve. Herm angled his body toward Penrose, an attempt at confidential communication. "You get to our age, Dick, you have to keep the batteries charged. No better place than south of the border."

"Ah," said Penrose, alarmed now. He nodded. "Lure of the tropics, that sort of thing." Pictures came unwillingly to his imagination, the little drugstore selling Coca-Cola and potions made of cactus and bull urine, Herm counting out pesos . . .

Herm dug a sheaf of papers out of his briefcase. "*Diatribe*'s going to take the new essay. I just found out."

The passing bell rang and Penrose was able to dodge the essay, which Herm seemed to want to gift him with. People attempted to squeeze around Herm, who still stood in the doorway. One of the junior faculty, a mop-haired young man in a velvet jacket, gave Herm a poisonous look. Herm, oblivious, began peeling off layers of outer garments and piling them in a collapsing heap.

"I'm off to class," said Penrose. "Have a great time in Mexico, if I don't see you."

"Margaritas!" Herm called after him, stepping out into the corridor. "Cerveza! Y mas cerveza!"

Penrose gave him a backward wave. You had to give Herm credit; he was untroubled by the new, supercilious regime in the department. They couldn't lay a glove on his cast-iron ego.

Penrose's classroom was ominously silent as he approached. It was always better when there was some sort of chatter or social noise. It meant they were less likely to sit in a sullen, unresponsive mass while he tried to jolly them into a discussion. There were days, too many days, when he felt like a television screen tuned to a channel they didn't want to watch.

"Good morning," Penrose said, bustling in and making a

busy show of unpacking his notes and books. A few drear and mumbling voices responded. There were twenty-five of them and only one of him. It was never a fair fight.

"Jason," said Penrose, addressing a boy in a stocking cap, with his feet propped up on the desk in front of him. "I'm going to ask you to put your laptop away."

"Aww, Professor Penrose." He was wearing a black sweatshirt with a picture of a cartoon man being dismembered by a cartoon explosion. "I'm a multitasker. My brain works better when I do two or three things at once."

Penrose held his ground until Jason sighed and shut the machine off. Penrose had only recently and reluctantly been introduced to all things computer. It was one more plague, students who wanted to send him their papers via attached files, who pestered him to put class material on an interactive website, and so on. And of course they all walked around plugged into headsets and cell phones, grooving and chattering away, while the knowledge and wisdom of the ages swept over a precipice.

"I have your papers to return to you," Penrose announced, to a general groaning. "Yes, well you might groan. I was not as impressed as I had hoped to be." He distributed the papers and waited as they flipped through the pages, past his careful, handwritten comments, to the circled grade at the end. They were aggrieved, most of them, he could tell. After all, hadn't they gone to the trouble of typing and printing and handing in an actual paper, when they could have been doing something much more enjoyable? Their lot was cruel.

"Professor Penrose?" One of the girls, a sophomore majoring in Wardrobe, made complaint. "Why do we have to put down the acts and scenes?"

"So I can tell if you're citing the play correctly."

"But you know the play already, you know exactly where stuff is."

"No, Alexa, I don't know what 'the part where Hedda Gabler goes all mental' refers to. You need to be more precise and follow the standard format. If you have other questions about your papers, please come see me during office hours after class. Let's get started on today's material."

They sagged in their seats. Make us, their body language announced. Like we care.

Patiently, he began to woo them. It was the last play on the syllabus, O'Neill's *Long Day's Journey into Night*. It still kindled something in him, this great family drama, the four damaged souls in their slowly darkening cage. He'd seen the Broadway production with Jason Robards Jr. as James Tyrone and Colleen Dewhurst as Mary, and he remembered it with near holy emotion. How could he make them feel any portion of that? How to make them love the thing he loved? So much of teaching came down to just that. He needed to strike a spark in them. He needed not to stand in front of one more bored, tolerant class and have them drain the joy out of him.

He began with talking about families, how everybody's family had the potential for tragedy, as well as love and comfort. How none of us in real life had the opportunity to stage or to express our fears and feelings as eloquently as a playwright did. "This play of old sorrow, written in tears and blood," O'Neill had called it. And yet the play begins on a fine summer morning, breakfast just over, the day full of promise. When do the tears and blood start showing through?

The class stared down at their textbooks, the only safe place in the room to look. Penrose measured out the silence. There had been times, in this class and others, when he had been tempted to let a silence extend itself, Zen-like, all the way to the bell at the end of the hour. But always he dutifully picked up the thread, inserted himself, asked the follow-up question or called on one of them. Today he was saved, as he so often had been, by his best student raising his hand. "Yes, Roger."

"It's right there at the start. With James talking about how young he feels. His saying so implies the opposite. Later, when he's coming down on his sons and saying what a disappointment they are, that's all about himself, him feeling threatened and bitter because life hasn't turned out the way he wanted it to."

Bless the boy. "Yes, I would agree," said Penrose. "It's a conflict that gets developed later. What else is a conflict in the family?"

A few more hands ventured upward, struggling against gravity, and the discussion lurched ahead. Roger inclined his big, pallid, serious face toward each speaker, listening. He had crimped, dark red hair and wore glasses with black plastic frames, like those sold in joke shops attached to false noses. Penrose worried about Roger, worried equally about his awkwardness and his intelligence. One didn't want to see him head off to grad school as the path of least resistance; besides, he was too genuine and inquisitive to be a good fit in the new, glib order. He might make a good lawyer, or even a politician, if he could find himself a girl, someone to polish his geeky edges, give him a man's confidence. Of course the girl would have to do all the work. Where was such a girl, brainy but unafraid, who would make a project out of him?

All this passed fleetingly through Penrose's mind as he

directed the class discussion, which was finally starting to jell. All of them had families of one sort or another, and no matter how loving or well-intentioned, there had been times that family life had felt as confined and boxlike as a stage set. There was the usual fascination with Mary's opium addiction—to think, even a century ago, moms were getting high!—then they started in on the grandiose father and profligate brother, then Edmund himself, who was never quite the hero they wanted him to be. Because of course they wanted to be the ones who picked the scab, who revealed the flaws and hypocrisies of the others while making an attractive display of their own suffering. It was Penrose's job, or part of it, to convince them that self-loathing was not especially attractive or desirable.

"The mother is just gross," complained Alexa, flipping her hair from one shoulder to another. "She's like, shooting up!"

"Like, eww," said one of the boys, and Penrose gave him a sharp look, but it seemed he was only making fun of Alexa, and that was allowed, even tacitly encouraged.

Another student said that the drug use was all offstage, and that Mary was never unseemly or unladylike. "She's just lost in a fog, like she wanted to be."

Penrose got them started on the fog, the foghorn, and then the other physical artifacts—the lamps, the whiskey bottle— and then on to how character flaws were revealed by drama. James's stinginess, Jamie's failure, Edmund's weakness. And how there were also traits that softened our judgment and gave complexity to the portraits. The hour glided past. Penrose felt it was going well. He picked two of the boys to read Jamie's and Edmund's parts in the last scene, Jamie's best:

Never wanted you to succeed and make me look even worse by comparison. Wanted you to fail. Always jealous of you. Mama's baby, Papa's pet! And it was you being born that started Mama on dope. I know that's not your fault, but all the same, goddamn you, I can't help hating your guts—

The boys read well, thank God, and some of the wounding and passion came through, enough to turn the motley class into an actual audience, caught up in the play. Penrose himself picked up James Tyrone's part:

A sweet spectacle for me! My firstborn, who I hoped would bear my name in honor and dignity! Who showed such brilliant promise!

Penrose was enjoying himself. He had a touch of ham in him, though teaching was as close as he'd ever come to acting. Edmund answered, then Tyrone had another line, but just as Penrose was hearing the sound of it in his head, anticipating it, they were all startled by a low, grunting noise from the back of the room. It dropped into the lull between speeches, loud and unseemly, an ugly, honking noise. It took Penrose a moment to identify it as sobbing.

"Sarah?" Penrose took a step forward, peering at the girl in the last row. "Are you all right?"

She shook her head, meaning, Never Mind. She was redfaced, either from embarrassment or her mysterious grief. She waved her hands, waving him off. Never Mind. Penrose hesitated, then, not wanting to make things worse for her, went back to the play. But the air had gone out of it, the class now unsettled and distracted. Penrose stopped the reading. It was almost time for the bell. He began to wrap things up, reminding them of the date their final papers were due, of the review session for the exam. All the while trying not to stare at Sarah Snyder in the back row. Who was she anyway? Unremarkable B student, unremarkable presence bundled into a chubby parka, rimless glasses, straw-blond hair pulled back in a wad. She wasn't doing anything alarming now, just staring at the desk in front of her, the inflamed color of her cheeks fading.

The bell rang. Penrose dismissed them. He thought of trying to intercept Sarah Snyder—offer some word of concern or inquiry—but she was heading for the door on a bullet course, and besides, Roger was approaching with his usual intelligent questions.

Penrose spoke with him for a few moments, then they parted, and Penrose gathered up his books and went out into the hall. There was no sign of Sarah Snyder, which in some ways was a relief, but left him feeling bad, guilty, inadequate. There had to be a better way to handle such moments. Something intuitive and wise, involving human skills he did not possess. What did girls cry about these days anyway? Boyfriend? Pregnancy? How would he know? He could not now recall a single thing Sarah Snyder had ever said in his class.

He reached his office. The door was shut and locked. He went inside and put his hand to the heating vent. It was the cold of cold metal. It had not been a very good day for the Spiritans.

If there was an easy way to kill herself she'd do it this instant. She was crying again, snotty tears, disgusting, and the cold air made them sting. Could she be any more fucked up? What was wrong with her anyway? She was just a big stupid mess.

Sarah Snyder had escaped the English building and now she hurried across the quad, head down, hunched and shivering inside her big coat. She reached the end of the campus buildings without seeing anybody she knew, or anyone from her stupid class. God! How could she ever go back there? They probably thought her mom was a heroin addict or something.

She slowed her pace, blew her nose on a nasty piece of Kleenex she found in her coat pocket. Here was a coffee shop she sometimes went to, a place she liked for its deliberate shabbiness and the oddball music they played. But she might run into some-body there and she didn't want to have to act normal or explain why she wasn't. There was nobody in the world she could explain it to, because there was no real reason for any of it.

So she crossed the street that marked the boundary of cam-pus and kept walking. She had it in mind to get herself good and cold, though she guessed she wouldn't freeze to death or get consumption, like Edmund. It probably had to be dark for that.

The neighborhood was one of apartment buildings, hutches for students, mixed with small wood-frame houses, one or two stories, which she liked for much the same reasons she did the coffee shop, because they were old, eccentric, mysterious. There was a romance about their porch steps and shade trees, their gravel drives and tumbledown garages. At night their lighted windows were squares and rectangles of tender gold, as if the lives within them gave off a radiance. And there was always the chance that someone might open a door, start down their bricked path at just the time she was passing by, speak to her, ask her name, anything might happen . . .

A stab of remembering, her total spastic idiocy in class, *Christ*. Poor old Professor Penrose. He'd looked stricken, like he was the one who'd written the play on purpose to make people miserable. Now she bet he thought she had some tragic family she was boo-hooing about, when she had a perfectly normal one—mom, dad, sister, brother—who only drove her crazy in expected ways. She didn't suppose anyone would believe her, because it was too simpleminded, but it had only been general, goopy sadness, the unfocused sadness of her whole life, that the play had called forth. So that crying for the people in the play had been like crying for herself, but in a nobler way, as if some of the tragedy had rubbed off on her.

There were people whose lives were worth ending up in poems or plays, but she wasn't one of them. She was just an ordinary head case. So suck it up, Snyder! If her life was a play, she'd probably still be unhappy, but it would make sense, with stage directions and speeches. Why couldn't she be weird in some interesting way? The occasional car passed, overtaking her without effort as she stumped along. Why didn't she have a car? She could blast up and down the highway, smash into something.

Eventually she circled a block and doubled back, giving up on the idea of an adventure. She didn't want to go home just yet; her roommate had a new boyfriend, and while Sarah told herself they weren't trying to exclude her, sometimes she believed exactly the opposite, that part of the fun of couplehood was the exclusion of other people. It was all very ick-producing, the giggling and the furtive love chats, the hours spent behind the roommate's closed bedroom door with the music playing, the sounds the music didn't mask, the unerotic sight of the boyfriend's bare ass slipping out of its towel wrap as he visited the bathroom, not to mention the residue of those visits. Still, she was envious. She'd never had a real boyfriend, only an ocean's worth of hopeless crushes, plus the occasional guy you'd hang out with, and sometimes the two of you would hook up. But sex hadn't lived up to its billing, at least not so far, one more thing that she guessed worked better as literature.

When she was feeling low and ugly and hopeless, as she was now, she hated everybody: people in commercials made ecstatic by their purchases, politicians screwing up the entire world, anyone who hurt an animal, celebrities, the Walgreen's clerk who always told her to have a blessed day, people who looked into mirrors and smiled, anyone on MTV, anyone who thought MTV was cool, anyone who used the word "cool," anyone self-satisfied or loud or rude or whose cell phone ringer was a Justin Timberlake song, that being basically everyone in the whole school.

If she wanted to, she could drop out, move to Seattle or San Francisco or New York and get a real job. It was a big world out there and things were bound to happen to her as they never would here in the Land of Children. College, what was that for most people except a place to kill time before they went on to lead equally shallow adult lives.

She didn't want to be one of them and of course she was, the whole time she was hating on them.

Without thinking about it, Sarah had retraced her steps across the quad and was standing once more in front of the English building. She hesitated before climbing the stairs and going inside, telling herself it was more than an hour since the end of class, it was unlikely anyone was still around. More than that, she was afraid that if she didn't make herself go in now, face the scene of the crime, she might put it off forever. And that would be sad because she loved the old building, as she loved anything old and curious and worn, loved its white pillars and dormers and the curving twin staircases on the first floor with their railings rubbed down to the wood grain in places. She loved the stained wood flooring underfoot, as well as the odd cubbyholes, cloakrooms, dim passages, the classroom with the old-fashioned maps mounted on rollers above the blackboard, so that you could pull them down and behold, on crackling antique paper, charts of The Ancient World, or The Voyages of Magellan.

It was the lunch hour and the hallways were uncrowded. Sarah's nerve failed her at the door of the Drama classroom, empty now, and she turned quickly away. With nothing in mind, as before, she took the stairs to the second floor. Radiators hissed and clanked. Light from the colorless, high overcast sky came in through the stairwell windows. Some kids said the building was haunted, and while Sarah didn't believe that, she wouldn't have minded being a ghost there.

Because she loved reading, she loved everything she'd ever read, *Alice in Wonderland* and *A Little Princess* and every sappy girl book that had come her way from the third grade on, and *Dune* and Kurt Vonnegut and *Lord of the Rings* and Shakespeare (at least the ones she'd seen as movies), and Emily Dickinson and *Wuthering Heights* and Hemingway and Willa Cather and *Even Cowgirls Get the Blues*. But it wasn't anything you could impress people with. "I love to read." Try telling that to a guy at a party, watch how fast he decides he needs to go get another beer.

She was only going to make a circuit of the building and leave—it would be safe to go home soon, her roommate would have to detach herself from the boyfriend and go to work—but she'd pushed her luck too far, and *oh crap*, here was Professor Penrose, heading straight for her.

At first Sarah thought he hadn't seen her, since he was walking in that peculiar way he had, as if watching his shoelaces untie. Then, just as she thought she might escape, he raised his head. "Oh, Sarah. Were you looking for me?"

She said yes because no would have been rude, and besides she might have been expected to come looking for him, after her performance in class. And so she had to follow him as he turned around and led the way back to his office. He'd probably been on his way to the bathroom or something. He hadn't looked all that happy to see her, no surprise there.

He unlocked the office door and went in first, so that Sarah had a moment to look around, get her bearings. She'd only been in here once before, at the very start of the semester, and she hadn't remembered how beat-up the place was. Even for someone like herself, tolerant of, even enamored of, the secondhand and faded, the room was depressing. Its walls were a peculiar putty color, blotted and freckled like elderly skin. The books in the bookcases looked as if no one had opened them during her lifetime; the old-fashioned blinds at the window were cockeyed. It was cold in here too. It felt like a cell in the Bastille; really, all it needed was some straw on the floor and a few rats, but that was silly, she was the prisoner, the one called to account, and her stomach clenched as Professor Penrose, with his pained, antic smile, invited her to take a seat.

• • •

In teaching, as in anything else, there were sins of commission and sins of omission. Penrose had a store of wincing memories, all the times over the years when he'd said the wrong, the clumsy, the hurtful, the fatuous thing. But there had also been the missed opportunities. He had the foreboding that in sitting down with Sarah Snyder, he was about to trade one sin for another. There was likely to be more weeping. Right now she looked sullen rather than teary, but that could turn on a dime, and anyway there was nothing to do now but see it through. "I was worried about you," he said, after an interval of waiting in vain for her to say whatever it was she'd come to say.

Still she kept silent, a hopeless, obstinate silence, staring straight ahead of her, hands jammed in the pockets of her coat. She was not a pretty girl, which she no doubt knew very well. But surely she could have made a little more effort, or any effort at all, hair, makeup, something other than these hobo shoes, jeans, and an upper garment that could have served as a pajama top. Then, aware that he was not being the supportive, sympathetic elder he aspired to be, he checked himself and asked, "Did you want to talk about your paper?"

She bent over to rummage in her backpack, another unlovely posture, he was forced to notice, retrieved it, and handed it over. Penrose studied it, as if to refamiliarize himself with it. There was no need. It was the same as all her other papers. Dogged, mechanical, neither very good nor notably awful. The B had been a coward's grade. A C+ would have been more honest. "Characterization in *A Doll's House*." Oh, boredom. Penrose said, "I'm not sure you were all that interested in your topic."

"I wasn't."

Penrose waited, but nothing more came of this unpromising beginning. "Well then, my next question would be, why choose a topic that didn't interest you?" Why read the play, take the class, go to college in the first place?

The puffy coat wriggled, evidence of some bodily movement underneath. Shoulders shrugging? "I don't know, I guess I couldn't think of anything else."

The passing bell rang then, and there was a scattering of noise, distant doors opening, feet on the stairs, voices. The intrusion only emphasized the peculiar intimacy of the small room, and the two of them within it. Although times being what they were, Penrose was always careful to leave his door wide open, so that no hint of impropriety was conveyed, even by such an unlikely Lothario as himself. He began again. "Now you can do better than that. You have to. If you didn't care for a particular play—"

"I like it a *lot,*" the girl said with heavy vehemence.

Once more Penrose waited. "All right. What did you like about it?"

"When Nora leaves at the end . . . when she realizes that Torvald isn't worth it, that she has to go out into the world and be her own person . . ."

She broke off, and resumed her sullen silence. "Well," Penrose said, "I'm glad you can relate to the character." He was, of course, biologically disqualified from participating in feminist grievances, although that did not spare him from having to hear all about them. "But your enthusiasm doesn't really come through in the paper."

Another convulsion of the coat. "Writing, papers I mean, is really hard for me."

"Then you need to try and work on that." She looked

unconvinced. "There's nothing grammatically or organization-ally wrong with what you wrote. You just didn't come up with a strong enough—"

"I don't know how! I never know how to say I like stuff!"

"But you had reasons you liked the play. You need to start with those."

"Papers aren't about liking things! They're about showing how smart you are!"

And here were the tears again, or their angry cousins, though she was not, technically, crying. Her eyes were red and her cheeks mottled. "I really like *Long Day's Journey*, too, I mean, I *love* it, when you guys were reading it out loud it was like, the most beautiful, awful thing—"

She stopped for breath and Penrose, helpless, waited for whatever would come next. "Why does everything have to be about *reasons*, and making everything into *ideas*. I don't think that's why you're supposed to read anything, that's not why people write plays, so somebody else can come along and turn it inside out and find all different ways to show how important they are . . ."

She stopped and tried to inhale the tears. "I guess I'm just not a very good English major."

"Maybe not," Penrose said. He could tell from her abrupt, startled expression that she had not expected him to agree with her. "But that doesn't mean you're wrong."

"What should I do then, quit?"

"If there's something else you'd enjoy more. I wouldn't want you or anybody else to keep suffering through these classes. If that's what you're doing, suffering."

He let a silence settle. The Zen of silence. The pure space

of empty air. And this time he was rewarded. "I like the class," Sarah Snyder said, in a normal, deflated tone. "I guess I like all kinds of things that don't like me back."

"That's more common than you know. So I wouldn't—"

There was more to say, but he stopped himself, and the girl was no doubt suspicious of him, thinking him melodramatic or senile or both, but he was listening to the sound of water trickling through the ancient pipes behind the walls. Hydraulics! As faint as perfume, as a chink in the rampart of cold, he felt a wafting current of warm air.

Penrose turned back to her. "Do you have your copy of O'Neill with you? Why don't you get it out."

Another struggle with the backpack. "Good. Turn to the end of Act I, where Mary and Edmund are talking. Start here, where Mary says, 'I've never felt it was my home.'"

She looked perplexed. "What for?"

"For fun."

She pondered this. The concept of fun. "But I'm not a very good Mary. I'm not old enough."

"Do I look like your son Edmund?"

A shake of the head. She would have liked to giggle. "Right here," said Penrose, tapping the page.

A slow start, the girl still uncertain of him now as well as herself. By the end of the first long speech she had her wheels underneath her and was hitting some of the right inflections— exasperation, resentment. Penrose's irritable Edmund chimed in. Then Mary again, then Edmund, back and forth, guilt, denial, bitterness, all the paces of the addict's dance. It was the most beautiful, awful thing. An ember flaring up as they breathed on it. Old sorrow made new again. Sarah Snyder's free hand,

Penrose noted, had begun to drum and twitch like Mary's. She had the right instincts, underneath all that self-inflicted misery. He liked her, although she probably would not have believed it, that anyone would like or admire her for her own contrary self. She would not be happy, at least not anytime soon. She was too stubborn and full of grievance, her anger not yet a weapon she could wield. Penrose thought he should find a place for her in his book. He would make her a young acolyte or warrior, a foot soldier in the army of the righteous.

Wilderness

The train was finally in motion, creeping through the underground tunnels of Union Station, bumping onto a different track in the train yard, then making its slow progress through city intersections. In Chinatown it loitered on a siding, waiting for a freight train to pass. After that, some haunted-looking old factory buildings. It picked up speed to travel the wonderland of industrial waste at the Indiana border. Here was a field of above-ground piping and submarine-shaped tanks—pressurized natural gas, Anna guessed—and a little farther along, the marching towers and glittering wires of an electrical plant, like a field of Christmas trees as imagined by aliens. Here the chimneys of a refinery, sending out stinking soot.

Anna turned away from the window. It felt like being confronted with her unmade bed when she was a child. Guilty consumer of electricity and gasoline, user of hair dryers, microwaves, watcher of television, buyer of bottled water. She figured she was in the proper state of self-chastisement to read Ted's letter.

It was half a dozen sheets of paper, handwritten in thick, soaking blue ink. No one but Ted had time to write long letters anymore. No one else had time to read them. "Dear Anna Mae," it began, which was not her name. Sometimes he addressed her as Anna Banana, or Anna Livia Plurabelle. When English majors go bad.

Dear Anna Mae,

Now that it's fall, I'm starting to see more hawks. They ride the thermals through the canyons, silent, mostly, except for the occasional long, drawn-out hunting screech. It's a falling-away sound, a lonesome sound, and if you hear it at twilight, it tears out your heart, just the same as if the hawk itself had landed on your chest.

Anna put the letter down. The scenic view of Gary, Indiana, was preferable to Ted's inflated prose. Ted had gone to live on a ridge in the Ozarks, ten miles from the nearest paved road. "Wilderness," he called it, though it sounded more like economically depressed rural life. He was exploring the spiritual aspects of isolation and self-sufficiency. He was building a log house from a kit. He wrote in great detail about his solar panels, his generator, his well-maintained woodpile. The ink on the page had probably been concocted from wild berries and glycerin. This last was an unnecessarily mean thought, and she put it behind her. Thinking about Ted always seemed to require this sort of shifting of equilibrium from her, guilt replaced by scorn, then back to guilt again, with fondness leaking through the seams. Somewhere in the letter was probably another invitation for Anna to come live with him, since isolation and self-sufficiency had their limitations.

There were times when, in spite of everything she could imagine and dread—rusty well water, feeble organic soap, the failing vegetable garden, the equivocal prospect of Ted himself—she considered it. Run off to the woods, breathe fresh air, cleave to a man and have him cleave to you, come what may. But she had the suspicion that Ted sent similar letters and similar invitations to all his old girlfriends, trying to increase his odds. "Oh, I guess I didn't get a chance to tell you about Kathy" (or Lauren, or Beth), he'd say, once she showed up at his door, provisioned with flannel shirts, sugar, and a year's supply of Tampax. "I'd been meaning to write." The other woman would be feeding hens or processing a bucket of gnarled beans as Ted stood at the edge of the narrow, rutted road, shouting instructions to Anna on how to turn around without breaking an axle. In her rearview mirror, Anna would see him wave good-bye, then drape his arm around Kathy, et cetera, the two of them turning their contented backs to her.

She was too good at this part. Imagining her own defeats, dismissing possibilities without considering them. Her character was built on some bedrock of cynicism, or maybe that was only the smart-aleck variety of fear. The train tracks ran parallel to a section of highway, bare fields sprouting the occasional shopping center or blocky, prisonlike apartment complex. Another four hours to go. Anna picked up the letter again and scanned the blue smears. The part about hawks went on for awhile, and then there was something about fencing, the difficulties of stretching fence, and then:

What do you think about right before you fall asleep? I try to think of everyone I know in the world (you, Anna! You!),

name them and call them to mind. What are they doing,
right that minute, and when will I see them again, if ever?
I'm up here on my little piece of high ground, so far away
from everything that at night I have to squint to see a light,
but I tell you, I'm at the very center of a network of hum-
ming thought.

The train rocked and shimmied. Anna's Styrofoam cup of tea sloshed in an elliptical pattern and she reached out to steady it. She felt claustrophobic, both from the enclosure of the train itself and from the letter, hemming her in with its proclamations and its neediness. She drank half her tea and didn't want the rest, so she stood, wanting an excuse to move. The car was full and she braced herself on the seat backs, walking carefully. She deposited the cup in the plastic-lined trash bin and kept going the length of the next two cars, trying to look purposeful rather than aimless.

It was Thanksgiving week and the train was crowded with college students, families with kids, and one wary-looking elderly couple, banished, Anna guessed, from cooking their own holiday dinner, shipped off to some hyper-competent daughter-in-law's kitchen. In the club car, two dressed-up black ladies were comparing notes on their foot problems, the trials of fallen arches, bunions, heel pain. They appeared not to have known each other previously, but to have established some happy communion of ailments. "And you know," one said, "with the Lord we have all the help we need." "That's true, praise God," the other chimed in, not missing a beat. Anna felt a little pluck of envy. Where were her fellow sufferers, how would they recognize and console one another?

Anna was traveling to East Lansing, Michigan, to spend Thanksgiving at the home of her old college pal. Lynn, almost alone among their set, had achieved an intact and fruitful marriage. Her husband was a professor in the business school at Michigan State. Her two children had entered their surly teenage years, and Lynn was now free to get back to librarian work, as well as devote more time to her rewarding Audubon Club activities. For Anna, there was a Disneyland quality to the trip, a visit to Normal Land.

She imagined Lynn instructing her husband and kids, laying the groundwork for her arrival. "I don't want to have to tell you to be nice to Anna."

"Well duh, that's exactly what you're doing," one of the rotten kids would point out.

"Yeah, why do we have to be nice to her anyway?" the other would chime in.

"Because she's a guest here. And a dear friend of mine. And because she doesn't have anybody else to spend Thanksgiving with."

"Why not, what's wrong with her?" Yukking it up by now.

"Nothing's wrong with her. She just never stayed married long enough to have children."

"That's weird," the kids would chorus, delighted now at the idea of the visiting freak.

She really needed to stop this. Try a little positive attitude. Or a lot. It would be good to reconnect with Lynn, a free ticket to the family feast, without any of the encumbrances of family. Anyway, she wasn't some charity case; she could have organized Thanksgiving with friends or gone to her mother's in Missouri. In fact, going to Lynn's had been a way of avoiding her mother in Missouri. Most people had holiday destinations. Anna had escape routes.

Anna guessed they were in Michigan by now. The train made a series of stately curves, north, as far as she could tell, and there were stands of trees, dense and close-packed, and every so often they opened up to reveal a slatternly small town, gone in an instant, then more trees. She must have dozed off. The intercom woke her, announcing a stop in Kalamazoo. Kalamazoo! She hadn't believed there really was such a place.

She was forty-one years old. The wreckages of two marriages and more lovers than had been strictly necessary trailed behind her like a busted parachute. She had a job which, like most jobs, could have paid her more and aggravated her less. In the last few years, she'd had problems with allergies, dry eye syndrome, brittle nails, constipation, all the diseases of a skittery nervous system. She had, in so many ways, failed to meet expectations. And yet she probably had about half her life left to march or mope through, and she could go out and snag her some happiness if she chose. She was entitled. It was in the Declaration of Independence.

Now the view from the window offered munching black-and-white cows, actual orchards, billboards promoting unborn babies and gun rights. Tawny farm fields swelled under a brisk gray sky. Here was even a fruit and vegetable stand, freighted with pumpkins and bushels of apples. She began to feel mildly hopeful. Live in the moment! Visualize joy!

It's funny, Anna, because of course I came in part for soli-tude. I wanted the purity of it, I wanted to wake up in the morning and know that unless I chose to speak out loud, I'd pass the whole day without hearing a human voice. Well, that's a certain kind of solitude, this diving into the core of yourself and seeing what's down there under the water. But solitude is different than loneliness, and I'm here to tell you, the loneliest times I've ever spent have been in the company of other people.

Lynn had arranged to come to the Lansing station by herself to pick up Anna and drive her back to the house, "so we have a chance to gab." Anna marshaled her luggage and walked a little distance from the concourse, anxious, as always, that she might be forgotten and unmet. But Lynn stepped out of the waiting crowd, a familiar face among the strangeness, like an optical illusion. They hugged.

"Was the train awful? You're almost an hour late!"

"Fine, once we got going. Look at you. You are the very model of a modern Michigan matron."

"Cut it out."

"No, I meant, you have it down cold," Anna backpedaled, because maybe it had been a crummy thing to say. "You look really together."

Lynn sniffed. "I changed out of my sweatsuit. I have a really together sweatsuit too. Is that your only suitcase?"

Both the train and the station had been overheated and filled with lurking, unclean smells: bodies, perfumey lotions, the ancient contents of vending machines ground underfoot. They stepped outside and the sharp wind blew every scrap of it away. "Frigid," Anna remarked, pleased. Chicago had been unseasonably warm and un-holidaylike.

"A front's coming through, I guess. Here's the van. If you say 'soccer mom,' I'm going to smack you."

"It is a powerful, well-engineered vehicle. I like the decals. Are we going to have pie tomorrow? I want to wallow in pie."

"Apple and pumpkin, from the bakery. Jay's making a pumpkin cheesecake." Jay was Lynn's husband. "He has this whole menu of gourmet creations. Oyster dressing. Bourbon-glazed sweet potatoes. Onions baked with pomegranates. The boys and I said if we didn't have a turkey and mashed potatoes with gravy and cranberry sauce, we were going to a restaurant."

"I didn't know Jay liked to cook."

"He likes to compete. It's the latest thing he can do better than me. He watches those TV shows where people cook for prizes and he makes fun of them. He threw out all of our old pots and pans and bought clunky Le Creuset ones. While you're here, try to say something nice about his food."

"I will be ravished by gastronomy," Anna promised. She was enjoying the ride, perched up high in the passenger seat of the van. The elevation made the ordinary view of highway, office buildings, suburban homes, seem like a kingdom she surveyed. Carry on, she instructed her subjects as they went about their labors. I am well pleased.

She kept Lynn in the corner of her vision, biding her time, waiting for them not to feel strange to each other. The first words out of her mouth had been the truest, even though she regretted them. There was a kind of protective coloration people developed to fit their surroundings, so that in the suburbs one saw whole herds of fleece garments, turtlenecks, sporty shoes. Lynn had cut her hair short and permed it, some hairdresser's version of a casual, fun look. Now it had flattened, like the pelt of an animal. Lynn had always been the light and shiny one, the up to Anna's down. Something corrosive had been at work on her, but Anna was cautious about voicing any more opinions.

How long had it been since they'd seen each other? Three four five years? Lynn and Jay and their kids had been in Chicago for some kind of conference. Anna and her then-husband had met them for dinner at their hotel. The boys had been subadolescents, gangly, inarticulate, suffering through every minute in the presence of adults. The two men had sized each other up and hadn't much liked each other. Anna and Ex drank too much, gearing up for the fight they'd have once they got home. Lynn had been on alert about children's table manners ("Sit up straight! Don't put that whole thing in your mouth at once!"), and she and Anna kept up a false, sprightly banter, every so often giving each other private glances, meaning, they should have ditched all these unsatisfactory males and gone off on their own. "She does enough talking for all of us put together," Ex observed later, one more thing to fight about. But he hadn't been wrong.

Now they were setting themselves up for more of the same. Another reunion observed by bored family members. "We have to stop and pick up the pies," Lynn said. "Are you hungry? Dinner tonight's just sandwiches. The refrigerator's full of Thanksgiving stuff."

"Sure, let's get a bite." It was hard to sound enthusiastic when Lynn didn't seem to be. "I got another letter from Ted," Anna offered, thinking that might spark something. There were plenty of Ted stories. "He wants me to go live in the woods with him."

"Well if you don't, can I?"

Anna did turn around to look at her then. "Sure. I mean, I don't see any reason why not."

"Just a couple of weeks out of the year would do it. Like a retreat."

"Old part-time Ted," said Anna, reminiscing. "Not what you'd call dependable. Though he had his good points." She wasn't sure why she'd said this last part, except that it made her sound worldly, a connoisseur of men and their good and bad points. Which she guessed she was, but not in any way you'd want to brag about. "His heart was always in the right place," she finished lamely.

"I guess he could be an option for you. In case nothing else works out."

"Excuse me?" said Anna, a shocked half beat too late. "What, exactly, do you think I'm trying to work out?"

"Oh, you know. The man thing." Lynn wrestled the van into a parking lot, scanned for spaces. "Like you're always complaining."

"I thought I was allowed to complain," said Anna, feeling something new and dangerous cresting in her. Skittish anger, a willingness to lash out. "Even lacking, as I do, the advantages of a longtime spouse, always available to be complained about."

"Funny," said Lynn, making the mistake of not really paying attention. She was waiting for another van to finish pulling out and unclog the lane.

"You think I'm, what, desperate? Running out of time?"

"Don't be silly."

"Don't be dismissive. 'Poor old Anna. I mean after all, what does she expect?'"

"What?" Now Lynn was paying attention. "You know very well I didn't say any of that."

"And don't use your mommy voice on me."

"My what?" Lynn spun the steering wheel and the van heaved toward, then away from, a line of shopping carts. The teenage grocery clerk pushing them didn't register the danger until they'd passed him by. His mouth unhinged and he stared after them. "Are you flipping out on me?"

"I'm past my prime. Stale-dated. Don't you dare feel sorry for me."

"Right this minute? I'm feeling sorry for me. And what's 'modern Michigan matron,' huh? You get off the train and start right in sniping at me, and then you say you don't want sympathy when all I ever hear you talk about is how you're lonely, you're horny, you're broke, you're old and pitiful, *you're* the one feeling sorry for you. I'm just supposed to keep you company."

"All right," said Anna. "All right."

"Get over it. Please."

"Over it. Sorry." Her anger flared out like a match and the next instant she had undermined herself, seen herself as Lynn must see her: her black coat, meant to be urban and sleek, was rubbed and discolored at the collar and hem, her boots were scuffed, her jeans drooped and bagged, and God knows what kind of face and hair would present themselves in a mirror. "A little holiday tantrum."

"Glad we got it out of the way," said Lynn. But it didn't feel as if they'd put anything out of the way, only demarcated the distance between them.

They stood in line for the pies, and then stood in another line to get soup and salads, which they carried over to a corner table. Anna shouldn't have been hungry, after all the upset, but she was, extremely, as if she were venturing into unknown territory where sustenance would be hard to come by.

After awhile Lynn said, "I guess we're having some weird competition. Who can be the most bitter."

"Yeah, well, usually I win in a walk."

"There's some stuff going on with Jay."

"Ah," said Anna, nodding. Stuff.

"You can't be married almost twenty years without hitting some rough patches. I still love Jay. I do. At the end of the day, he's the father of my children. My long-term partner. But I need to not be the Great Mommy Satan. The reason for everything that's lacking in his life."

"He'd be lost without you," said Anna, wondering if this was true. She prided herself on having a store of empathy, of being able to figure people out, see them as if they were one of those clocks with transparent cases, the gears and cogs spinning and visible. But Lynn's husband always stopped her cold. He might be one of those men who walked away from a wife and family without much distress, or even much thought.

"Just as I guess he shouldn't be entirely responsible for everything that's lacking in my life. Like, for instance, sex."

"Uh oh."

"Maybe most married people don't, after awhile. God knows there's enough jokes about it." She looked at Anna. Her turn.

"It kind of came and went," said Anna. "Alcohol helped." She wasn't inclined, just then, to detail her sexual failures, and besides, she couldn't speak as to either children or marital longevity, both of them no doubt in play. She wondered why Lynn didn't compare notes with some other mom. Maybe she did. Or maybe she didn't want that kind of information loose out there in her world. The dinner guest, looking Jay over with knowing eyes. "But you love the guy, that's the important thing," Anna said, aiming for encouragement.

"There's all different kinds of love," said Lynn, breaking crackers into her soup bowl.

I know you think I'm out here getting by on roots and grubs and squirrel stew, but in fact I eat pretty well. I've got my basics—rice, flour, cornmeal—stowed away in critter-proof containers. I make the world's best granola and I store that too. I'm good with anything in a can. Working on a root cellar for potatoes and onions, not having much luck, what with all the mud. Someday I'll set up shop to do some smoking and pickling. Do you know why Johnny Appleseed planted apple trees up and down the frontier? Because you can ferment the juice and make vinegar. Applejack too, I guess.

Anna hadn't seen Lynn's house, this new house, before. Lynn pulled in the driveway and Anna said, "Hey, this is nice. This is top of the line." It always surprised her when people she knew owned real, actual houses with grown-up mortgages. "Is that Jay up there on the ladder?"

"Yeah, he's installing gutter guards."

"Oh," said Anna, not knowing what a gutter guard was, and figuring she didn't need to know. She waved at Jay, but he gave no sign of seeing her.

The boys were out playing basketball, Lynn explained. The boys' names were Tim and Dan. They were the complete monosyllabic family. Lynn took her through the house room by room, like a Realtor. She stood aside at doorways so that Anna could peer in, assess, compliment. "The boys' rooms," she said, indicating two nests of disordered bedding and strewn clothing. "You'll have your own bathroom. Be thankful for that."

The backyard was a wonderland of bird feeders, birdbaths, and birdhouses. There were whirligigs and platforms, hoppers and Plexiglas tubes, bird condos decorated in Cape Cod and rustic styles. "These birds have it good," said Anna, thinking it was all a little crazed, so much effort, like those folk artists who constructed homemade temples out of bicycle wheels and aluminum foil.

"The best thing about birds is, they don't ask for anything. You put the seed out, they show up. Forget to fill the feeders and they scram. Simple."

Back inside, Anna went upstairs to unpack and go through her remaining clothes, see if anything she'd brought held up to scrutiny. She was always doing this, packing with care, then discovering that everything was wrong. She liked the little guest bathroom with its blue tiles and soft towels. She didn't dwell on her own untidy reflection, except to note that she was the only accessory out of place.

In the bedroom she opened her suitcase and selected the good sweater she'd meant to reserve for Thanksgiving dinner. She was pulling it on when a sound close by startled her, made her panic with her head still stuck within the sweater's inside-out complications. She flailed about, bra and bare stomach exposed, and finally freed herself. Jay was on his ladder outside the window, not five feet away, scraping and shoving at the gutters. He was wearing a baseball cap that shaded his face and Anna supposed it was possible he hadn't seen her—the light outside was getting dim, the room was unlighted. But then, it seemed unlikely that he *wouldn't* have seen her, at this distance. Maybe he was pretending not to, just to avoid embarrassing them both. Or, since Jay was so hard for her to figure, he might have positioned the ladder for the express purpose of leering in at her.

Unnerved, she went back downstairs and found Lynn standing in the kitchen, absorbed in reading a piece of mail. She didn't look up when Anna came in, and Anna was left to direct her guest's hopeful smile at empty air. Scanning, she didn't see any evidence of the next day's Thanksgiving dinner, except for the pies in their bakery boxes. Nothing stewing or soaking or toasting. Her stomach snarled.

Lynn tossed the mail aside. "Wine," she said. "Cheese and crackers."

"Yes please," said Anna, happy now that there would be something to do, sit and drink and feed, while domestic life churned around her. "Red, if you have it."

Lynn poured them two oversized glasses and set them out on the counter. Anna claimed the stool in the corner, head wedged against a cabinet. Back to the wall, always safest. Jay came in at the kitchen door, making a lot of foot-scraping racket.

"Hey Jay!" Anna greeted him with such apparent delight that he stopped short and gave her a startled, hooded look. Creep. She bet money he'd been spying on her.

Then he rearranged his face into indifference. "Hi," he said, not looking at her. Instead he sought out Lynn. "That silver maple? It's leaned in and rotted half the shingles over the west dormer."

"You should probably cut it down, then," said Lynn, nodding over her glass. "Bad tree."

"If you think it's funny, the roofing bill's going to be a real scream."

"Oh honey, I promise I'll get all kinds of upset the day after tomorrow, but this is Thanksgiving. Thanksgiving Eve."

Jay went to the sink to wash his hands, and Lynn came up behind him, patted his back. "You hungry? Want some soup? Want me to brine the turkey or anything?"

"I decided not to brine it."

"There's chicken noodle, pepper pot, and tomato. We should probably save the tomato for Tim."

"If nothing else, that maple needs to be cut way the hell back."

"Or maybe they already ate at Connie's. Pizza or something."

Anna drank more wine. It dulled her appetite (she was still unreasonably hungry), as well as giving her the appropriate off-center vantage point. She couldn't decide if Lynn and Jay were any more discontented than any other married couple, if there was some baseline of low expectations that set in after a time. From her perch in the corner she noted that they were still a good-looking pair. That counted for something. Lynn was still recognizably the pretty blonde of their college days, minus the smile that had been her armor against the world: Don't hurt me! I am a friendly, approachable girl! And Jay was still tall and straight and comely, even as his neck and chin had thickened, his profile taking on a florid, petulant aspect, the same progression seen over time on the coins depicting certain Roman emperors.

"So, Jay," Anna began, wanting to make some minimal polite social noise, "how are your classes?"

"I don't teach classes. I do research and I supervise the thesis and doctoral students."

"Oh, that's nice." Or not. She couldn't detect any perceptible job satisfaction in him. She wondered if he was this arrogant and unforthcoming at work, or if he unbent, came alive there. Some men were like that, treating their home life like an annoying series of chores to be accomplished.

There was the thundering noise of the garage door rolling up, then down. Tim and Dan (she could never remember which was which) filed in, dressed in their uniforms of sweatshirts and shorts and sneakers. Their bare legs were red with cold. They were tall, like their father, and there was something unsettling about the sheer amount of skin displayed. What must it be like to be a man, take up so much of the world's volume and acreage? Lynn fussed over them, got them to agree to microwave chili for their supper. The older boy went straight to a cabinet and took out a box of cereal and began munching handfuls of it. The younger fixed himself a glass of chocolate milk. Thanksgiving, Anna could tell, was going to be a special occasion if only because everyone would be sitting down together instead of foraging for themselves.

"You remember Anna, don't you?" Lynn prodded, and the boys acknowledged her without changing their remote, fixed expressions. "She lives in Chicago. Tim's always been nuts about Chicago. He's thinking of applying to Northwestern. Well, that's Evanston, but close."

So Tim was the older one. He gave Anna a brief, appraising glance. "What is it you do? In Chicago?"

"I edit a newsletter for the building trades industry and another for a realty group."

The boy nodded. He'd been right all along. She was boring.

Lynn said, "Anna wrote a humor column for the school paper. All kinds of wacky fun stuff."

"You had to be there," said Anna. The humor threshold in this family seemed pretty high.

The younger boy, Dan, said, "So, what was Mom like? In college?"

"Some tales," said Anna, "are best left untold."

"Oh, thanks." Lynn got up to refill the wineglasses. "Thanks heaps. I was a perfectly nice, normal girl."

"No, really," the boy persisted. "I bet she did all sorts of stuff she pretends she never heard of."

"They're on to you," Anna told Lynn. "Might as well deal out a few crisp facts, right here at the kitchen table."

Both boys were now regarding Anna with probational approval, as if she might offer some entertainment value after all. They were nearly identical, two imperfect copies of Jay, brown-eyed, taciturn, equipped with Adam's apples and jutting wrist bones. Anna didn't see much of Lynn's leavening spirit in them, which might have been why they were so intent on hearing naughty stories about her. They wanted some other heritage. How grim it must be, to see your genetic destiny walking around in front of you on a daily basis.

"How about just one little anecdote," said Anna, enjoying herself now, thinking she just might win them over. She noted that Jay was paying close attention, even as he pretended to be engrossed in a cookbook. He and Lynn hadn't met until after graduation. "The secret life of Mom."

"She's going to make something up," said Lynn.

"How about the blind date story? They know that one?"

Lynn groaned her martyr's groan. The boys looked nearly jolly. "Okay. The dorm we lived in freshman year always had signs taped to the bathroom mirror: '5'8" boy from Scott Hall needs date' '5'10" ATO needs date for mixer.' That was always the big thing, not wanting to be taller than your date," said Anna, turning to Tim and Dan. "You guys would have been like, kings.

"Anyway, your mom, being such a shrimp, always ended up with the shorties. So when the 5'5" dude turns up, plus you figure these guys always added a couple of inches to their advertising, she gets the call."

"Why did they need somebody else finding them dates?" asked Dan, who seemed to be the more lively of the two, Prince Harry to his brother's Prince William. "They couldn't just hang out, go to parties?"

Lynn said, "Oh honey, everybody was so terribly *dumb* about things, and I know we were older than you guys but we seemed so much younger, and here we were at this big new place and every minute we were excited and every other minute were desperate not to be left out, and there'd be some girl who had a boyfriend and the boyfriend would have friends And you'd set it up and the guy would call from downstairs and you'd go out and have a perfectly awkward time. That's how we did it."

"So this really short guy," prompted the relentless Dan.

Lynn was drinking too much or too fast or both, Anna thought. She had a blurred, flushed look that meant sentiments of one sort or another were likely to be dredged up to the surface. "The short guy is your mom's date, and I'm set up with his friend, who's some normal height, and we're all going to a dinner at this frat house."

"Dad? Were you in a fraternity?"

"Hah," said Jay, by way of a negative.

". . . and yes, the guy is seriously short. Like a hobbit. But not as cute. And with a yappy attitude."

"Short man's syndrome," Jay put in. She couldn't stand the guy. Really.

"My date just isn't that into it, or not into me. They were pledges, they had to go to this awards dinner, they had to have dates, no matter how lame. Short guy made gross jokes about the spaghetti looking like worms. Sophisticated repartee. Afterward, we all go down to the make-out room—"

"The what?" She had the boys' complete attention.

"Well that's what it was, all the houses had them, though they called them things like the Pit or the Cave. See, unlike you lucky youth of today, we couldn't have company of the opposite sex in our dorm rooms." Anna was immediately aware of a current of parental alarm or caution, as if these might not be suitable observations. She began to hurry her story. "Oh, it was just a big ol' dark TV room, and we were all sitting there, waiting for something thrilling to happen, and I got up to find the bathroom, and when I came back, your mom and my date were in a lip-lock."

"Eww, Mom," the boys chorused.

"It was a youthful indiscretion," said Lynn carelessly. She drained the last of her wine.

"You were like, passion's plaything."

"I guess I'm never, ever going to be allowed to live this down."

"Never," said Anna cheerfully. Of course that was not the entire story. Left to themselves, Anna and the shorty had made the best of things by groping and mashing with each other. Once he was seated and not talking, he hadn't been so bad.

Lynn hadn't even noticed. The room had been that dark. And Anna had never told her. A mean little secret.

The microwave chimed. The boys loaded up their bowls of chili and took them upstairs. Lynn announced that she was going to lie down for awhile. Anna and Jay, abandoned, looked at each other, then away. Jay started opening cupboards, hauling out casseroles and flour bins. She decided against making any insincere offers of assistance, and instead filled a bowl with the remainder of the chili and retreated to the den. The backyard light was on, illuminating the patio. Lynn's bird feeders, she noted, were almost out of seed. They cast elongated shadows that Anna tried not to think resembled something fanciful and inappropriate, like gallows.

She was remembering Ted, back in the old days, back when she and Lynn had shared an apartment and Ted had been her boyfriend, or a certain kind of boyfriend, one who mostly hung around smoking your pot. She couldn't remember any extravagant sentiments being exchanged, though Ted had extravagant opinions about all manner of things, books and politics and religion, and drugs as the door to perception, and the benefits of going off the grid. She guessed he would have been voted most likely to live in a tree. Just as Lynn was a sure bet to end up married and settled, and Anna herself . . . she didn't like to think of her future as foretold. Not then, not now. She'd wanted to keep all her options open. Glamorous possibilities which still eluded her. Quirky individuality, fading over time into eccentricity. She crept upstairs as quietly as she could.

I've determined to try and get to know some of the locals,
who I can see when I go into the post office and the lumber-

*yard. Right now we seem stuck at the nodding and grunt-
ing stage.*

It smelled like Thanksgiving. Anna woke with her nose curling around the tickling, teasing smells of onion, roasting meat,
cinnamon, sage. It was reassuring that Thanksgiving was still
Thanksgiving, no matter how far afield you might go. She
showered and dressed and felt some of her hopefulness return,
or maybe it was just the hope of being hopeful. Good attitude!
Smiling face!

The boys were eating cereal in front of the television in the
den. She gave them a comradely wave as she passed by. Stopping to make conversation would have risked ruining the fine
rapport they'd reached the night before. The kitchen was empty,
though the oven was on and the turkey was sending out its good
smells. A stock pot burped and simmered on a back burner,
while smaller saucepans, some with crusted edges, crowded the
rest of the stovetop. Complicated preparations were strewn over
the counters: the leafy ends of celery, dark little bottles, packets
of raisins, knives and cutting boards, vegetable peelings, measuring cups, wadded sheets of aluminum foil. The garage door
activated, and, crossing to the front of the house, Anna saw
Jay backing out of the driveway in his black, Dad-sized SUV.
Heading out to get currant jelly or leeks or something other
perfecting ingredient, she guessed.

There wasn't any coffee made, so Anna found a packet of
cocoa, then helped herself to a carton of yogurt, pleased at her
resourcefulness. She wondered if Lynn was still asleep. With
nothing else to do, she washed the dirty pots and pans and
sieves and spoons that had landed in the sink, stacked them

neatly in the dish drainer. Even Jay shouldn't see that as inter-
ference. What was the etiquette for guests these days?

She heard Lynn coming down the stairs, then she appeared
in the doorway. "Christ," she announced, surveying the wreck-
age of the kitchen.

"The turkey smells great," Anna offered. Lynn didn't answer,
just set about making coffee. She was wearing pink flannel
snowflake pajamas and she looked like something awakened
too early from hibernation. "You sleep okay?" Moody shrug
from Lynn. "I'll take that as a no."

They watched the coffeemaker chug and cycle. Anna said,
"Are you mad at me for telling that story?"

"My mom, the make-out slut."

"You were always popular."

"It's such a pathetic little story. I kind of wish you'd told
them something racier."

"You never did anything racy."

"My point exactly."

The coffeemaker finished its heaving and Lynn poured them
each a cup. "What's the game plan for dinner?" Anna asked.
"Should we be fasting? Carbo-loading?" Maybe she should
squirrel away some granola bars in the guest room. "I guess Jay
went out to get something," she added.

"He left?"

"Yeah, ten, fifteen minutes ago."

"Oh fuck him. Fuck him to death."

"Lynn?"

Lynn was shaking her head, but it was more like twitching,
something she couldn't help, and Anna crossed the room to her,
alarmed, uncertain, but Lynn put up her hands to ward her off.

"Okay," she said. "Right." She turned and scrabbled in the corner desk. "Keys," she said. She lifted a coat from a hook by the door and headed out into the garage.

Anna said, "What are you—" and then, "Wait a minute, wait a minute." She hurried upstairs, found her own coat and purse, then down the stairs again, past the lounging, incurious boys, detouring to grab her coffee mug.

Lynn was already behind the van's wheel. She was having trouble with the garage door opener. The door came up partly, then banged down again, up down, up down, "...fucking thing," Anna heard through the van's closed window.

"Hold on." A snow shovel had gotten wedged in the door track. Anna straightened it and the door rolled up. She hoisted herself into the van. "Will you tell me what's the matter?"

"That asshole. I know where he is." Lynn started the van and they lurched out into the street. "He's been screwing one of his grad students. It's supposed to be over. Hah. Even on Thanksgiving he can't stay away. Goddamn him."

They were zooming through suburban streets laid out in curves and circles so as to hinder zooming. Anna held on to the door handle. "Wow. Are you sure? I mean . . ." She found herself thinking of the combat-zone kitchen they'd left behind them, the bubbling stock pot, the turkey in need of basting. She hoped the boys would notice if something actually caught on fire. "It could just be an errand." Not wanting to defend Jay as much as calm Lynn down.

"Oh, he'll come back with a pound of butter, or some other alibi. We've been in counseling for almost a year now. I found a bunch of their emails, he thinks he's so clever. She's twenty-three. I've seen her, she's a little business slut."

"Business—"

"You know, the whole hair-and-makeup package, sits on the desk, shoves her tits in everybody's face. Business slut."

"I'm sorry. What are you going to do?"

She'd meant it in the general sense, as in, do about your marriage, your life, but Lynn hit the accelerator in the two-block stretch between stop signs, then slammed on the brakes, sending Anna's coffee slopping over into her lap. The engine stalled and she cranked it viciously to restart it. "Don't think I don't know where she lives. I'm gonna block his car in her driveway so he has to come out and face me. Goddamn his eyes."

Anna considered that Jay would be facing her too, unless she asked to be dropped off at the corner. They peeled out onto a four-lane road, past apartment complexes, expansive gas stations, through sparse holiday traffic. Sunlight came down in a slant but the rest of the sky was piled-up clouds. The van's heater was roaring, making her head feel clogged. She said, "I don't suppose there's a bar open, anywhere we could sit and talk."

"I'm in my pajamas."

"Oh, yeah." That would look nice in the police report. "Do you want me to talk you out of this or egg you on?"

"I wasn't going to tell you. It's too stupid and embarrassing, it's so *common,* the cheating rat husband. It's like getting hemorrhoids."

"You sort of told me. I knew you weren't happy."

"You're like, psychic, right?"

They turned off the larger highway onto a smaller one. The university district, Anna guessed, since the businesses were named Spartan this or Spartan that: dry cleaning, liquor, shoe repair. Anna's stomach began to curdle. She hoped that Jay wasn't really at his girlfriend's, or if he was, that he'd hide in the house and not come out. "Hey, Lynn? I don't think this is your best move. Seriously, we should go home."

"Just this once? I think I get to do something really trashy and sordid."

"Okay, then. We're good."

At the next stoplight, the van's engine stalled and died. Lynn cranked it; it made a stubborn noise and failed to catch. She tried again. And kept trying, until the starter only clicked.

"You probably flooded it."

"Crap."

"I would look on it as a sign from God."

"Holy crap, then."

The innards of the car ticked, the engine cooling down. It was going to get very cold very fast. "Do you have AAA or anything?" Anna asked.

Lynn patted at her coat pockets. It didn't appear to be her coat. "I don't have the card. Did you bring your phone?" Anna handed it over and Lynn fumbled with the keypad. "Your phone sucks."

"Don't throw it," said Anna, because Lynn looked capable of one last petulant, thwarted act. "Here." She retrieved the phone, cleared the screen, and handed it back. Lynn punched in the number. One of the boys must have answered, because she asked if Dad was there.

A space of listening, then Lynn said, "All right, here's what I need you to do."

Afterward she gave the phone back.

"Was Jay there?"

"Yes. But that doesn't prove anything."

"I guess you don't trust him."

"No shit."

"I haven't heard you swear this much since, like, forever." Lynn shrugged. "You deserve better. You know that."

When Lynn didn't answer, she went on. "I don't know what to tell you. I don't think either Steve or Terry was stepping out on me, or if they were, I didn't know about it, anyway, that's not why things didn't work out." She sounded glib, false to herself. "Didn't work out," what did that mean, it was shorthand for wretchedness, mortal combat, loss, failure, grief. She had the sensation of shouting down a well, sending her words into some echoing, absent space. "I mean, God, you guys have all these assets, we never did. You could probably kick him out, keep the house, get him to pay for the kids' college. Everything."

"I don't want a divorce. Jay doesn't want one either. At least, that's what he says."

"But if you have to check up on him every minute . . ."

"If that's what I have to do, I'll do it. You think I'd get some kind of great settlement, forget it, you don't get bonus money just because the other guy's screwing around. Assets, forget it. He'd still have his income and his fuckee, or the one that'll come after this one, or the one after that, and I'd end up all by myself in some crummy little apartment."

"Like me."

"I didn't say that. I didn't mean that."

"It's okay," said Anna, although it wasn't.

"You know I didn't—"

Anna held up a hand. "Let's just drop it." She was afraid she might cry, furious, squalling tears. She forced them back out of pure self-loathing. They sat without speaking until Tim pulled up behind them in the SUV.

Lynn popped the van's hood and Tim applied something from a spray can. "Try it now," he told them, and the engine turned over.

Anna got out of the van and watched him let the hood down, blowing on his bare hands. What was it about boys that made them avoid protective clothing? "All right if I ride back with you?"

You could count on people saying yes as a reflex, if you caught them by surprise, and so Anna climbed into the SUV and waited for Tim to finish talking with his mother. She figured Lynn could explain anything she felt like explaining.

They followed the van on the way back. "Did you guys have a fight or something?"

Anna thought this must be what it was like to be a parent, some part of parenting. When you had to explain to children those things you did not wish to explain to yourself. That it was possible she and Lynn had never really been friends, that over time they had become a reproach to each other, and that people would do almost anything, contend with all manner of injuries to the spirit, just to keep from being alone.

Anna said, "Neither of us is in a very good mood today. When people know each other for a long time, they sort of wear each other out."

The boy nodded. He was a serious kid; she thought she had been right to talk to him seriously. "Mom wears her*self* out. I wish—"

He stopped, and Anna was left to wonder what it was he wished, this serious, half-grown creature, and how much the boys knew about their parents' troubles. Plenty, she guessed. It was even possible that one or both of them, Lynn most probably, had sat them down and made an earnest, awful speech about Mom and Dad having to work some things out, but nobody should worry.

Anna thought she had never had children because she wasn't optimistic enough. Wouldn't you have to be deeply hopeful to believe that your own children would end up happier than you were?

Lynn's van nosed into its spot in the garage and Tim maneuvered the SUV next to it. Following her inside, Anna beheld the kitchen, now tamed and ordered and bristling with edibles. The dining room table was set with a white cloth, with cheerful, harvest-patterned dishes, a centerpiece of tall, yellow candles, grapes, pomegranates, apples. "Oh honey," Lynn was saying, "this is all just perfect. It's yummy-scrumptious."

Now don't laugh, but I'm thinking of getting a dog. Something big and furry and friendly that's always, by god, happy to see me.

It just worked out better for Jay to drop her off at the train station, and Anna said that was fine. She and Lynn had made up, or at least they'd said the words necessary for making up. "You big goof. I didn't mean anything, you're so silly sometimes." Oh yes, ha ha, said Anna. Famous for her silliness.

During the drive, Jay played a talk radio station that substituted for actual talk. Fine with Anna. At the train station, he alarmed her by parking and announcing that he was coming in with her.

"Honestly, you don't have to. I'm fine."

Jay opened the back of the SUV and hoisted her suitcase. You could almost admire how good he was at ignoring other people, how words, requests, instructions rolled right off of him. "Let's just make sure your train isn't going to be late."

As if she wouldn't sleep in the station, rather than go back home with him. She followed him through the doors, scanned the waiting crowd. "Looks like everything's good to go," she announced, hoping that would be enough to make him leave.

Jay walked her suitcase up to the head of the straggling line of people waiting to board, a minor rudeness. She supposed she could go to the back once he left. "Well, thanks for everything. The dinner was great." It had been great. In that, at least, she thought Lynn had nothing to complain about. "And thanks for the ride."

It was his cue to leave. Still he lingered, looking around him peevishly. Or maybe that was just his face in repose, its natural settled expression. He stood out, too tall, too prosperous for the semi-shabby group of travelers. Was she supposed to shake his hand? Embrace him? He said, "That's really something, you and Lynn knowing each other for so long."

Anna said yes, it was. Cautious about agreeing with him on anything.

"I don't know anybody who goes back that far. College or high school. Growing up. I don't even know where any of those people are anymore."

"I'm trying to imagine you as a little kid. It's not coming to me."

"I wanted to be an archaeologist. I had a map of the world with pins in it, all the important sites, Egypt, Greece, Peru,

China. I did an archaeology badge in Boy Scouts. I don't know why I quit on it. I don't know why things stop being important, they just do."

She couldn't stand the thought that he might be lonely too. She couldn't stand having to feel sorry for him. "Hey, could I ask you something? When I first got to your house, and you were up on the ladder outside? Were you looking in at me while I was changing clothes?"

"Good God, no." He was genuinely startled, distressed. "What kind of person would do that?"

He did leave then, and in due course the train came, and Anna boarded and found a seat next to the window. The train nudged forward on schedule, the promise of a smooth ride. She was thinking about Ted, laying in his supplies against the winter. There would be the hunting hawks, and mornings of ghostly frost, and the scouring wind, and the great theater of the sky. In such a bare and gorgeous place, the soul's ache would find its proper home. What did you need in the wilderness? A kinder, braver heart. When she got home, she would write Ted a nice letter.

Mr. Rat

I was hanging out at the window by the coffee area, watching the construction crews going at it across the street. They were working on another gigantic office building a lot like ours. We'd watched them from the hole in the ground phase and now the scaffolding and rebar framing was up to five or six stories. Pretty soon they'd get as far as ten, where we were, and we'd be able to practically look out and wave. We all liked watching them. In our jobs we worked with words on computer screens and numbers on paper. There were plenty of times when I thought it would feel good to be out in the open air, getting my back into it, with an actual physical *thing* you could point to as a product.

I had a pretty good view of them, looking across and down. A construction crane was lifting big sections of girder up to where the ironworkers, I guess they were, little bugs in yellow hard hats, guided it onto a big stack of girders. We'd watched them do that over and over these last few months, and we always got a kick out if it.

But today something went wrong, big-time. The crane arm swung too wide and hit one of those industrial-grade extension ladders, and there was a guy on the very top of the ladder who paddled and flailed as it tilted at a crazy angle, then the whole thing went over.

He landed somewhere below my line of sight. The other little bug guys scattered. The next minute you couldn't see any of them.

Just then Brian, whose work space was next to mine, came by and asked me what was up.

"The weirdest thing just happened. A guy fell off this really tall ladder and probably pancaked himself."

Brian peered out the window. "I don't see anything."

"You had to be looking right at it."

One of the supervisors came by and we got moving. There had already been a few remarks passed about window time.

Our work areas were not equipped with windows. We had a lot of bleary fluorescent lights that somebody at corporate was experimenting with. They were supposed to prevent eyestrain, but they made you feel like you were breathing something other than air. A full day of them made me groggy. Walking from the window back to my chair was like submerging. I sat down but I wasn't able to pick up my work where I'd left off. I wondered if the guy who'd fallen was dead or alive. It was like a part of me was still looking out the window. That's how peculiar it felt. Like I'd seen it all happen on some outer space TV channel. It wasn't like me to get worked up about some strange guy, even if he did take a header onto concrete. I'm just not famous for things like that.

I went out to the reception area to bullshit with Steph. She's my age and we kid around a lot. Steph had her earphones in and was bopping around to her music. I was pretty sure she wasn't supposed to do that. I had to stand in front of her and wave to get her attention.

"Hey Matt, what's up?" She still had one of the earphones half in. I could hear the scratchy, miniature music.

"Not much. Did any ambulances pull up around here, anything like that?"

"Unless they came up on the elevator, I wouldn't know. Why, how come?"

"Nothing." I didn't feel like going into it. Instead I asked her what she did over the weekend, and she told me and told me. There's times I think that Steph wants to be my girlfriend, and I have to be careful about that. She's a nice girl, but it's not going to happen. I could just sense she was way ahead of me, like she was already telling her relatives at the wedding reception how we met while working at the same place.

I finally got into the work groove and knocked out my day's quota. None of it's that hard, to be honest. A sheltered workshop could probably handle it. I was always tired at the end of the day, but that was probably from boredom. That night I watched the news, flipping back and forth between channels, but nobody mentioned the guy who fell. I bought a paper the next day and turned to the part where they had the car crashes and stray murders. Nothing there either. I couldn't believe the guy wouldn't have hurt himself pretty bad, enough to be noteworthy. If it was you, wouldn't you want your own square inch of ink? I'm just saying, it was weird.

Our group leader had called a morning meeting, so that was the first order of business. We all filed into the conference area. There was a coffee setup and some of those disappointing healthy snack cakes. Corporate was trying to direct us into better lifestyle choices. The group leader got right down to it. She said that we were not performing up to expectations. "Productivity has remained static, as opposed to the five percent increase that was projected. I don't have to tell you the consequences of being a consistently underperforming unit, except to say that they would be serious."

I was trying not to look at Brian. He never managed the neutral, attentive expression required of an employee who was getting his ass kicked. Brian has a narrow face that just naturally settles into a smirk. I knew if I even looked at him, he'd have me rolling my eyes right along with him at the horseshit the group leader was dishing out. Five percent, what did that mean? These people had no souls.

Instead I used my trick for getting through meetings, which was to rehearse detailed sexual fantasies while I stared at the group leader. The fantasies weren't about her. That would have been, well, unpleasant. No, just your ordinary porn stuff. See, I'll admit to things like that, things guys really do. Those girl magazines with articles about how to figure out what men really think, or want, or why he's not calling, or letting you move in, or whatever the program is? Believe me, you probably don't want to know.

I snapped out of it when the group leader began passing out papers, one for everybody. Employee Responsibility Checklist, it read, and beneath that, a series of questions:

1. Have I established ownership of team objectives?
2. Have I implemented best practices?
3. Have I learned from my mistakes?
4. Have I looked on each new day as an opportunity to excel?

There was more, but before I could finish, a piece of paper nudged into my lap from beneath the table. On the back of his Employee Responsibility checklist, Brian had written:

1. Have I gotten anything like a raise in the last year and a half?
2. Have my best accounts been outsourced to Malaysia?
3. Do any of you assholes even know my goddamn name?

I didn't dare raise my eyes from the page.

The group leader was saying we were supposed to answer each question on a one-to-five-point scale, with one being Needs Improvement and five being Exceptional. We were supposed to do this daily for six weeks, then plot our responses on a graph. In this way it would be possible to chart the trend of our deficiencies.

Honestly, there were times I wondered why I worked here.

The rest of the day I put my head down and just cranked. I was like the poster boy for Employee Responsibility. Sometimes that happens, they'll get me mad enough that I decide I'll show them, and I blast through all the crap like a comic book hero putting his fist through a wall. But I do it for me, on my own terms, not because of their cheapo motivation games.

So it wasn't until the end of the day that I made it over to the coffee area. Just to stretch my legs, because by that late the coffee turns into sediment. I couldn't tell if they'd made any progress on the building across the street. The workers were gone by then; they started early and knocked off early. It was one of the those gray days that made it hard to judge distance, like I could have moved my hand just beyond the glass and practically touched the other side of the street.

I heard the elevator chiming in the distance as people from the office left for the day. I guess it was later than I thought. After awhile I could tell I was the only one there. It was a feeling, a particular kind of quiet. But I didn't leave yet, even though I could have. I was trying to clear my head, travel between work and not-work, when your mind unties the knot of itself and comes floating back to you.

Maybe the guy I'd seen fall was really all right, maybe he had a safety harness or something. I hoped so. You wouldn't want the guy's family to have to think about him cashing in every time they looked at the building. It would be like a tombstone twenty stories tall.

I don't do real well with heights. Most people don't know that about me because, think about it, how often does it come up? But I never went off the high dive when I was a kid. Never climbed a tree or a water tower, never even liked sleeping on the top bunk. All this is to try and explain what happened next: I fell.

Not actually; it just felt like it. One second I was standing at the window, and the next it gave way and I was clawing at the gray sky. My stomach somersaulted. The speed pushed the air out of me and all I could manage was a strangled yelp before I landed, feet first, on the exact piece of floor where I'd been standing all along.

The back of my shirt was damp, and it hurt to breathe. Have you've ever had one of those dreams when you're falling and you scramble around and wake up in your own bed? It felt like that, except, of course, I'd been awake the whole time.

I got myself out of there pretty quick, I can tell you, and

went to a bar and drank a beer, and then I drank another one. I was beginning to feel really stupid. It was a good thing nobody had been there to watch my little performance, or else I might have gotten a call from HR to come in for one of their friendly chats where they try to determine if you're a mental health risk and should they start giving you bad job evaluations.

Maybe it wasn't the brightest idea to call my old girlfriend who doesn't like me very much. But I still felt shaky, hollow underneath the beer buzz, and I didn't want to be alone, and at least with her I always knew where I stood.

So I called. She let it ring awhile. "Hey, pretty lady."

"Who's this?"

I hate that. Like she didn't have Caller ID. "It's me," I said.

"Oh, Mr. Rat." That's what she calls me. Matt the Rat. I think that's cold. "What do you want?"

"I was wondering if I could buy you a drink."

"Hah."

"Dinner, then. Come on. I've been thinking a lot about you." Technically true, if you counted the last fifteen minutes.

I could hear her working it over, looking for angles. "Dinner but no dessert," she said, which meant, no sex, and I said, Fine.

She walked into the restaurant half an hour later, totally done up, hair, shoes, the wicked makeup. Like she spent her evenings by the phone, all primed and ready for when a call came in.

I stood up, like a gentleman, and wondered if I should try to kiss her on the cheek just so she could have the satisfaction of shoving me away. But she sat down across from me before I could make any move and looked around. She said, "I was here once before and it wasn't that great."

We ate some food. I pounded back a few more beers. Everything in my head had become complicated. I'd been afraid of something, which shamed me, and I couldn't remember exactly what, which made me mad and was probably her fault.

One of the things she said was, "How's work these days?"

"Why is that always the hot topic of conversation? Why is work the only thing that people ever ask about?"

She was eating this salad she'd ordered, the kitchen sink kind that has everything in it except a cheeseburger. "Okay. How's everything aside from work?"

I said something like great, everything was great, but I couldn't come up with any particulars.

After a minute she said, "Why don't you tell me what happened at work?"

I started out with the bullshit meeting, because that was the ordinary part, and then I told her about working myself into some kind of fit so I spaced out standing at the window, and then about the guy who did fall, the construction worker. "Can you imagine falling what, twenty-five, thirty feet, and maybe the ladder lands on top of you? I mean, what wouldn't you break?"

She was mopping up the last of her salad. I waited for her to say, that's terrible, or some other normal response. Instead she said, "It's like there's some part of you missing, isn't there?"

"Excuse me?" I said. Very polite, in case she had suddenly turned into a mentally disabled person.

"I mean, that's what it takes for you to notice another human being. A tragedy happening right under your nose."

We were on familiar ground here. My old girlfriends, this one and I guess all the others, were always accusing me of not noticing things. Their bad moods, which they called their needs.

Their absences, and occasionally, their presence. I said, "Yeah, but think of all the other great working-condition parts I have."

She wasn't impressed with my humor, but by now I was just trying to piss her off. I didn't much like it when she started in on the medley of her greatest hits, all the things that were wrong with me. Was it too much to ask, if you paid for somebody's dinner, you got a little pleasant company in return?

She said, "When's the last time we talked?"

I knew that this was a test, and that I wasn't going to do very well. "I don't know. Not that long ago. Two, three months."

"Six. I remember because my mother was in the hospital having heart bypass surgery."

"Oh yeah, I remember." I didn't. "How'd that turn out, how's she doing?"

"She died two weeks later."

"Oh man, that's terrible. I'm really sorry." And I was, I felt bad for not calling back, like she meant me to feel bad. But it also seemed like, excuse the pun, overkill, using a dead mom to beat me up. I mean, I never even met her mother.

She said, "You never called about my mother, but some gruesome accident has you all excited. Excuse me if I'm not impressed."

"And here I was sure you would be," I said, sarcastic again. I couldn't win, she wasn't going to give me a break. Next time I'd be sure not to mention anything heartrending. She wouldn't understand, it was precisely *because* I didn't know the guy that it was so freakish. Like any of us could go that fast, zap, a bug hitting a bug zapper. Like it could happen to me! But what did she care? She was too caught up in her own head games. I never set out to make her, or anybody else, unhappy. More like, they had this idea of who they wanted me to be, then they blamed me for not living up to it.

I walked her out to her car. And I admit it, I tried to get something going. Is that so terrible? Does anybody look down on birds or bees or monkeys or whatever, just for doing what comes naturally? And believe it or not, it was my way of trying to make it up to her, apologizing for the dead mom and everything. Sometimes it really does work that way, making love: you get past all the bad history and hard words and you're happy with each other again. Anyway, it was what I had to offer just then.

Of course she wasn't having any of it. "Thanks for dinner," she said, once she'd pried herself loose from my unwelcome advances. "I hope that one day you decide to upgrade to actual human status."

Yeah, and she could just bite the back of my knee. I went home and fell asleep on the couch without taking my clothes off. The next morning I woke up unfit for duty. It felt like my skin shrank a size overnight, like my tongue had warts on it. It was truly ugly. But there was no calling in sick these days, not unless you wanted some gimlet-eyed supervisor coming around and expressing fake concern for your health once you got back. You had to figure they all knew the symptoms of brown bottle flu.

So I showered. Applied caffeine. Et cetera. Steph was already at her desk when I got off the elevator. "Mattie, you look terrible."

"And top of the morning to you too." Talking made my teeth hurt.

I told Steph I was probably coming down with something, and she knocked herself out fetching me vitamin C, throat lozenges, hot tea. She thinks that all I really need is the love of a good woman.

When I got to my work area, I looked over the wall for Brian, but he wasn't there. I figured he was in the john or something. I opened my computer and stared at the screen. It was like staring at a goldfish in a bowl and waiting for the fish to do something.

I had my choice of rotten thoughts this morning, except I didn't want to be thinking about anything. Last night had been a total disaster. Next time I wanted cheering up, I'd call one of my old drinking buddies, not that I'd done that in awhile. I wasn't even sure I had their numbers anymore. Well, anyway, I'd learned my lesson. No more sniffing around girls when I was at a low point. You should only take them on when you were primed and ready, like going on safari.

I did a little bit of feeble work. The hands of clocks moved backward. I think I slept some, right there in my chair. Then a wad of paper hit me between the eyes. Brian had thrown a note over the partition. It said, "Meet me at noon at Subway. Tell no one."

I wasn't in the mood for Brian's fun and games, but by then I was hungry. I got there first and ordered a sub with a lot of mayo and a lot of bacon. It sounds bad but trust me, your hangover craves it. When Brian showed up he said, "You look like, I don't know, a hit-and-run victim maybe." He got his sandwich and sat down. "Guess what Brickhouse did to me." Brickhouse was our group leader's boss, and serious asshole.

"Invited you home to do his wife."

Brian held up one finger while he worked on a corner of his meatball sub. "Put me on probation," he said, his mouth still half-full.

"You're kidding." Brickhouse putting you on probation was like Darth Vader putting you on probation. "How come?"

"They're using some new point system. It's not real clear. I think you get points for poor telephone manners. For using too many office supplies. Not returning a salute. Liking dogs instead of cats. They're making it up as they go along."

I didn't know what to say. If I was Brian, I'd probably start sending my résumé out.

Brian said, "So, I just wanted you to know, if I don't hang out with you like I used to, goof around, it's because I'm trying to save my ass."

"Oh sure. Jeez." I shook my head, commiserating. Brian looked sort of serious. I guess he really was worried. "But hey, worst comes to worst, there's other jobs, right? When one door closes, another opens."

"Yeah, that's what they say."

"People with our skills, we've got it made. We're like the top of the food chain."

I was just giving him shit, trying to screw around like we always did. We didn't have any skills. He didn't even crack a smile. He said, "No, man, we're like, the bottom."

"Duh?"

"We can't do squat that's really useful. Can't grow our own food or hunt for it, or build a shelter, or make our own clothes. Just think about shoes. What the hell would you do for shoes? We couldn't keep ourselves alive for a week if they turned us loose in the woods."

"Then it's a good thing this ain't the woods," I said. I didn't know what his deal was. He was tripping.

We finished our sandwiches. It wasn't like Brian to be so

uptight about work. He was always the one who had the big bad attitude, even more than me, and I wondered what was up with him. But I didn't ask, in case it was something I'd be embarrassed to find out, like, he needed the health insurance because he had AIDS.

We went back to the office. I got through the day, but not in any fashion I'd brag about. The rest of the week I just did normal stuff, watched TV after work, cooked up some pork barbeque that turned out great. People always act surprised when I tell them I can actually cook, like they think I live on cold pizza with bits of the box stuck to the crust. Work was pretty boring since Brian really did turn into Mr. No Fun. I hardly ever saw him, and I missed things like him hoisting a little skull-and-crossbones flag above his desk, or texting me during meetings with comments about the group leader's poor wardrobe choices. Was I supposed to be the bad influence, or was he? It was probably a toss-up.

Meanwhile, the building across the street got taller. It did that from time to time, had some kind of growth spurt. It was easier to see what they were doing now. A few stories down, there were walls and windows, and you could see the workers walking around in there. They were putting in the plumbing and electrical and heating and air-conditioning, all the things that make a building a building. Actual skills. Brian was probably right about us, we were pretty useless when it came to practical, regular-guy knowledge. I couldn't so much as rewire a lamp. If my car didn't start, I called a mechanic. I bet the guys across the street had whole garages full of automotive tools.

I tried to think positive. I had to believe there was something I was good at that maybe nobody else was. I took a quick inventory: music arts sports, nope nope nope. Academic achievement, back in the day, better not go there. Big financial success, still coming up craps.

It was getting to me, and I felt, no lie, pretty dismal. Maybe that's why I let Steph talk me into going out after work. Happy hour, she said. I didn't think I could get all the way to happy, but crawling into a big glass of alcohol sounded like just the thing.

Of course Steph acted like it was a date. I saw that right away. She steered us into this fancy place, little tables, low lights, a piano playing lush cocktail music. She probably wanted to be able to brag to her girlfriends about it. And here I'd been thinking sports bar.

Never mind. I made the best of it. I paid for our expensive drinks and watched Steph wiggle around in her chair trying to see if anybody she knew was there. "Nice place," I said, being totally sarcastic, but of course she didn't get it. "Very uptown."

"Oh yeah, it's great." She babbled on for awhile and I smiled and nodded. Steph is one of those girls who dresses kind of slutty but really, it's just a fashion thing. There were times when she pushed the envelope for business clothes, and today was one of them. She had on a corset-type top, and I guess there was a jacket over it for the office, but now that was gone and we had the tits-on-a-plate effect. Who was I to complain about that, it's not like I find the view offensive or anything. But that's our Steph. Always trying a little too hard.

We talked about work for a while. Exciting. I hit the bottom of my glass. I started shifting my weight around, getting ready to pick up and leave, but before I could, Steph's waving money at the waitress and we have two more drinks. "Oh relax,

Mattie. You aren't some old fossil who objects to women paying for things, are you?"

"No," I said truthfully. "I just don't want to get too sauced and spend tomorrow at my desk with Apache mouth."

She hit me on the arm. "You are seriously the funniest guy I know."

"Thanks." My elbow had cracked against the table where she shoved me and I was trying to rub it without her noticing.

"Deirdre's always saying how funny you are. Deirdre in the processing department," she prompted me, because I was drawing a blank.

"Oh, Deirdre," I said, still not knowing who the hell she was talking about.

"She thinks you're hot." A pause, where I guess I was supposed to react, but nothing came to me. "So what do you think of her?"

"Honestly, she never crosses my mind."

Steph sat back, looking pleased. I guess there was some kind of girl war going on that I wasn't aware of. Whatever.

I got up to go to the john and when I got back, there was silverware on the table, and napkins folded into shapes, and a couple of plates. "I got some appetizers," Steph said. "In case you were hungry."

I see where we're headed here, down your basic slippery slope, but I decide to play along with it, at least for a little while. Be Steph's trophy date. In her mind, I mean. It wasn't like I had other big plans for the night. And I have to say, my bad mood was long gone. She bought the appetizers and I bought the next round of drinks. Then she wanted some ice cream drink with a stupid name and I bought that for her too.

"Bottoms up!" she said. "Arrr!" We were talking pirate talk.

"Gold doubloons for your pantaloons." I don't know where I came up with that one. It started her off on a championship giggle fit. I was afraid she'd squeeze herself right out of her top.

Here's where things start to get fuzzy. I guess we had some more drinks, and since we were having such a good time, we decided to leave the fancy bar and go somewhere more pirate-like. I threw a bunch of money on the table. It was probably enough, and anyway I'm sure they were glad to get rid of us by then. We staggered out on the sidewalk and the world was a hilarious place.

Steph said she lived just a few streets over and we could chill there, she had stuff to drink. I didn't mind the idea of not spending more money and besides, I was losing altitude fast. I wasn't sure I could make it all the way home just yet. Of course I should have seen a big crane arm swinging my way. Should have felt that ladder rocking. What can I say, I was drunk? I mean I was, but so is every other poor slob who ends up standing in front of a judge.

Steph's place was okay. She liked IKEA. She liked stuffed animals. Do I have to say anything else? She had a roommate but the roommate wasn't around. Right away I had to excuse myself to the restroom and that was a little weird, being in this girl bathroom with makeup and worse spread all over it. I came out and flopped on the sofa and Steph brought me a beer I didn't much want by then, and she sat down next to me. It's not like there was a big choice of places to sit, but I was reminded that I didn't really know Steph all that well. She'd put on some music and I nodded off listening to it.

I woke up because Steph was wedged right under my arm and it was kind of uncomfortable. I tried to work my arm free and she must have misunderstood the gesture, because she started nudging up against me, kissing my neck.

Now I'm getting actively concerned. I patted her head, pat pat pat. Friendly, not encouraging. I was embarrassed for her. Girls shouldn't come on like that. "Hey matey," I said in my cheeriest voice. "I have to be shoving off."

"Naaww." She wasn't as drunk as she was making herself out to be. Don't ask me how I knew that, but I did. "You gotta stay an be a pirate."

"Not a good idea," I said, in a burst of brilliant thinking. I was trying not to panic. I made a sudden move, designed to detach Steph from my neck, where I swear, she was trying to give me a hickey. I knocked her off balance and she slid all the way off the sofa and landed bump on her ass.

What she did then was grab on to my knees. "Whoa," I said, keeping it all light and easy, just two old pirates messing around. Avast. Shiver me timbers.

I'd like to say, *before I knew it she was giving me a blow job*, but who's going to believe that. Here's the truth: I froze. Like when people see a train or a charging lion coming straight at them and they can't move to save themselves? Something like that. I just couldn't fathom it at first, why she was pulling at my belt and zipper.

Am I saying she raped me? No, but pretty close, and if you're thinking heh, heh, bet you enjoyed it once she got going, yes and no. For one thing I seriously had to pee again by then, ask me how good that felt. And then there was the whole bizarre, bad dream part of it, I'm in some place where I've never been, and the music's too loud, and there's this girl pumping away between my legs where I never expected her to be, did I say bad dream? Christ, it was a nightmare.

It just kept getting worse and worse. I grabbed her shoulders and tried to pry her loose, but she was on a mission, and I was actually afraid she might hurt me, you know, do serious, sexual-function damage if I made a wrong move. By now I had to piss so bad I was practically crying, there was no getting around that to any successful conclusion, she was going to keep going until my dick fell off. Which is why, when my cell phone rang, I answered it.

The phone was in my jacket pocket. I didn't think about it. I didn't even look to see who it was. "Hello?"

It was this guy I know, though it took me a while to realize who it was. He said, "Hey, Matthew! What up?"

"Not much." Trying to sound, what, nonchalant.

"Yeah, same old same old."

"You know it."

"Talk to Daniels lately?"

"No, what about him?"

All this time Steph was keeping on with the chore, like she wasn't going to let a little thing like a third-party conversation stop her, but the guy on the phone was still talking, telling me a story about the other guy, and every so often I said "Uh huh," or "Sure," and finally she stopped abusing me, thank God. I kept my eyes on the ceiling, but I could feel her sitting back and watching me.

"Mattie," she said. "What are you doing?"

"Really," I said into the phone. "No shit."

Steph got up and ran into her bedroom and slammed the door. I have to admit, I stayed on the phone a little while longer, then I have to admit the first thing I did was duck walk into the john, my fly still open, and thanked God I'd lived long enough to take a piss.

I straightened myself up as best I could. I was trying not to look at all the crap in the bathroom. I'm not one of those people who go through medicine cabinets; honestly, I'd rather not know people's private business. But I couldn't help noticing this huge tube with For Facial Use on it. I turned it over and it was hair remover, which gave me all these unpleasant thoughts like, maybe she was really a wolverine or something.

When I came out I could hear Steph in her bedroom, crying. I knocked on the door. "Hey, Steph?"

"Oh God."

"Steph, I should probably get going."

"I'm going to kill myself!" She was still blubbering and her nose was all stuffed up: *Ib going to kill byself.*

"Come on," I said. "Don't talk like that."

"You hate me!"

"No, come on. I don't hate you. I think you're a really nice girl."

She didn't say anything else, just more of the blubbering, pretty loud now. I didn't think the door was locked. Maybe she wanted me to go in there. But I didn't see how that was going to make anything better in the long run. "Hey," I said, practically shouting to make myself heard. "Take care of yourself. You're a peach. See you tomorrow."

I don't even know what time it was, pretty late, because the streets were all dark and quiet. I got myself home and pulled the covers over my head and I slept like a baby. Woke up feeling not as bad as I might have expected, aside from a little souvenir dick soreness. But at least I woke up alone.

Of course I was a little nervous about seeing Steph at work. I decided the best course would be to act like nothing had happened. Be absolutely normal, and pretty soon things would be normal again.

Except Steph wasn't there. Usually she was at her desk all bright and shiny early. I guess she needed a little time to pull herself together. I didn't seriously think she'd killed herself or anything. Girls are always saying things like that to get attention, and anyway, she had a roommate.

Meanwhile, I had a new worry. There was an email waiting for me. The group leader wanted to see me at my earliest convenience, which would be now.

I started toting up all the things they could hang me for. Nothing big, but they didn't need big once they had it in for you. Hell, they didn't even need real.

I chewed some peppermint gum in case there was any stink on me. No use putting it off. I set out on the death march that led to the group leader's office. She had an actual office with a door, probably so no one could hear your screams. You had to go through a long corridor to get there, lit with the same godawful fluorescent lights, except these were half-burned out and making fire hazard noises. Somebody was headed toward me coming the other way, but because of the freaky lights I didn't recognize Brian until he was really close.

"Hey man," I said. "What's going on in there?" Because he couldn't have come from anywhere else.

He muttered something and I swear he tried to walk right past me, but I wouldn't let him. "Hey," I said again. "Talk to me."

Brian just stared at, I was going to say, his shoes, except I just then noticed he was barefoot. "Man, what did they do to you?"

"Nothing," he said. He could have used a shave. "Look, no offense, I have to get back to work."

I just stood there watching him. The door behind me opened. "Matthew?" the group leader said in her happy voice, like it was time for milk and cookies.

I put on a smile and marched inside. The group leader was sitting behind her desk, and Brickhouse, the old horror, was there too, looking like a toad in a business suit. There was a window behind them but they had it all covered over with curtains. Now that was just sad. "Good morning, Matthew," the group leader said. "We're conducting some training exercises and we hoped you'd help us out."

Like I had any choice. "Sure. Happy to help." They waved me to a chair facing them and I sat. Still smiling. The important thing was not to show fear.

The group leader said, "If we could ask you to watch the screen." She was wearing a giant pink dress. I mean, we're talking tent.

I hadn't noticed the computer setup a little to one side. I hitched my chair toward it.

"We're going to show you a series of images and we'd like you to indicate a response to them, positive or negative, by moving either forward or back."

Well okay. That didn't sound so hard. There was a keyboard and a joystick. I gave it a few test moves. Things started off easy. Pictures of kittens, daisies, chocolate chip cookies, forward. Dead fish, car wreck, nuclear holocaust, back. Brickhouse still hadn't said anything, just watched me out of the corner of his puffy toad eyes. He creeped me out. I couldn't believe they were spending time on something so simpleminded, but then, this was the same outfit that had us play rock, paper, scissors as a leadership exercise. Sunset on the beach, good. Starving African children, bad.

The screen went blank and I eased off the joystick. The group leader said, "Thank you. Now that we've established a baseline, we can move on. We're interested, Matthew, in questions of incentive and motivation. That is, how they optimize, or hinder, employee performance. For this next series, the goal is to complete the course as quickly as possible. Are you ready?"

I said that I was. The screen brightened and one of those highway scenes appeared, like a video game or in driver's ed. There was little red car, that was me, idling at the start of the track. Then it started moving. I set a good speed, steering wide around the curves. A duck with her ducklings was crossing the road and I slowed down. Then a lady pushing a baby carriage jumped into the lane and it took some fancy braking to get past her. Other cars cut me off and I had to hang back. A clanging railroad signal made me stop entirely and wait.

Over the computer's sound effects, its zooming and squealing, I heard Brickhouse talking to the group leader. "... average ... already knew ... rather limited."

Oh yeah? Talk about incentive. Hatred coursed through my blood like gasoline. They wanted fast, I'd give them fast. I bore down on the joystick with a heavy hand. I sideswiped a school bus. I mowed down a puppy. I took on a speeding semi and forced him off the road. Pedestrians threw up their hands and vanished beneath my wheels.

Sweat was flying from me. My hands shook. My teeth were

bared and I wouldn't have been surprised to find some kind of virtual bug stuck in them. I mean, I was into it. I was almost disappointed when the road ended at a big red Stop sign. It seemed a little anticlimactic.

The computer sounds ceased, and the screen went blank. The room was silent. Then the group leader said, "Thank you, Matthew. Give us a moment, please."

I was still breathing hard. My upper lip twitched. Of course it had been part of their plan, pushing me to some kind of edge. Everything was part of one big experiment, which was still going on. I should have seen it from the start. This was how they ran things. These people just like screwing with you. You had to put up with so much shit to get your food pellet.

Brickhouse raised his evil head and blinked at me. "Room for improvement, Matthew. Definitely room for improvement."

I nodded. It wasn't like I expected them to say anything positive.

"We're going to be doing some belt tightening, Matthew. It's come down to that. Tough times call for tough choices."

Here it came. From out of nowhere I remembered something I'd read once, that if you were going to have your head cut off, you should relax your neck muscles so it wouldn't hurt so much. I don't remember how you were supposed to do that.

Brickhouse said, "And as one component of our decision-making process, we're soliciting peer reviews. Entirely confidential. We expect your absolute candor." Brickhouse stopped and fixed me with one of his favorite nasty looks that he probably practiced in a mirror. After you saw it a few dozen times, your sphincter didn't automatically clench. "Tell us what we need to know about Brian."

That was when it all started to make beautiful sense to me. The thing I was so good at, my special skill. I was a genius at self-preservation. I would do whatever it took. I guess they knew that now. I had my eyes on the prize, which was me. You could even say I was a triumph of natural selection.

And so I made a point of hesitating, and looking reluctant, like the truth was being dragged out of me in spite of myself. I said, "Actually, I've been a little worried about Brian."

Afterward, I walked back to my work area. Steph still hadn't come in. Brian wasn't anywhere either. I did another lap around the place, just to make sure. I knew I was going to have to say something to him and I wanted to get it over with. But it looked like that was going to be put off until tomorrow, or maybe never.

I stopped at the window. The construction guys were going at it, all busy-looking, as industrious as hell. Another week or so and they'd be up to where we could wave. I wasn't envious of them anymore. Let them knock themselves out. Let them die a bug's death. Once they were through, it would be people like me moving in, drinking our coffee, sitting in the nice chairs, taking advantage of everything they'd built for us.

I went out for my lunch break, and on the way back I decided to call my old girlfriend, the one who didn't like me very much. I was full of confidence. I knew exactly how to get things right between us, make it work out the way I wanted.

The phone rang and rang. "Who's this?" she demanded, once she finally picked up.

"It's me," I said. "Mr. Rat."

Little Brown Bird

The people across the alley were spending their Saturday morning sitting in the bed of their pickup truck. The man, the woman, the three children—it was difficult to think of them as a family—had emerged from their squat little house and climbed into the truck more than an hour ago. And there they had stayed, as if this were a new amusement, the truck itself a destination. Their backyard was scattered with toys, with tricycles, wagons, and plastic items in ugly, cartoon colors: a playhouse, an oversized baseball bat, a basketball hoop on a stand, different broken-looking odds and ends of games. But these had been abandoned in place when the children lost interest in them. Beate thought that the truck was probably a better idea, if only because it was more durable. From time to time the two youngest children stood up and stamped on the truck bed, making satisfying metal noises, or ran from side to side, trailing their hands along the rails. She couldn't hear anything they were saying from her second-floor window. What did such people say among themselves? She had no power to imagine them.

As if it was any of her business! Such a snoopy, idle old woman she was becoming.

Downstairs, her husband made his racket. Wood ripped and groaned. A saw started up, then stopped in mid-whine. Every so often something heavy collided, or dropped, and Beate waited for the noise to begin again so as to reassure herself he had not had a heart attack. He was rebuilding the front door and entryway, installing new molding and etched-glass side panels. He had been remodeling the house in one way or another for the last five years. She had lived through the dismantled staircase, the floors stripped down to their joists, ceilings peeled away to the rafters, drywall dust, dishes washed in the bathtub, rooms navigated by flashlight, ladders tangling her feet when she went down to do the laundry. Always there were heaps of debris and supplies, his scattered tools. Someday, he said, they would want to sell the house and move on. The upgrades would make a huge difference in the asking price, and who could argue with that?

But this room was hers, her sewing room, and he was not allowed to interfere with it. Here was her cutting table, the big Bernina sewing machine, her quilting frame, the thread caddy, the cupboard set aside for knitting, the dressmaker form her children had long ago nicknamed Miss Swanky. Here she had good light and a comfortable chair, some framed prints on the walls, a radio for company. Here she spent her time, aside from house chores, and the eating and sleeping that too often felt like chores. She could close the door on the infernal noise and destruction her husband was intent on making, and if that was what the two of them had come to, each of them retreating into their separate spheres, well, they were used to each other, they didn't fuss or argue, they were able to talk about normal things. There were worse marriages. You heard about them all the time.

She was working on a quilt of special complexity and magnificence, twelve appliqué blocks, each with a different pattern, pieced together, then bordered and bound and quilted. Three of the blocks remained to be completed. The finished blocks were pinned onto the flannel sheet that served as her design wall, where she could study them and decide their final arrangement. Intricate wreaths and vases of flowers and leaves, perching birds and twining vines. Pretty cascades of weaving waving blossom, more lush and artful than anything found in nature.

Beate smoothed the fabric of the tenth block. Tracing and cutting and pressing the fabric pieces had been the difficult part. Now she was ready to place and stitch them onto the background fabric. It was slow, meticulous work of the kind she liked best. She moved between the pattern diagram and the fabric square, comparing the two. Little Brown Bird, the blocks were called. They had a prim, somewhat antique look. So in places she had changed the pattern, added free-form elements, and there was some anxiety about how these might turn out.

Her husband's noise rose and fell, rose and fell. She was used to it, it did not distract her. But the sound of a car horn honking in a cheery, shave-and-a-haircut rhythm made her put down her fabric and go to the window.

The children had climbed down from the truck bed and were playing a new game, tearing around the backyard in some giddy version of tag. The man sat behind the wheel and honked whenever one of them approached the truck, sending them shrieking and fleeing. The children's mother must have gone inside, though Beate wasn't certain. Her view allowed her to look straight down into their yard, although a portion of it was blocked by the fence line. She saw the smallest child, a girl of four or five, wearing her usual costume of grubby pink shirt and a pink tutu. There was a sturdy little boy who might have been a year older, and a long-legged girl who Beate guessed to be seven or eight. They ran and screamed and the truck's horn blared, egging them on.

All the commotion had roused Beate's ancient collie, Franklin; he stood at the fence, his plumy tail batting from side to side, adding his hoarse barking to the mix. She would have to go down and see to him. It was almost time to fix her husband's lunch anyway. She was glad the children seemed to be having one of their good days, since children like these, through no fault of their own, began life with two strikes against them.

She called Franklin inside from the back door and he came reluctantly, hoisting himself up the steps and settling into his bed in the corner of the kitchen. "Bad dog," Beate said, not meaning it. She cut bread from the bakery loaf, toasted it, layered on cheese, tomatoes, lettuce, the ham from their dinner two nights ago. For her own lunch she ate some of the ham and cheese without sitting down.

She went out to the front hallway, where her husband was rubbing sandpaper over a section of wood molding. The walls in the entryway were taken down to their studs and the floor was covered with a tarp. "Your lunch is ready," she said. "I'll leave it on the counter, unless you think you won't get to it for awhile."

"I'll eat in just a bit." He put the sandpaper down and looked around him for something he couldn't find.

"You look like you're making progress."

"Ah, it's slower than I'd like . . ."

Beate watched him lean the molding carefully upright, then

search the floor for whatever it was he needed. She went back to the kitchen, covered the sandwich with a clean dishtowel, and climbed the stairs again. There was never any point in interrupting him when he was in the middle of something, although she had always put her own work aside when someone needed her attention. She did not really resent it; it was just the difference between men and women.

She was pleased with the way the quilt was turning out. Leaf and vine, blossom and bud. The finished, splendid quilt already existed in her mind's eye. She would probably enter it in a quilter's show, but after that she was unsure what to do with it, beyond storing it away with so much else she'd made. The house was already full of her quilts and coverlets and fancy work. Beate supposed that her daughter would eventually inherit much of it. Her resolutely unmarried daughter who did her best not to live the kind of life that made space for heirloom quilts. But neither would her son and his family welcome it. Beate imagined the unpleasant daughter-in-law looking askance at the quilt and declaring it hopelessly old-fashioned, unsuitable, and what in the world were they supposed to do with it? Beate tried to be nice to the daughter-in-law for her grandsons' sake. They lived far enough away that Beate and her husband only saw the children on long-planned and exhausting holidays. That was not really the daughter-in-law's fault, even if other things might be.

The next day, Sunday, her husband was still busy making his virtuous and necessary mess. Beate took Franklin for a walk. He was not yet such an old dog that he didn't enjoy a walk. It was a fine summer's day, with a blue sky and sailing white clouds. She should take walks for her own health more often, just as she should watch her blood pressure, remember her vitamins, and so on. Had age always required such vigilance, such scolding self-reminders? Were you ever allowed to simply let yourself be?

Several of her neighbors were out doing yard chores, mowing and weeding and sweeping their walks clean of grass clippings. She and Franklin stopped to chat with them and to allow Franklin to flirt and have his ears scratched. At the end of the block she intended to double back, but it was so pleasant to be out—really, she could make more of an effort to exercise—that she decided to walk a little farther and cut through the alley to her back door.

The alley was a clear line of demarcation. If Beate and her husband went out of their front door, their neighborhood was handsome and prosperous, lined with houses much like their own: older, well-kept, some with remnants of Victorian fretwork or gables set off by careful paint jobs. The plantings in the yards, hydrangeas, lilacs, rose hedges, grew leggy over the years and were pruned back with the same sternness that maintained porch stairs and railings, roofs, window frames, foundations. Without this shared vigilance (her husband surely did his part!), the street might lapse into shabby decline.

The view from their back door was less encouraging. The district on the far side of the alley had once held small workingmen's cottages, built at the same time as their own house, although they had not fared as well. Here and there it was possible to make out one of the original structures beneath the added-on porches and carports and bedrooms. But most of them had given way to the cheaper kinds of rental property, duplexes and apartment "villages" and stand-alone houses, all of which had begun to fall apart as soon as they were occupied. Rust dripped from the gutters, siding buckled, front doors were kicked open until they sagged on their hinges. Beate supposed she was a snob. She was wary of her less fortunate neighbors, of their shoutings and honkings and slammings, their lives so unnecessarily on public display, the occasional police cruiser moving slowly along their streets.

The alley held refuse cans and prowling cats. Older children sometimes gathered there to smoke and set off firecrackers and get into other semicriminal mischief. But this was Sunday morning and no one else was about. Birds piped. Tree branches hung over the back fences, and the fences themselves were thickly covered with honeysuckle and orange trumpet vine. Sections of pavement gave way in places to gravel and the gravel to dirt. If you blurred your eyes, you could pretend it was a country lane. She thought about nursery rhymes, their landscape of milkmaids and stiles and shepherd boys. Then she tried to follow the thought back to its origin, why it had come to her. Things that were not what you wanted them to be. Something about what it must have really been like, country life all those centuries ago, the smells, the mud, the pestilence, not some jolly rhyme.

She was almost at her own house when a man stepped out from the gate opposite hers, and Franklin, startled, began to bark and tangle himself in his leash. She recognized the man as the tenant, the owner of the pickup truck, who presided over the household of children. She had never spoken to him but she knew him by sight. He was tall and thin and hunched, with a wedge of slick blond hair and a sharp-edged moustache. He did some sort of shift work, and Beate saw him most often in the late afternoon, arriving home and climbing out of the truck in his dark blue workshirt, the fabric sweated through along his back.

Since it was the weekend, he wore other clothes, a white

T-shirt and jeans. Whatever he had come out into the alley for, he stopped and waited while Beate tried to quiet Franklin. He was still barking and turning in circles, binding the leash around her knees. "Sorry," she said. "He just gets carried away."

"Here now," the man said to Franklin. His voice was oddly high and nasal. "You quit that."

"He's actually very friendly," Beate said. Franklin, excited by his own noise, was caught in an endless loop of ecstatic barking.

"He doesn't listen good, does he? You give him to me for a week and I'll teach him to mind."

"He's an old dog," Beate said, unsure whether she meant it as an explanation or an apology or a reproof. She got herself free of the leash, unlocked her own gate and pushed Franklin inside. She felt the man staring after her.

By the time she got Franklin into the house and settled, and went back upstairs, she couldn't see him from the window. The brief, unpleasant encounter stayed with her. How she disliked such men, who believed that the firm hand was the answer to everything, who regarded all forms of womanish coaxing or reassuring or soothing with contempt. There had been times in years past when she was forced to intervene with her own husband, who was not by nature at all angry or intemperate, persuade him that the crying, misbehaving child needed comfort rather than punishment.

She had to wonder about the children in the neighbor's house and how they fared in his surly company. But then, who else but he would have bought them all those toys?

For some months the man had been the only one living in the house, and Beate had paid him no particular attention. Then the woman had become an occasional presence, her old brown sedan parked next to the truck some nights, the two of them walking out together in the mornings and driving their separate ways. The woman was tiny, with the kind of narrow, childish figure that made it hard to believe she had borne children herself. She had long, heavy black hair that she usually piled on top of her head and covered with a scarf, making a peculiar stovepipe shape.

She did not like to think of herself as nosy, but it had been difficult not to notice.

At some point the two youngest children had begun spending time at the house, mostly on weekends. Their mother would arrive with them midmorning and drive them back after supper. Who minded them when she spent nights away from them? A grandmother, or maybe the children's father? Families these days were so distressed, so fragmented and badly rearranged, there was no telling. Then the woman and children had moved in, for all intents and purposes, and about that time the older girl began to make an appearance. A different car dropped her off and picked her up. School had still been in session then: it was likely that she had some living situation that was organized around school. Now that it was summer she had joined the others in the house across the alley, which scarcely seemed large enough for all of them.

"The mother almost never goes outside," Beate told her husband that night at supper. He didn't know who she meant, and she had to explain. "Don't you think that's odd? Sometimes she sits in her car and talks on her phone. Talks and talks. And sometimes it's just the two little ones out there by themselves, and they're simply too young to be without supervision."

Her husband took another bite of his beef with horseradish

sauce, chewed and swallowed it down before he answered. "Sounds as if you're doing a pretty good job of supervising them."

"Oh, thank you." She only pretended to be offended. "I just wonder what she does in that house all day. Watches television, most likely."

"Maybe she sews," her husband said, another joke at her expense, but still nothing she had to take seriously. He was in a good mood because his work was going well.

Whatever misgivings Beate had about the man, it was true that he was the one who spent more time with the children, at least, in organized outdoor play. He'd come home from work, go inside briefly, then come back out to start tricycle races in the driveway, or pitch a foam baseball for the children to swing at. Whenever they connected and the ball went airborne, he led the cheering as the child ran imaginary bases. She really was a terrible snob. Why couldn't she give the man some credit? People did the best they could.

Her husband still went to his office during the week. Someday soon he would retire for good, and there would be no peace or quiet under her roof. But for now she could enjoy having the freedom of the house. She lingered in the kitchen after the breakfast dishes were done, reading a magazine.

Once again it was the dog's barking that interrupted her. She rose and went to the back door. He was standing on his hind legs, his front paws against the fence. It was a six-foot board fence but there were cracks in it, and someone in the alley was manipulating a long twig through one of them, wiggling it back and forth.

Beate went out to him, shushed him, unlocked the gate and opened it wide enough to see out. It was the girl from across the alley, the older child, her face pressed up to the boards while she poked at Franklin with the twig.

"Honey," Beate said, and the girl stopped and gazed up at her, open-mouthed. "Don't tease the dog. It's not good for him."

"I was just playing." She had a small, snub-nosed face, freckles, two wings of lank brown hair. She wore a cotton shirt and shorts, and her bare legs had a couple of scabs that looked like scratched mosquito bites.

"That may be, but it gets him upset, and he's too old to stand up like that."

The girl let the twig drop, as if pretending it had never really interested her, then scooped up a small white teddy bear from the ground beside her. "Want to buy my bear?"

"I don't think so."

"Two dollars." She wiggled it invitingly.

"No, I don't need a bear. Why are you trying to sell it?"

The girl didn't answer. She didn't seem shy, only disinclined to speak. She picked up the twig again and put it to work tracing lines in the dirt. "What's your name?" Beate asked.

"Kyra." She spoke without looking up.

"Well Kyra, it's nice to meet you. My name is Beate."

She did look up then. "That's not a name."

"Yes it is. You see, I was born in Germany and I came to this country when I was just a little girl."

The child looked dubious, as if Germany too might be something Beate had invented.

"How old are you?" Beate asked.

"Eight."

She looked small for eight. Thin little legs and arms. "I was only five when I came here. I had to learn a whole new language." She sensed Kyra wavering, reluctant to show any real enthusiasm but still loitering. "My dog is named Franklin. Would you like to pet him?"

Kyra said that she would, and Beate took hold of Franklin's collar and let him stick his long nose through the gate. Kyra touched his nose, then pulled her hand back. "See, he's a nice dog, you can play with him if you're gentle."

"Roger used to have a dog," Kyra informed her. "It was black. His name was Tweaker."

"Oh? Who's Roger?"

"My mom's boyfriend."

"I see. Is your mother home now?" Because surely the child should not be out in the alley by herself.

"Shelly's not my mom."

Beate paused a moment to process this. "Then where is your mother?"

"In Tennessee with Roger."

She was beginning to lose track of the names, but persevered. "Does Shelly live over there?"

"Yeah. She stays with my dad."

So the surly man was Kyra's father. "Who else stays in your dad's house?"

"Petey and Michelle."

Beate thought she might have sorted it out, finally, except for the possibly vexed question of Pete's and Michelle's paternity. "Well Kyra, it was very nice to meet you. Why don't you go back in your own yard now, so Shelly doesn't worry about you."

"Okay."

"Don't forget your bear," Beate reminded her, and Kyra

turned to pick it up before she opened the gate to her own yard, squeezed through and let it bang shut behind her.

Funny little creature. Not so much unmannerly—though eight was not too young for manners—just unwilling to put much effort into a conversation. But she was being unfair. Children that age were very much in their own worlds. And this little girl seemed to live pillar to post as it was, shifting between parents and whoever the parents' cotenants happened to be at any given moment. What could you expect?

That evening Beate's daughter called. She lived in a city that was nearly as far away as her son's but in the opposite direction. Her daughter was, as always, vague about how she spent her time, and with whom, and anything else that might allow for personal knowledge. But she was full of prodding questions about Beate. Was her mother still drinking coffee even after she had been advised not to? Was she still having trouble sleeping? Well no wonder. Was she getting out and doing things, seeing people, not just shutting herself inside with her sewing?

Beate asked what was wrong with sewing. "Nothing," her daughter said. "You just can't make it your whole life."

"It's not my whole life."

"You know what I mean."

"I'm sure I don't," said Beate, beginning to be sorry she'd answered the phone. There was a point when one's children began to bully and manage you for your own good, but surely she had not yet come to such a pass. What would her daughter know about her life these days, either in its entirety or its parts? What would anyone?

"You could do volunteer work," her relentless daughter

went on. "You could take a class at the community college or somewhere."

"What sort of class?"

"Whatever interests you. Music. Art. The Y here has a course in memoir writing. A lot of older people do that, write down their reminiscences. Even get them published."

"Since nobody ever wants to hear about them, I doubt anyone would read them."

"Never mind," her daughter said. "I think it would be nice if you had some kind of more social hobby, but never mind. Is Daddy there?"

Beate called her husband to the phone and hung up. She heard him talking for some time, although she couldn't make out what he said. Every so often he laughed. If she asked him later what they were talking about, he would say nothing, nothing in particular. Let them have their jokes and secrets. She would settle for being left out, as long as they didn't fuss over her.

She had been a good mother. She'd taught them Christmas carols, made pancakes in the shape of bunnies, checked their homework, taken them for vaccinations and eyeglasses and braces. Love measured out by the teaspoon, built up over years and years, a reservoir. Why did so little of it flow back her way?

Kyra returned the next day. This was not surprising. Beate figured she was a novelty, or perhaps Franklin was the real draw. When he started pawing and whining at the fence, Beate went outside, knowing what she'd find. "Hello?"

"Can I play with your dog?"

Beate opened the gate. Kyra had a red popsicle in one hand and was sucking on it. Her mouth and tongue were stained a startling cherry red. Not the sort of thing Beate would have given a child at nine-thirty in the morning. "Why don't you finish your popsicle and go ask Shelly if it's all right with her. And wash your face," she added.

She waited while the girl scooted across to her own yard, emerging a little while later without the popsicle, her mouth a rubbed-looking pink. "Did Shelly tell you it was all right to play here?" Kyra nodded. "Good, because you know you shouldn't go visit people you don't know without permission."

Beate stepped aside and Kyra entered. Franklin rushed to cover her with sloppy dog kisses. Kyra giggled. Beate found a couple of his old toys, a ball and a squeaky man. She sat on the stairs and watched them play, Kyra giving him detailed instructions, Franklin, uncomprehending, following along as best he could. After a while Beate got up and went into the kitchen, poured out orange juice into plastic glasses, and set out some cheese and crackers and apple slices on a plate. She called Kyra over the picnic table (Franklin needed a break by then), and the two of them ate their snack in the shade of the old linden tree. Kyra, once talking, chattered on in hectic fashion. She liked dogs and she liked horses. She was going to be in the second grade. Her teacher last year was Mrs. Singer and she was "all right." Petey and Michelle didn't go to school yet. She liked Petey but she didn't like Michelle but she wouldn't say why. Her mom sent her a postcard from Tennessee. It had a picture of a horse on it.

"Sometimes Petey hits me and I hit him back," she volunteered.

"Well that's not very nice. You shouldn't hit him."

"He hit me so I hit him and then I tied him to a chair."

This seemed unlikely, but Beate let it pass. "When is your mother coming back from Tennessee?"

"I don't know. Roger has a motorcycle. And two rodeo horses. And a million dollars."

"You like to make up stories, don't you? Will you live with your mother or your father when school starts?"

Again Kyra said she didn't know, and Beate didn't ask any more questions. After an hour, Beate sent her back across the alley. No one had called or come looking for her, but it was best to pretend that someone might be.

She returned the next morning. Beate was ready for her and had a note prepared: Would it be all right if Kyra visited at my house? I enjoy her company but would not wish to worry you.

At the bottom she signed her name and included her address and phone number. Beate sent her home with it and almost immediately Kyra was back. "OK" was written in scratchy blue ink at the bottom of the page.

This was probably the best you could hope for. Beate sat and watched Kyra and Franklin play, as before, and once that ran its course she told Kyra she had work to do, but that she could come inside and watch if she wished.

She did, and Beate led her upstairs to the sewing room. Kyra was transfixed by the dressmaker form. "What's that for?"

"If you're making clothes, you can fit them on her."

"What kind of clothes?"

"Anything you like. Pants, shirts, dresses."

Kyra looked uncomprehending. Beate realized that this was a new idea for her, that ordinary people made clothes, they didn't just come from a store. "Her name is Miss Swanky."

"What does swanky mean?"

"Fancy, like showing-off fancy."

Beate gave her a tour of the room and all its features, let her touch the skeins of yarn in their basket, run her hands over the rainbow spools of thread. She showed Kyra a picture of the appliqué border she had selected for the quilt, a pink and green pattern of stylized, trailing roses. "Do you see the little brown bird?"

Kyra shook her head. "Try again," Beate told her, and when Kyra spotted it, tucked into a green curlicue, she smiled her first full, unguarded smile. She might well grow up to be pretty. Up until now it had been difficult to say. "You see," Beate told her, "the bird was right there the whole time. You just had to look carefully. Would you like me to show you how to embroider? First let's go wash your hands."

Beate provided an embroidery hoop and a square of white muslin, showed her how to thread the embroidery floss and roll a fat knot at the end of it. She taught her how to make a crossstitch in yellow, then they picked red, Kyra's favorite, for blanket stitches, then blue for stem stitch, and pink for French knots. "You practice those for a while. When you are good enough, if you like, we will find a project for you."

She started in on her own work, one eye on Kyra in case she grew bored or frustrated. The light from the window lit her silky hair as she bent over the hoop, quiet for once, absorbed in pushing the needle in and out. Her thin, summer-brown legs were planted wide apart, her feet in their old plaid tennis shoes flat and splayed out. Still, she made a nice picture. A little girl learning to sew; what was more charming than that? "Let me see," Beate said after a while. "Very good job," she pronounced. "You can take it home with you and show everyone." If nothing else, she thought, the girl had learned how to thread a needle.

Beate fixed their lunch—chicken salad, bread and butter, milk—and again they ate it at the picnic table in the backyard.

Children's high, indistinct voices reached them from beyond the fence. The two younger ones must have been playing outside. Beate closed her eyes. Her childhood in Germany existed only as scraps of much-handled memories. There had been a cherry tree outside the front door and her father had lifted her up on his shoulders so that she was surrounded by the glowing fruit. There was a song they sang when they went to feed the ducks in the park: *Alle meine Entchen schwimmen auf dem See, schwimmen auf dem See, Köpfchen in das Wasser.* She had tipped over the blue bowl of sugar and her mother had been cross. How much was remembered, how much was lost? Who had she been, that long-ago girl child? Now that it was almost too late, she reached back, trying to reclaim her. Perhaps childhood was always a foreign country.

From across the alley one of the children, probably the little girl, raised her voice in a sudden, piercing shriek. Beate opened her eyes. It was time to send Kyra home.

She came again, not the next day, but the day after. And she did not appear on the weekends when her father was home and presumably keeping better track of her. But she visited often enough for the two of them to fall into a routine: the simple sewing tasks Beate set for her, Kyra's mile-a-minute observations on the people in her world ("Shelly has a rash between her toes"), the lunch eaten at the picnic table. She was a flighty little thing, Beate decided, but also inquisitive and anxious to please. She might have interests and aptitudes that would reveal themselves over time. All any child really needed was encouragement.

Beate told herself not to make the girl into a pet. There were not very many weeks left in the summer, and once school began, she might be reclaimed by the mother and the legendary Roger.

But say she stayed here, with her father. It might be possible for Beate to assume some place in her life. She would introduce herself to the adults in the house, make arrangements. Provide her with some of the supervision and attention she seemed to lack. Help with her schoolwork. And what a pleasure it would be to have a little girl in the house, teach her how to knit, how to bake cookies . . .

Here Beate stopped herself, since she was surely getting too far ahead of herself. And she had to wonder what Kyra herself wanted.

Beate began by asking her if she liked school, if she was looking forward to school starting up again. "Uh huh," Kyra said, unconvincingly.

Beate persisted. "And what do you like about school? Do you like reading stories? Spelling? Arithmetic?"

"Roger lets me ride his motorcycle."

"That sounds like fun." Giving up her attempts to steer the conversation.

"Yeah, and I got to put the gas in it."

Beate said that was a good thing to do. She couldn't help noticing that Kyra's own father was never mentioned with any similar enthusiasm. Then again, it would be hard to compete with a motorcycle.

She made a surprise for Kyra, a little sundress she stitched up out of red bandana fabric, red being Kyra's favorite color. She had to guess at the measurements if it was to be a surprise, but she put smocking across the front and made straps with adjustable buttons to allow for anything off in the sizing. It turned out well and was certainly more attractive than her stretched and faded play clothes.

"I have something for you," she told Kyra, the next time she came over. "Here you are."

She held it out but Kyra wouldn't take it from her. Something blank and dull settled over her face. "Would you like to see how you look in it?" Beate prompted.

"No."

"Kyra, if someone gives you a present, you should thank them."

Almost inaudible: "Thank you."

"Why don't you go into the bathroom and try it on?"

"I don't want to."

"All right, but why don't you want to?" Her feelings were rather hurt, although she was not really entitled to such feelings.

"I don't want to! You can't make me!"

"Kyra, I would not make you do anything you don't want to. I'll wrap the dress up and you can take it home with you." Quickly retreating, since what choice did she have? Maybe the girl didn't like wearing dresses. She wondered if it would ever be worn, or if it would end up shoved into the corner of a closet. Kyra left that day with the dress in a brown paper bag, the bag drooping from one hand. It had clearly been a mistake, but she had no idea why.

That night after dinner, she asked her husband if he thought there was an age when children became self-conscious about their appearance.

He looked up from the computer where he was researching his next grandiose project, a complete replacement of the house's heating system. The front entrance was still a bare and dispiriting mess, but he liked to think ahead. He seemed surprised that she would ask him such a question, as well he might, but who else did she have to talk to?

"I guess so. I couldn't say what age. Probably when some other little kid starts making fun of you."

"That starts young." It was how she had come to think of Kyra's near-tantrum about the dress: she had interpreted the gift as criticism. And she had hardly been wrong to do so. Was that why she didn't seem excited about school, because she was teased there? "Or maybe there's a phase when they aren't sure what they want to be, girls or boys, you know, pulled both ways . . ." Ride a motorcycle? Thread a needle? Her son when young had played with dolls. Her daughter, well, she had never had any use for normal girlhood.

"Who are you talking about, your little orphan friend?"

"She's hardly an orphan."

"All the more reason not to get involved in her affairs."

"There are parents and then there are parents," Beate said, but their conversation was at an end. How little comfort they were to each other. How many more years life might go on in this way, until one of them died and the other fell entirely silent.

She might have worried about Kyra staying away, but she reappeared the next morning just as before. Beate welcomed her inside. The new appliqué square was now finished and she pinned it to the design wall and asked Kyra to help her decide how to arrange them. "This one on top of this one on top of this one," Kyra declared. "Then this one and this one." Beate laughed and said that then it wouldn't be a quilt, only a long piece of cloth.

Their lunch that day was peanut butter and jelly sandwiches

and vanilla pudding. Franklin sat at their feet in the shade, panting. The weather had turned hazy hot. "You know, Kyra, I like your idea of making a long embroidered panel. A kind of tapestry. That could be my next project, you could help me." It wasn't even the skills themselves she wanted to teach the girl, but the principles of craftsmanship, the ethic of excellence, how doing a thing well could absorb and sustain you.

"My daddy sleeps in Michelle's bed."

Kyra held the last peanut butter and jelly square in one hand, though she seemed uninterested in eating it, and was intent on squeezing the filling out through the flattened edges of the bread.

"What did you say, Kyra?"

"Sometimes he does."

"Does what?"

Kyra drummed her heels against the bench. "Sleeps in her bed," she repeated, patiently. There was no sense that she felt she was communicating anything remarkable.

Beate felt her insides revolving. "Do you mean, when Michelle is sick or has nightmares?" Please God that there would be some such an explanation.

Kyra shrugged. "I guess so."

"And what does Shelly say about this?"

Another shrug. "I don't know."

"Finish your milk," Beate said automatically. She made herself sort through the different possibilities. Kyra was mistaken. Kyra was being untruthful, or exaggerating. Children often did, and certainly Kyra's statements did not always seem reliable. It was something ordinary and innocent. Bedtime stories. A child afraid of the dark.

She remembered something she'd once seen from her window, some time back, in the spring, before Kyra had come to live in the house across the alley. The man's truck had pulled into the driveway and he'd gotten out and lifted up the little girl in her soiled pink ballerina outfit. He'd carried her inside and they had not come out again. The woman's car had not been there.

None of this was evidence of anything. But once the thought entered your mind, it pulled other thoughts and suspicions along behind it. And all the toys, the backyard games the man arranged for them. What if he did it not to court and appease the woman, or because he genuinely liked children, what if the woman was just the excuse for him to gain access to the child?

Such things happened. She had no doubt. The close heat of the day bore down on her and she lifted her glass of ice water to her forehead. "Why did you want to tell me about your daddy sleeping in Michelle's bed?"

"I don't know."

"'I don't know' is not a good answer."

The girl said nothing, just picked at the piece of sandwich that was now so smeared and flattened as to be inedible.

"What does he do to Michelle?"

"Tickles her."

"And does Michelle like being tickled?"

"I have to go home now," Kyra announced. She put the sandwich back on the plate and hopped down from the bench.

What to think? What to do? She stood at the gate a long time after Kyra had disappeared across the alley. If it was an invention, a falsehood, a misunderstanding, it would be a catastrophe to set the ponderous machinery of the state in motion, police, social workers, the child welfare agency. Nor might they intervene on such a scant account. They would look at her and think her a meddler, a troublemaker, wonder why she didn't keep her nose on her own face.

Yet how easy it was to ignore or disbelieve a child, simply because it was the habit of adults to ignore and disbelieve children.

It was the weekend again. The man's pickup truck stayed in their driveway, and Kyra did not visit. Beate's husband returned to his attack on the front door and enveloped himself in sawdust and noise. Beate, frankly spying by now, kept watch from her window on the neighbor's backyard. But the weather had turned rainy, the children did not come out to play, and there was nothing to see.

Only this: there had been occasions when Kyra's father and the children's mother stood outside by themselves, talking. Beate could never hear them, or even see their faces clearly, but she knew the look of a couple who had serious things to say to each other, things best said away from the children. Now here they were again, out in the driveway in the mild drizzle. As always, the woman, Shelly, had her hair wrapped up in that peculiar unflattering way, as if she were hiding a length of pipe beneath her headscarf. They stayed there a long time. Should she even hope that it had to do with the little girl? What if Kyra had said something to someone else, what if the mother really had not known or noticed until now? It was possible, anything was possible, though God knows there were enough other reasons for any couple to have their difficulties.

On Monday morning the truck was gone by the time Beate woke and looked out her window. None of the children came out into the backyard, although the rain had cleared and the day was fresh and cool. Kyra did not visit. The woman's brown car left at some point, although when Beate looked again it had returned.

Things happened quickly after that. The truck stayed absent that day and the next day and the next. A car Beate had not seen before pulled into the driveway. A man got out and began loading cardboard boxes, laundry baskets, clothes on hangers into his trunk. The children's mother filled her own car also, with blankets, backpacks, children's jackets, paper sacks. Clearly some major dislocation was in progress.

As she watched, the two younger children were led and carried out to the brown car, the little girl clinging, the little boy dawdling, there was another driveway conference with the strange man, then both cars started up, backed out into the street, and were gone. The whole process had taken less than an hour.

At night she kept watch, and in the daylight hours she went from window to window, as if she might see Kyra in some unexpected place, the next street over or the far end of the alley. What would her father do to her if he suspected her of telling tales? Such men were unpredictable, possibly violent. The child might be in real danger. How high would you have to climb to see the whole city laid out beneath you, find the one small moving piece that was dear to you? How horrible people were, what an ugly blotched patchwork life made. What a lie a pretty picture in thread was when your own life was just as sad, as torn, as misshapen as anyone else's. . . . "What's the matter with you?" her husband asked, and she said, Nothing. Nothing was the matter. Turning her back to him in bed. She felt him hesitate, wondering whether to say more, then he settled into sleep.

On the third day, the pickup truck was back. Around midmorning the man emerged from the back door, hauling out pieces of furniture and wrestling them into the truck bed. Nightstands, mattresses, bed frames, chairs, a dismantled exercise machine of some sort. He squared the load and roped it in and drove off.

She made up her mind to go speak to him, ask him where Kyra was. Demand information, some way to get in touch with her. Surely he would be back, the house would hardly be empty. Perhaps this evening, when her husband could go with her. She would make him, he didn't have to be happy about it. There would be an advantage in having a man on hand.

But when the truck returned in the middle of the afternoon, she couldn't bring herself to wait. He might leave again for good, and then how she would reproach herself. What was she afraid of, anyway? So he was rude, unpleasant, perhaps worse, *a creep,* as her children used to say. Her children, anybody's child. She had a mother's heart. She would face him down.

It would have been easiest just to cross the alley—she was certain their gate was left unlocked—but walking through the yard might aggravate him, and why begin that way? She went the long way around, down to the end of her own block, then past the alley to the unfamiliar street with its line of battered mailboxes on posts, its feral-looking cats skulking under fences, its sagging front porches. She'd never seen Kyra's house from the front, and it took her a moment to recognize it. The driveway was unpaved. Grass had grown up in the center path between the tire tracks, then scorched and dried to yellow weeds. The house looked as if something heavy had once settled on it and knocked its every right angle askew. A ceramic wind chime was nailed to one of the porch supports. The front windows were covered over with blowsy curtains, or perhaps they were bed sheets serving as curtains.

Beate walked a little ways up the drive. The truck was pulled up to the back door. The man came out, dragging one end of a sofa. He guided it up a ramp to the truck bed, then shoved it into place from behind. He turned and stared at Beate. His face was dark red from exertion and his hair was damp.

She couldn't tell if he remembered her or not. "Hello," she said. "I saw that you were moving and I came to ask about Kyra."

"What about her?" Flat, belligerent. None of her business.

She had not rehearsed what to say. "I haven't seen her in awhile. I wanted to . . . I wondered if she was all right."

"She's fine."

He wasn't going to give her anything. Beate said, "Oh, is she with her mother?"

He made a barking sound, a laugh. "Not likely."

"And why's that?"

"There's a word that fits her mother. Her and them like her. But I won't say it. It's not for delicate ears."

It was his longest speech yet. It seemed to animate him to recall his grievances. Beate said, "I wanted to tell her good-bye."

"How about I tell her for you."

"No. That's not good enough."

"And why's that?"

"Because I don't trust you."

He seemed to find this funny. "Well it's a good thing you don't have to." He stepped to the back door. "Kyra! Get on out here!"

She came out slowly and loitered on the porch step. She wore a blue party dress made out of some stiff, glossy fabric, the cheapest kind of fancy garment. The skirt stood out unevenly, already draggled. Her old plaid sneakers had been replaced by new pink ones, the laces printed with red hearts.

"Hello, Kyra," Beate said, once she found her voice. Kyra gave no sign of recognition. She was absorbed in scratching some substance off the screen door.

"Come here," her father said, and she hopped down to stand next to him. He held out his hand and she took it. "Whose girl are you?"

"Daddy's."

"That's right."

"Where are you moving?" Beate asked. The sun beat down on the center of her head, a beam of pure heat.

"Someplace where the neighborhood watch ain't so busy."

"Kyra?" Beate bent down, trying to meet the girl's eye. "You remember where I live. You can always come visit me."

Her father picked her up and set her on the sofa in the truck bed. The horrible dress twisted around her, too tight beneath the arms. He said, "I guess it'll be awhile before that happens."

He was waiting for her to leave. She walked past them through the backyard and its broken, discarded toys, opened the gate and crossed the alley to her own house.

She sat in the kitchen until she heard the truck's doors slamming, its engine starting up. Then she climbed the stairs to her sewing room. She had two more blocks of her quilt to finish. After that there was the border to piece, with its roses and curving stems, the little brown bird that was there all along if only you knew to look for it.

Liberty Tax

We were broke, Bobby and me. Both separately and together, as a marital unit. It had happened without warning and without our consent. It had all taken place at a distance, in offices and institutions far from us. We had been notified by mail. We still had the house and the cars. We didn't seriously believe we'd lose the house and the cars, but what if belief was just one more thing that would fail us? Along with equities, interest rates, collateralized debt obligations, auction rate securities, bundled loans, and all the rest of the financial gimcrackery that had laid us, and so many others, low.

Bobby said, "We're upside down in the house."

"What? What are you talking about?"

Bobby took a hard swallow from his wineglass. We were still buying wine, although not of the same quality as before. "It means we owe more on the house than it's worth."

"I don't understand how that can be. The house is practically brand new."

"Every house in the neighborhood is worth less than it used to be. We bought at the top of the market and now the market's in the crapper." Bobby got up and fetched the wine bottle from the kitchen, set it down in the middle of the dining room table. I worried that the bottle might mar the wood finish, but maybe the table wasn't worth what it used to be either, and what would it matter. I was still confused about how something as big and solid as a house, a really nice, desirable house like ours, could spring a leak and start dribbling money.

"I love you, honey," I said to Bobby, and he said, "I love you too," and we kept saying it, often and at different times as we came to terms with our bewildering new condition. For love was meant to be both our anchor and our buoy in times of trouble.

There was still reason to be hopeful. We had each other, for whatever economic good that would do us. We were still young, although not quite as young as we had been. We were both employed, although our jobs too had been nibbled down at the edges and were not the jobs they used to be. We had been married four years and five months, and up until now, our life together had unrolled as smoothly as a bolt of cloth. Bobby was so handsome. Every once in a while I'd catch women looking at him with this lost expression, just poleaxed by the sight of him. And me, I kept myself up. I had a nice figure, everyone said so. I smiled a lot. At store clerks, strangers on the street, small children of the appealing sort. It knocked them for a loop. We made a sharp couple, a good-looking young couple with the world at our feet, and if that sounds prideful, just stick around. The world was setting us up for a fall.

We'd borrowed against the future because we thought we had one, and because the future was always supposed to be better. More brightly colored, new and improved. We felt entitled to it, although we could not have explained why. It was one more assumption that might not bear weight when tested. Maybe we were none of the things we thought we were: well-intentioned, generous, enterprising, fun. Maybe we were stupid.

It wasn't as if either of us had grown up with money, far from it. My dad was a union pipe fitter and he earned a good enough living when times were good and a lesser one when times were not. We didn't want, but there weren't any extras. My mom served up Tuna Surprise often enough that it was no surprise, and if you didn't like what was on your plate, you were told fine, more for the rest of us. Bobby and I got married in the Laborer's Hall and our reception was a potluck.

Bobby had it a lot tougher because his father was a famous deadbeat and ne'er-do-well, a Big Idea man whose ideas were all about how to get money without working. There was a scheme for marking up imported shrimp and selling them to restaurants, there was another for hawking overpriced and soon-to-be-defunct vacation packages, and other semilegal or outright criminal manipulations of wagers, loans, and skims. If I hadn't known the old man was dead, I'd suspect him of being a Wall Street genius these days. Anyway, Bobby grew up in the shadow of all this, the boom and the bust, the father's lurking, creepshow associates, the phone ringing in the middle of the night, the patched-together family life of a hustler.

So we were self-made, me and Bobby, because that was part of the future's promise, that you could make yourself up, or over. We'd worked hard, we'd latched on to jobs that we rode like a fast wave, up to a pretty decent living and then some. Of course our mistake was in not seeing it as a wave, with a break point coming after the swell. We thought it was just life, the way life was once you finally climbed up high enough to have a good view of it. Can you blame us for going a little giddy, well, yes, of course you can, but could you understand it?

The things we had spent money on! Furniture! Manicures! Orchids! An entire room full of video entertainments! Every service, commodity, and luxury item had been available to us, the resources of the planet spread out for us to browse. Now, of course, we cut way back. No more shopping-for-fun. We got rid of the cleaning service, we stopped looking at brochures for time shares. We packed our lunches, we ate dinner at home. We were stern with ourselves, and we took some actual pleasure in the process, like going on a rigorous diet. "At least I'm not a crook like my old man," Bobby said. "We'll get out of this pickle fair and square." I said of course we would. But it was hard not to think of the crooks and semicrooks who were making out so well these days, cashing in on the rest of us.

We canceled the health club membership and instead took long walks in the evening through our pretty, devalued neighborhood. We learned to read the signs of others' similar distress. Sometimes they were literal signs: For Sale. Price Reduced. Motivated Seller. Sometimes it was more subtle. A lawn grown ragged, a basketball hoop knocked askew and left to rust, or a long-empty bird feeder with an optimistic squirrel still grubbing around beneath it. Other people were in trouble too, we knew this from the television news, though it was not a topic for polite conversation. We were all diminished in our own eyes. We hoped to keep up what was left of appearances.

In November I came home from work to find Bobby in the breakfast nook, eating a bowl of cereal. "Hi there, how was your day?" I said, all cheery and casual, but it was as if I already knew. He never got home before I did.

Bobby didn't answer right away, just kept eating. The milk and the Sugar Frosted Flakes box were still on the table, and he was downright gobbling, working that spoon for all it was worth. He gave me the strangest look, like you'd get from a dog guarding its food, like I was going to grab the cereal bowl away from him, like he was ashamed of his own hunger.

"Babe," I said, "what is it, what's wrong? Will you stop eating for a minute?"

Finally he left off the spooning and the gobbling and wiped at his mouth with the back of his hand. "What do you think's wrong?"

"Oh." That was all I said.

"Four months' severance, outplacement service, and I can buy into health insurance for the next year. And it's nothing personal."

"Four months is pretty good," I said, already shifting gears, adjusting everything downward. "That's a reasonable arrangement."

Bobby still had that hungry dog look in his eye. He said, "Let's not try to be big about this just yet, huh? Let's just wallow."

"Sure, wallow away." I figured Bobby was entitled, that this was one of the unwritten rules of being fired, you got to behave as unreasonably and childishly as you wished, at least for a little while. But I would have appreciated it if he'd made some sort of an effort at being a grown-up. My job was now the only slender lifeline we had. And since it was a girl job, of course it paid less than his. We were going to be back to the land of Tuna Surprise if something didn't break our way. I knew it was the wrong time to bring up baby year.

We'd always said that once we'd been married five years,

we'd have a baby. Five years was supposed to be enough time to lay down a good financial foundation, also to get all the self-indulgence out of our systems, take the kind of exotic vacations that only childless people can. Belize! Fiji!

How firm a foundation? How many vacations were enough? Those had been important questions, but now we would have different questions, further calculations. And yet I was determined that a baby be something other than a budgeted purchase. You were supposed to want a baby in a different way than you wanted a Jacuzzi. Maybe we should just go for it, a reckless leap of faith. A throw of the cosmic dice. I didn't discuss any of this with Bobby. Like Mary in the Bible, I kept these things and pondered them in my heart.

We began noticing an increase in the kinds of ads and solicitations designed to separate us from our money in imaginative ways. This was a great time to invest in film production or purchase franchises in tortilla restaurants or mattress stores. Our vehicles were in need of extended warranties, we qualified for loans with special rates, we were invited to explore the untapped potential of overseas currency markets. We heard radio promotions telling us there were terrific opportunities to purchase foreclosed properties, a real buyers' market. And maybe it was, but as our loan payments continued their climb, as Bobby's résumé continued to languish unread at places that should have fought to hire him, we were less and less charmed by the notion that there were always ways to make even a bad business climate work for you.

We got through our downsized Christmas well enough. We couldn't stop noticing that there were fewer and fewer of those big gaudy energy-slurping light displays in the neighborhood.

"A little less holiday overkill isn't such a bad thing," I said. I was wrapping (sensible, thrifty) gifts for our families in off-brand paper. "There's so much excess and pressure and ostentation."

"Yeah. We could do like, Christmas on Walton's Mountain. Whittle presents for each other."

I gave him a quick glance, but he wasn't being snotty, just making a joke. He said, "You know, we didn't exactly have the big happy holidays when I was a kid. Some years we just skipped Christmas."

"Oh honey. That's so sad."

Bobby shrugged and picked up his Santa mug. We were using them for our coffee, in an effort to feel more festive. His wallowing phase was over and he was just low-grade depressed these days. I felt so bad for him, my handsome husband, the way you might feel bad for a beautiful golden retriever with a hurt paw. It was painful to see him make the circuit of the mailbox, the answering machine, the email account, with less and less expectation of any good news. It wasn't doing anything for our sex life, either, I can tell you.

Of course I was patient. Of course I was understanding. I wasn't some horrible accusing-type person and I didn't intend to become one. I kept taking my birth control pills (no matter how seldom they might be required), because I wasn't going to trick us into a baby. Even though a baby would be the next best thing to going back in time, find that little boy Bobby had been and spoil him like crazy, give him all the Christmas presents he'd ever wanted.

In January I said, "We could go somewhere else. Sell the house, eat the loss, move on."

Bobby propped himself up on one elbow from his spot on the couch. He was watching a basketball game, which was a normal enough Sunday afternoon thing to do. I never nagged him about how he spent his downtime, since I understood this would be demoralizing. The TV was never on when I got home from work, although once, picking up something that had been left on top, I couldn't help noticing that it was still warm. Bobby said, "Go where? And do what, exactly, once we get there?"

"Oh I don't know. Gosh. Live on the ocean, run fishing boat charters. Go to Maine and open a bed and breakfast. Any old thing."

"Be our own bosses. Dance to our own tune."

"That's the idea. Sure."

Bobby raised his chin to look out the den window at the backyard, which at this time of year wasn't a view to lift up your heart. Sad, sad brown grass, bare and undersized trees that we'd only recently installed. "Babe, I don't think the world lets you operate that way anymore. They got all the screws tightened down. You can't make a move without somebody lighting on you, crossing you up. Everything you've ever done is in a computer somewhere, ready to be used against you. All your bad debt and preexisting conditions and anything you ever signed off on. We're like damned cows or pigs, they figure out how much profit per pound they can get out of you. Pot roast and sausage and boil up the hooves for glue."

"That's putting it a little strongly," I said, trying to hide my alarm. "Who's 'they' anyway?"

But Bobby was through with his talking. He turned off the TV and said he was going out for awhile. I didn't ask him where. The truth was, it was a relief not to have him underfoot every minute.

This was about the time I began to worry about the Liberty Income Tax guys. I saw them every year, but only now did they strike me as depressing and sinister. Liberty Tax is one of those franchises, a little shop that sets up in strip malls and does a brisk walk-in business from people too confused to do their own returns. Their big gimmick is hiring guys who dress up as the Statue of Liberty and Uncle Sam to walk back and forth on the sidewalk, waving potential customers inside. It was sad, I tell you, really corny, plus they were out in all weathers, toting signs and jumping around to keep warm. The Statue of Liberty was an especially pitiful getup, a kind of green plastic shower curtain with an inflatable spiked crown that was always in the process of deflating and flopping over.

They had a shop practically across the street from us, at the entrance to our subdivision, so that I saw them every time I came or went. I'd never paid much attention to them, except a brief, occasional opinion that it was a pretty annoying, tacky idea, then to reconsider that it might still be smart advertising for those exact same reasons. Now I wondered about the Liberty Tax guys, what kind of down-and-out person you'd have to be to hire on for such a stunt. Bums, I'd always thought, when I'd thought about them at all, bums who'd look on it as a way to get a day's drinking money. They were often pretty rough-looking characters, what you could see of them underneath their costumes. One of the Statue of Liberty guys in particular just plodded along scowling, like he dared somebody to mock him, like he'd lived a life that equipped him to make people spit teeth. But what if they were the normal unemployed and hard-up people like our neighbors who had fallen on hard times? What if that was me, Miss Liberty, and Bobby, Uncle Sam, all pride gone, whooping it up out there on the sidewalk?

Of course that was just where worry could bring you to, just such a foolish point. I don't want to give the impression that I lost sleep over it or considered it an actual possibility. More like a symptom of my general dread. I spent my days at work trying to be the essential, non-fireable employee, then I came home to the limited good cheer that Bobby afforded. And the bad news of the world went on and on, with one thing or another closing down, broke, or defaulted. The stock market might go up for awhile—we still had some investments—but really, it was like one of those cartoon characters, Wylie Coyote, maybe, climbing a ladder, while the Road Runner chopped off the legs. It was as if the entire country had been turned upside down and shaken. There was something creepy about Uncle Sam and Miss Liberty prancing around, inviting you to drop what remained of your money. Come on in! Line up, sign up, we got one more bad investment for you: the American way of life!

By now we were actively trading down. I bought groceries at the discount store, shuffling through coupons and loading up on the specials. I missed my old, ridiculously precious food store, with its fresh gnocchi and caramels with sea salt and stuffed chicken breasts, its uncrowded aisles and cheerful young clerks. Everybody at the discount grocery seemed blighted somehow. They had withered arms, or a walleye, or they overflowed the motorized carts they used to chug around the aisles. Oh, I know that wasn't literally true, it was just me being a snob and feeling sorry for myself, and anyway, who was I to hold myself above anyone? Hadn't I grown up on peanut butter and saltines and cans of fruit cocktail, the kind with gooseberries and maraschino cherries and those pale, pale, almost unidentifiable bits of pear?

I didn't want to believe that who you were was a matter of money, its presence or its lack. But maybe it was truer than I wanted to admit. Maybe I was going to look into the mirror one of these fine days and see the girl I'd always been, just equipped now with better hair and clothes: anxious about the world having room for her, not even knowing how much she didn't know.

There was something about the discount grocery that turned people chatty, made them initiate long, personal conversations with the checkers. "This is my third marriage," the woman in front of me said to the turkey-necked man scanning her purchases. "Number One don't count, and the one after that was just a mean son of a bitch. But this one now is my honey bunny."

Maybe they couldn't afford counseling. Maybe it was just the lonely lives most of us lead these days, or maybe talk radio and daytime TV had done away with any silly notions about private trouble staying private. For whatever reason, I heard all about their heart attacks and their parents' heart attacks, their knee replacements and diabetes, all the complications of their lives. It wasn't even eavesdropping, because they weren't just talking, they were broadcasting. "My son went into the Army and we got his little girl with us now because her mama run off to Arizona." "Once we get that carburetor fixed, we'll be in business, yeah, Camaros hold their value pretty good." "These minute steaks? You ever try them? We had some the other night while we was waiting for the vet to call and tell us if the cat died, and he did."

The checkers just kept on passing groceries over the scanner, blip blip blip, and putting them in sacks. Every so often they offered a little noncommittal agreement or acknowledgment, but really, they'd heard it all before and they were going to keep hearing it. Times were tough all over. One of these days it would probably be my turn, watching the register to see that the frozen potatoes rang up correctly and confiding my domestic problems.

We were getting close to the end of Bobby's severance checks and still nothing had come through for him. We were going to have to make some kind of move pretty soon, get rid of one of the cars or liquidate the last of our stocks or whatever else we could do to play things out awhile longer. And I didn't want to be the one to call the question. I wanted Bobby to make some kind of forceful decision, act the man's part. It wasn't good for either of us to have him so droopy and sad sack. A man is his job, often enough, and if he loses that, it just hollows him out. Women are the practical ones. We put our heads down and pull the load any way we can, and too often that load includes a man's broody feelings.

Then one night I came home from work and walked in to the smell of cooking, I mean real cooking, aromatic and high style, not burgers or chili or the usual supper Bobby threw together if he was in the mood. He sat me down at the dining room table and poured me out a glass of the good stuff, the like of which we hadn't seen for some time. "What's the occasion?" I asked.

"A little money coming in," he said carelessly. He darted back into the kitchen to yank a tray of stuffed mushrooms out of the broiler. "Watch it, these are hot."

"What money? Coming in from where?"

"Pennies from heaven." He made a show of pretending to burn his fingers. "Hot, hot, hot."

I put my glass back on its coaster. "Bobby, what's going on?"

"A project I've been working on is finally coming together."

"What kind of project? Bobby?"

"Speculative. Profitable. Don't give me that look. It's solid. It's idiot proof. It's going to turn things around for us."

"Tell me about it."

"Can't just yet." He mugged at me, giving me a big wink. "Maybe later. Tonight let's just be happy. Pretend I'm a caveman and I just brought home a dead mastodon. We'll have meat and hides. Our cave will be warm, our tribe will prosper."

"Oh Bobby."

"What? You think I haven't thought this through? I've had however many months it's been. I've studied it from every angle. There's no happy-ever-after option. I'm doing what I need to do for the both of us. So, quit asking me. You don't need to know any details. Better you don't. Anyway, it's just a onetime thing, not a way of life."

I quit asking, and we ate our nice dinner, and that night we made love like one of us was going off to war the next day. You'd think that sex would be one of the last great free pleasures, and technically that's true. But often enough, nothing in the bank means there's nothing in the tank. One more way that men let things get to them. I was just glad we had the comfort of each other again, for however long that would last.

As for Bobby's new source of income, I saw no evil and heard no evil. There's a sense in which I just gave up and gave in on everything. Maybe it was the long burden of worry that had worn me down. Or maybe I'd never had any real principles to begin with. Judge not lest ye be judged, is all I'd say in that regard. Call me when the same thing happens to you and we'll swap stories.

Of course there were occasions when, in spite of myself, I tried to fathom what Bobby was up to. I snooped around on the computer and kept an eye out for mysterious paperwork. But Bobby might as well have been one of those Godfather guys, and I was the wife who reminded him to bring home the cannoli. We just didn't talk about it. I had my own notions. Some kind of Internet flimflam or hacking job. Bobby was always clever that way, always messing around on the computer and coming up with outlandish stuff. It really was amazing, the way computers ran everything now, and how much power they might give to the criminally inclined. Newfangled varieties of plain old-fashioned crookery. About all that was left of my morals was the hope that he wasn't ripping off anybody who couldn't afford it. I hoped he was targeting some big fat plum of a corporation, which I know is just as illegal but would be less personal.

Every so often Bobby gave me cash money, one or two or five or six hundred dollars, and it was understood that I was to use it for our day-to-day expenses. Everything off the books. I assumed he kept his pockets full as well. In this way we caught up on the mortgage and even began to make some payments on our heap of debt. Now whenever I saw the Liberty Tax guys, I felt a new kind of dread. No doubt our tax returns were going to be fiddled and faddled to the nth degree.

You can get used to most things, and so there was a space of time when I did just that. If Bobby was to mention that on such and such a day he wasn't going to be answering his phone, and therefore not to bother calling, I said all right. If he gave me money one day and asked for it back the next, I let it go by. One night, while I was doing the dinner dishes, he leaned up against the refrigerator and said, "I took out an insurance policy today."

"What, another one?" He was still covered under his old work plan; we just paid for it ourselves now.

"It's a different kind. Here." He was holding something small, a key. I dried my hands and took it from him, the question in my eyes. "Safe deposit box," he said. "I wrote down everything you need to know on the wall next to the phone."

"I'm not happy about this, Bobby," I said, meaning, everything. It was the closest I'd come to making objections.

"Just a little while longer." And that was the closest he came to any sort of explanation.

When I look back on it, the wonder is that none of it lasted that long. It didn't seem that way, since every day brought its full load of worries, and every hour was taken up with sorting through them and deciding which ones you could get away with ignoring. But in fact Bobby had only been a criminal mastermind for a few weeks when the wheels started coming off. It was early March, the first soft spot in the weather, with sunshine and birdsong and puddles soaking into the ground, when I walked out to my car after work and found myself the object of official attention.

He popped up when I was still a few yards away, a puffy-looking young man in a blue sports coat and a tie like a noose. "Mrs. Crabtree?"

He was between me and my car. I stopped right where I was. "Who wants to know?"

He flipped open one of those badge things. "Agent Kyle Roorda, Federal Bureau of Investigation."

"Wow." My heart was beating up in my throat, but I kept my cool. "Is there a terrorist alert or something?"

"No, ma'am, nothing like that. I wonder if we could have a word with you."

"We?"

Agent Roorda nodded in the direction of a black Town Car parked across the lot. The windshield was shiny with sun and I couldn't see anything, but an arm was visible at rest on the open window. "Agent Tate."

"What about?" I was going to make him go through his whole script.

"I was hoping we could go somewhere more private." Agent Roorda looked a little self-conscious saying this, like he was asking me for a date. There was a patch of rash along his jaw from shaving. His eyes were a light, washed-out blue. Although he was younger than me, he might have been one of the under-bred kids I used to play with growing up, the ones who had pinworms from going barefoot all summer long.

"Well," I said, "it would take more than a badge to make me go off somewhere with two strange men." But I smiled, because I wanted to keep him off-balance. He didn't look like a guy who got many full-bore smiles from pretty women. "Maybe you should just tell me what I can help you with."

Agent Roorda waited until one of my coworkers passed by on the way to her own car, giving me the scrupulous, none-of-my-business averted gaze. He said, "It concerns your husband."

"Bobby? Is he all right? Oh my God." And of course I really

was anxious, but I was also putting on a show of being anxious, as an Innocent Spouse.

"There's no emergency. Sorry to alarm you. But we're making inquiries into some possibly fraudulent transactions."

"What kind of transactions?"

I was hoping he'd tell me, because of course I really didn't know. But Agent Roorda only blinked, as if the light was too much for his pale eyes. His jacket was too tight across the back, I could see the seams pulling beneath his arms, and his white shirt was too white and stiff, like he'd just unwrapped it from a shrink-wrapped package of three. I wondered if he'd been on the job all that long, and why I wasn't getting a real, grown-up agent to menace me. My mind was skittering around the way it does when you're trying not to think about what's really happening. He said, "Mrs. Crabtree, you need to be aware that you might be implicated if we determine that your husband has been involved in any criminal activity."

"I haven't done anything. And if you think Bobby has, he's the one you should be talking to. I'm sure he could clear all this up."

"Our investigation," said Agent Roorda, coloring up a little, even as his face remained impassive, "is ongoing."

I was figuring some things out. I said, "If you can prove something, you should go ahead and do it. But don't put me in the middle of it."

"You are in the middle of it, Mrs. Crabtree, like it or not."

"Possibly fraudulent. That doesn't sound real convincing."

"There's ways of going right up to the edge of the law, Mrs. Crabtree. There's people who think they're so clever, they won't trip up. But they always do."

"You want me to help you send my husband to jail."

"I want you to do the right thing."

"Which is what, exactly, in this day and age? You check the price of gas lately, Agent Roorda? You want to call your friendly neighborhood mortgage broker, ask them to do the right thing? Right and wrong, it's all gone corporate. Now I have to get home and start dinner." I hit the button on my car's opener and it flashed its lights. "Excuse me."

"I'll be seeing you around," said Agent Roorda, once I was settled in the driver's seat with the engine running.

"Not if I see you first." I pulled out of the parking space smartly, shifted into drive, and accelerated so fast that he had to take a step back.

Was it a right or a wrong that I didn't say anything to Bobby? I chased the ideas round and round through my tired head. Right to stand by my husband? Wrong that he was defrauding somebody or other, when so many laws had been arranged to allow for legal fraud? Right or wrong to want to save myself? It all collapsed into a big heap of doing nothing. And of course by then I'd gotten pretty good at ignoring things as a way of life.

Still, I hoped there was some easy exit we could take. "Bobby," I said one night in bed, "I think we should make a clean start. Be done with your project—" That's what we called it, like something he was putting together for the school science fair. "And have you get some sort of regular old job. It doesn't have to be anything much. Enough to tide us over until times turn around again."

Bobby yawned. We'd just made love and he was drifting off to sleep, maybe not the ideal time for such a conversation. But sometimes heavy things roll out of you on their own. Bobby said, "Only a little while longer. One or two more golden eggs."

"No, Bobby. Now."

"Soon. Few loose ends to tie up."

"Soon soon. Promise."

He had been fondling me, in a drowsy, afterward way, and now his hand stopped. "What's up with you?"

"It's too risky."

"Babe, there's risk in everything. Including the stock market. Okay, bad example. Hey, we'll be back to Mr. and Mrs. Clean Upstanding in no time. You think I want to end up like my old man?"

I said of course not, and he gave me another friendly groping, and then he was asleep.

I didn't see him first. Agent Roorda. It was a Saturday and I was at the Sav-A-Lot, checking detergent and Kleenex and whatnot off my list, when he rounded a corner, blocking his cart with mine. "Oh, hey there, Mrs. Crabtree. Wait a sec, I'll back up."

He was no doubt the only man in the place wearing a tie, though he'd at least shed his sports coat. The only item in his cart was a packaged angel food cake. "Picking up a few things," he said. "My mom used to make angel cakes. I don't expect this'll measure up to homemade."

"Where's Agent what's-his-name?" We were right in the middle of the store and it was crowded with families and shrieking children. I couldn't believe he was here.

"Tate. That's him over in the coffee shop." Agent Roorda pointed him out, and I could see right away why Agent Roorda was the one doing the legwork. Agent Tate looked to be about sixty going on eighty. He was hunched over a paper coffee cup, and he might as well have had one of those electric signs over his head, running down the months, days, and hours until he reached retirement. "He's got some cardiac issues," said Agent Roorda, as if reading the thoughts on my face.

"You guys work weekends. I'm impressed."

"Whatever the case requires. Sure."

It put a chill on my heart, thinking of Bobby as a "case." I wondered if our phones were tapped, or if people were going through our garbage, or worse. I scanned the grocery list in my hand to steady myself, and pushed my cart down the aisle. Agent Roorda made a U-turn to follow me. "Mrs. Crabtree, I'm thinking you're just a victim of circumstances here. I'm thinking none of this was your idea. Unfortunately, the law doesn't see it that way. If you benefit from the proceeds of illegal activity, then you have a liability."

"I'm sorry, I wasn't paying attention. Do you see pancake syrup?"

"We need the hard drive from his computer."

"Get a warrant."

"Help us so we can help you. This is a limited-time offer."

I'd led us to the big wall coolers with the milk and eggs and I stopped, not remembering what I'd come for. Agent Roorda and I were dimly reflected in the glass surface. We stared into it as if we were having our picture taken. I was startled to see how likely a couple we looked. Same light hair (mine more artful with its streaks and highlights), same pale, stolid faces. We could have been the couple in *American Gothic*, dressed up for a day off the farm.

I turned away from the glass. "Where did you grow up, Agent Roorda?"

"Paris, Illinois," he said, not missing a beat. "My parents still live there."

"No kidding. I'm from Olney. We're practically neighbors."

"You could say that." He was cautious about where I was taking this.

"So we're both a couple of hicks who made it to the big city. Worked hard. Bettered ourselves. A toehold on the American Dream. Why do you think me or anybody else would want to give that up?"

"Nothing in any American Dream says it's all right to bend the laws until they break."

"I wouldn't be so sure about that," I said, and I left him there to contemplate the price of milk, which had gone up twice in the last month.

At the checkout, the girl asked me how I was today. "The FBI followed me in here," I told her, and she asked me if plastic was okay.

On Wall Street, giant investment banks rocked on their foundations. Not literally, but something close to it, and when that very week a twenty-two-story construction crane came loose from its moorings and pancaked a New York condo building, filling a city block with rubble and the innocent dead, well, it seemed like a sign. People whose job it was to make pronouncements about the economy argued over the different gradations of Bad. If we'd been told that a giant asteroid was hurtling our way through black and frozen space, it would have seemed par for the course.

"Look around and you can always find somebody else worse off," my dad used to say, whenever we were faced with some reversal or privation. "Yes, and somebody better off too," my mother would chime in from her place at the kitchen table, sorting through our bills as if they were a jigsaw puzzle with a missing piece. And I have to say, that was pretty much the way I saw the world, going back and forth between the two views. There but for the grace of God go I, and Why shouldn't we have a new SUV? I'm not claiming it was admirable, just another part of contrary human nature, our better and worse angels. I think that all those months, I kept trying to hold on to something that wouldn't change, some bedrock certainty I could count on, be it a job, a future, love, or who I'd chosen to be in life.

The day after I'd encountered Agent Roorda in the Sav-A-Lot, a Sunday, Bobby and I took one of our walks. The last cold spell was behind us and the grass had greened up, the trees were budding, and a few damp spring flowers had begun to uncurl, crocus and daffodils and those little blue stars I don't know the name of but they always break my heart, each one so small and so perfect. We were surprised to see a Realtor's sign in front of one of the grandest houses in the development, an oversized nouveau-Victorian with turrets and balconies, scrollwork, fanciful windows. Or maybe we were not surprised, once we thought about it.

As it happened, the Realtor was having an open house, so we went inside. What a staircase! Such acreage of shining wood floors, so many luxurious appointments in the kitchen, in the near-decadent master bath! We gawked and envied, as we were meant to do, but the sadness that was never too far out of reach rose up in me as I considered that people used to live here, no one we knew, but human lives no different from our own, and now all traces of them had been erased. It was too easy to imagine our house, mine and Bobby's, emptied out and wiped clean, as if we'd never been, and strangers' feet echoing on the bare floors.

When we came outside, a black Town Car was idling at the curb, and Agent Roorda was extracting a flier from the plastic sleeve attached to the For Sale sign.

I turned the other way and set off for home. Bobby hurried to catch up with me. "What's the deal, huh?"

I told him I was catching a chill.

What to do? What to leave undone? I didn't seem to be able to bring myself to be an FBI rat fink, but I'm not going to throw any flowers at myself. I just thought that process would be every bit as terrifying as waiting to get busted. And I was still hoping that Bobby would pull it off. Not just because of money, wanting the money. That had been a deal with the devil, and the devil could have it all back, as far as I was concerned. But I wanted to believe in Bobby. I wanted him to triumph, be the hero in the movie that was my life. You always want a man to come through, live up to all the things you saw in him back when you were first in love.

A few days? A week, two? I was eating bad and sleeping worse by then, and time had a bleary, jerky quality. Easter was in there somewhere, with its chocolate rabbits and potted lilies. But it was still tax season. I know that, because one morning on my way to work, I was waiting at the traffic light and watching Miss Liberty and Uncle Sam doing their thing on the sidewalk in front of the tax shop, and the hair on the back of my neck rose. The light changed and I pulled into the strip mall's parking lot and got out of the car.

"Uncle Sam wants you!" Agent Roorda greeted me, strolling across the lot.

"I don't believe this."

"It's only for a day or two." Agent Roorda removed his starred and striped hat, which made him freakishly tall. He patted at his forehead with a handkerchief. The day was already warm. "It's actually kind of nice, getting out in the fresh air. Usually on a stakeout we're cooped up in cars or some kind of trailer."

I pointed to Agent Tate, who made the world's saddest Miss Liberty. He'd stalled out and was sitting on a bench as if waiting for a bus. The green plastic sheeting sagged between his knees. "How did you get him to do it?"

"There was some comp time he'd been negotiating. Now he's going to get paid for it."

I guess I said something like that working out well for him. I was still in a state of stupid disbelief, as if I'd gotten up that morning and found the world turned into some scary cartoon. Then I said, "A day or two."

Agent Roorda gave a perfunctory wave at the passing traffic. He was too big for the costume and his ankles protruded from the striped pants. He wore what I guessed were regulation FBI black socks and shiny black wingtips. "I shouldn't have said that, Mrs. Crabtree. But make no mistake, major bad-type things are in the pipeline. I've tried to tell you that all along."

"I have to get back to work." But I didn't move. I said, "It must be nice to have a job that's all about truth and justice. No, I mean it. Good guys, bad guys. You always know where you stand."

"I don't decide those things, Mrs. Crabtree. I follow orders just like anybody else. But I serve my country, and I'm proud of that."

"Well, it used to be a better country."

He was distracted by Agent Tate, who had fished a pair of binoculars out from under the green plastic and was training them in the direction of our driveway. "That's not for me to say."

"Good-bye, Agent Roorda. Keep in touch."

"Count on it," he said, turning back to the busy traffic. But in fact I never saw him again.

That night in our bed I put my mouth up to Bobby's ear and whispered. I felt his body next to mine shiver and then grow rigid. That was almost the hardest part, right then and there, feeling all the sick-making fear pass through his skin, both of us knowing how sundered we were now from the life we'd led. A few days later, the FBI raided the house. It was another first for the neighborhood. Agent Roorda wasn't with them. I like to think that he had some choice in the matter and decided not to join in out of his personal feelings for me. It would have been too embarrassing for us both, having him poke around through our dresser drawers and the refrigerator's freezer compartment. They really do look through the freezer. I guess people stash drugs or money there more often than you'd imagine.

Bobby was long gone, of course. There was some more unpleasantness to get through, but by then I had a good criminal lawyer, the kind who slices and dices the law so that you're left with some odd-shaped piece of it. There were ways in which I was innocent and ways in which I was guilty, so I guess staying out of jail was enough of a good deal.

The bank foreclosed on the house and I moved to another city. They still keep tabs on me, waiting for me to show up with some of Bobby's ill-gotten loot, but we've been clever about that in ways I won't go into. Uncle Sam still wants me. Bobby too, though I expect he can keep one step ahead of them for quite some time. I'd like to think I'll see him again someday, now that I know for sure I'm pregnant. My last dishonesty was not telling Bobby I'd gone off my pills, but I can't say I'm sorry.

Meanwhile, times in general have improved, a modest up cycle after all the down. But it's as if the whole world's slipped a notch. No more happy dollars filling the air like flocks of birds. We're all sadder but wiser, as my mother used to say darkly, when one or another bad thing had come to pass, just as she'd predicted. But I'd rather hold to my dad's favorite saying, which was about never missing the water until the well runs dry.

Smash

It happened the usual dumb way these things happen: driv-ing along, driving along, then, smash. The voices of metal shrieking, the angels of automotive death.

I was on my way to work. I wasn't paying any more or any less attention than usual. Commuting as I do—much as every-one does—you zip along inside your enclosed space with your coffee and your radio and the rest of your personal comforts, and the world outside is like wallpaper, almost, in a room where you have to sit for a time. Just get it over with, go on to the next thing. Zone out. Twenty or thirty or forty minutes you'll never get back. Maybe if you're a champ at meditation, a guru or something, you can devote your life to sifting through con-sciousness a grain at a time so that nothing is lost. Whole days spent watching lotus flowers drop into a pond. Nice, but it's not the way most of us live. Nope. We have to get to work.

Instead of lotus flowers it was a twenty-five-foot aluminum extension ladder come loose from its rigging and lying like an orange slash mark along both lanes of the interstate. It must have just landed. It had my number and nobody else's. I saw traffic in the passing lane veering wide, then I was right on top of the thing. I braked, tried to swerve onto the shoulder, clipped the ladder with my front wheels and threw it underneath me. There was a grinding racket as the car shook and thumped and the steering wheel was a broken toy.

Someone else hit me from behind, hard, sending the car shooting off the road, briefly airborne. It turned around 360 degrees in the ditch, with a noise as if it had been dumped whole into a blender.

When everything was over, I waited for the great Announcement that would tell me I was dead. It didn't come, but that was when my heart started flopping around in a panic, wondering if I was gravely injured but didn't yet know it. Neck or spine broken, or the soft parts inside of me burst open, and then a whole new fear, that my face might have been split or gouged, ruined. There was by now a great deal of broken glass around me.

I touched my fingertips to my face, registering also that I had the use of my hands, and was relieved to find no new seams or leaks. Just the same tidy arrangement of eyes, nose, et cetera, as before. And there were people crowding around the car door, peering in and tapping at the window, and a thick, burnt smell, and in the distance, like a wasp sound you'd bat away, a siren.

"Sir? Sir?" the people outside kept saying, but that was not my name so I didn't answer. With difficulty, they pried open the door. I was extracted, led to a spot on a green embankment, wrapped in a blanket, and made to sit. How was I, was I all right? Everyone wanted to know. It was thrilling to think that so many people, all of them hitherto specks on the traveling wallpaper, had stepped out of the wall, so to speak, to make these solicitous inquiries on my behalf. But I couldn't say anything. I felt abashed, unworthy.

Someone said, "Whoever dumped that ladder sure as hell didn't come back for it."

"Would you? Tickets, court appearances, fines, all that?"

"I'd like to think I would."

"I'm pretty sure I'd keep on going. If I have to be honest about it, which I guess I don't."

My car had died and gone to car heaven. The funeral was being held right then and there. A wrecker made its untroubled way down the side of the ditch, like a tank on a battlefield. A man got out and attached a hook to the car's undercarriage— the bumper had been bitten off—and began the noisy, officious process of winching it up. I can't say I felt sad, watching it, or felt much of anything else. It was only one more remarkable thing, a car aimed skyward and ready to launch.

All this time people had been doing things to me with rubber gloves and flashlights and probes of different sorts. These were the necessary examinations before you were declared officially Alive, and so far I had not satisfied them. Either I had lost the power of speech, or perhaps I'd never possessed it in the first place.

A small pile of my personal belongings had been assembled on the grass. Wallet, phone, briefcase, insulated and insulted coffee mug. Someone picked up my wallet and flipped through it. "Mr.———. Is that your name? Can you tell us your name?"

It seems like such an easy thing, but it was beyond me. My name no longer fit me. It had been bent out of shape and flung aside, like the car's bumper.

"He looks familiar," someone else said. "Like he was on TV, maybe."

"I don't think so. He's too ordinary-looking."

"I didn't mean like a star. More like somebody who was on the news."

"Well if he wasn't already on the news, he might get there now."

The air was full of whirling colors, like the beating of giant shimmering wings. When I identified these as the flashing lights, red and blue, on top of all the clustering official vehicles, I thought, Oh, sure. But even then, the mystery taken out of it, I liked the idea of breathing colored air.

A woman came up to me then, an older woman with a face that looked like flour had been sifted into its cracks. "I just wanted to make sure you were all right," she said. Her hands fluttered up and she seemed to want to touch me. I shrank away. "Oh well," she said, and I could tell she was a little hurt. "I guess, under the circumstances . . ."

Someone said to her, "It was an unavoidable accident. Even insurance companies allow for such things."

"Not my insurance company," the woman replied glumly. "There are no acts of God for those people."

"And here you have to buy coverage, you've got no choice. They get you coming and going."

"Death or Dismemberment. Now there's a choice."

"Shh."

The crowd stepped back. An officer of the law appeared in the cleared space. His sword and shield were burnished, his face radiated glory. "Mr.————? We're going to hand you over to the boys here. They're going to take you the hospital. You understand?"

I tried to indicate, with my humble posture, that I did.

"We've talked to your wife and she's going to meet you there."

I didn't want to think about my wife. She was not the same woman she'd started out as, all those years before. Time had gotten into her veins and made her anxious. I figured she was already hightailing it for the hospital. My cell phone there on the ground made yipping noises, and I knew it was most probably my wife, but I didn't pick it up.

"Should we answer it?"

"I guess not. I mean, where do you start explaining?"

They put me in the back of an ambulance but they had me sit up, like an ordinary passenger. One of the ambulance guys sat across from me. "Still a little shook up? You got to expect that. I mean, one minute you're solid, you're wheels up, in a manner of speaking, well on your way to another day of Normal, and next thing you know, it's all catawampus. Total befuckedness. I've seen it many a time, and friend, I'm here to tell you, the little ride we're taking is easy-breezy. You just got your soul pulled a ways out of you and now we got to stuff it back in. The things I've seen! The times we've had to coax a soul back into a body, or practically whack it with a broom to get it down from the walls. Our whole bag of tricks: defibrillator, fluids, epinephrine, oxygen. IV Valium for those seriously nervous moments. Sometimes it's enough, sometimes not. And when it's not, we are your ambulance of last resort, Your Ride To The Other Side. Discreet. Professional. Caring. But you, friend, are only going partway, a short hop, an excursion. A dry run before the big fun. How are you feeling? Any pain? Difficulty breathing? Nausea? Dizziness? Ennui? Dissatisfaction? Anger, sloth, envy, and so on? Are you paying attention yet?"

We reached the hospital and I was unloaded. This time they strapped me on a gurney and whizzed me through the hallway so that I saw mostly ceiling, a checkerboard of tiles interrupted by white fluorescent tubes. I couldn't see who was pushing me, couldn't see their faces. Nurses, I guess. They smelled like baby powder. They were talking but I couldn't understand their speech, which was like the speech of birds. The white fluorescent tubes ran together into a single track. Then there was a terrifying lurch as the gurney came to a halt. "The doctor will see you now," the bird chorus announced.

I couldn't see the doctor's face either, because the room was dark and he wore one of those headlight things, a light strapped to his forehead radiating brilliance in all directions. I lay still as he picked and sorted through my body. I knew he could tell what was wrong with me without my having to speak. After a time the light withdrew a little and he said, in his doctor voice, stern and wise, "I think what's needed is a course of electro cortical magnetic absolution therapy."

I opened my mouth but it just stayed open. There was no force of words behind it. I knew the doctor was right. Wasn't he always? Then another mouth-shape opened before me and I knew it was the machine, into which I was inserted like a tray of cookies into an oven.

The door closed and a pulse started up, a throbbing just below the threshold of sound. Nothing more happened. The arched roof of the chamber, only a little ways above me, was ribbed with dark and light bands, light enough to make out the nothing that surrounded me.

I felt inclined to fidget. For the first time in the proceedings I began to have practical, worried thoughts. The woman who had hit me from behind: Had anyone taken her name, her phone number, license and registration, insurance information? Were there witnesses? What sorts of calls would need to be made, and my poor poor car, ah, better not to think of that, the car thing, although I did not think I had been At Fault. I wondered if the woman who hit me was At Fault, in the way these things are reckoned, hitting from behind being one of the criteria of Fault. I knew she had been worried about the looming possibilities, including my own injuries. If I had been damaged, or even inconvenienced, if I was some unpleasant and litigious type—and I very well might be, I couldn't yet say—there could be a lot of trouble.

I imagined her going home from the accident scene, driving in some overcautious, rigid, shell-shocked way. She lived alone and kept a cat. She was the kind who would keep it all together until she was safely within her own four walls, the car garaged, her purse and keys set down on the kitchen counter. But when the cat came up to greet her, making its plaintive noise, its tail held up like a question mark, that's when she'd break down, weeping because there was no one else to weep for her.

And what about the criminally negligent owner of the ladder, the immediate cause of all the trouble? It was harder to get a picture of him—surely it was a man—some contractor or painter who loaded up his truck or van every day and set off for work. There was probably something like clamps that held the ladder in place, clamps on the top rack of the vehicle. I'd seen such things, without really seeing them or paying attention, any number of times. I didn't do that sort of work, building and repairing things. I didn't have a clue, and not much curiosity. Something broke, and you made phone calls, and men came with ladders and all sorts of other gear to set it right. You paid them and they took themselves off again.

Always there had been myself, and then there was everything outside of myself, and whatever effort I had to make to deal with it. With other people: get what I needed from them, work around them. A clear boundary that was turning soft and blurred, or maybe it was my own self that had gone so blurry. The machine throbbed. The light was the blue of thunderstorms. A man with a ladder wasn't anyone I usually cared about. But the ladder was the last thing I remembered with perfect clarity—orange, battered, unexpectedly solid—and the rest of my mind, my self, my own name, my *soul*, was still floating somewhere out of reach. I thought I might climb the ladder up to where I could get my hands on them. And of course there was still the question of Fault to be resolved.

He'd been careless about the ladder. Hadn't taken the time to fasten it down securely. Or else the mechanism that held it in place was worn, balky. Sooner or later it would have to be replaced, like everything else he owned: busted, coming apart, crapped out. That was his luck. But the ladder had always stayed in place just fine, right up until today, and besides, he had other things to worry about this morning. He was behind, off to a bad start. In arrears. Overdue. His late payments were late. This job he was on wasn't going well. There had been complaints. Work always took longer than people wanted it to, nobody understood that. They rode your ass like it was a train. The truck's engine balked when he tried to start it and he cursed it, but without real energy or imagination.

Traffic was in his way. There were people on the roads who drove like old ladies, in fact a lot of them actually were old ladies now that he got a look at them. A whole herd of prissy women taking to the road in their Kias or Geos or Sunfires, cheapo cars that even they should be ashamed to drive. Riding the brake, clogging the passing lane. They had him hemmed in. His own escort of slow-assed old babes. The one in front of him drifted back to the scenic lane where she belonged and he finally got his speed up and a chance not to be any later than usual and that was when the racket of dragging metal started up, and the noise and the panic traveled up his back as if his spine itself was a ladder, and by the time he figured out what it was, the thing had detached itself entirely and bounced away.

He kept on going. It wasn't really a decision, just inertia, maintaining speed. Motion took up the space that would have otherwise been occupied by dread. Then he thought about doubling back, driving a little ways on the opposite side of the freeway to see if anything had come of it, but he was already late and he didn't want to know.

He did pull over when he reached his exit, went around back to see if his license plate or anything else identifiable had come loose, but it hadn't, and he felt a coward's relief at that, yes he was a damned coward and a lot of other names he could hang on himself. He would have to buy a new ladder but not right away, and not anywhere close by, in case the cops started making the rounds of Home Depots, checking out suspicious ladder purchases, now that was a genuine paranoid thought but he couldn't shake it. His armpits were cold with sweat and he told himself to get it together, for Christ's sake. He couldn't show up at the job looking like he'd killed somebody even if he had.

I didn't know his name any more than I knew my own. But I saw him clearly enough now. The clothes that he wore:

you'd think there was no pride involved in their selection or care, but there was a kind of pride in how little thought or effort was devoted to them. Because he had more important things to worry about. He smoked, he'd always smoked, he didn't give a rip what anybody else thought. If I get a notion to swim out in the ocean, ain't nobody's business. And he drank his share, but only after work and on weekends, and that too was nobody's business. The rest of the time he worked his nuts off. What else did people expect of him? He wasn't born rich and he'd made his own luck, and if the luck was usually bad, he got up the next morning and started in all over again. He'd like to see some of these smart guys with their cell phones and their Starbucks coffee spend even one day doing the work he did, year in and year out. Like to see them try.

So that if a ladder were to come loose on the highway and bust up somebody's big-deal day, well, they probably had it coming. They were probably in too much of a hurry, they had an attitude about what the world owed them because life had been pretty good so far, hadn't it? Huh, buddy? All those pissy little problems you squalled about, who cared? Like you had it so rough. You could have been born without some important component part, a mouth, or even less of a brain than you already have, or feet! What would you do without feet? What if you weren't even human, but some large, patient animal beaten regularly with a stick, a water buffalo, for instance, with a ring through its nose, a beast of burden yoked to a plow, one slow foot ahead of the other all your life, until one day you sank down in the mud and didn't get up? What if you were a bird in the wood, a fish in the flood, a gnat, a fly, a speck tossed by the wind, a thought, a kiss, a prayer? Would you still think that you had suffered insurable losses? Could you forgive the man who let the ladder fall, or the ladder itself for falling? Could you forgive the world for its suffering?

I opened my eyes. My wife was holding my hand. She had a brave look on her face. "How are you, honey? Can you hear me?"

"Yeah," I said. I fell off the ladder and straight down into myself. "Oh boy."

"Don't try to talk, honey, just rest. You're going to be fine. You're going to be good as new."

I was finer than fine. Newer than new. I was wheels up. I was paying complete attention.

Do Not Deny Me

Julia's boyfriend had a cough he couldn't shake, a wet laboring in his lungs that irritated her even as she exercised sympathy and concern. On nights they spent together she kept waking up to his convulsive racket. "Honey," she said, attempting patience, "you really need to get to the doctor." The boyfriend was not a big fan of doctors. He prided himself on his vitamins and his workouts. Still. The doctor diagnosed bronchitis. Unsurprising, since it was winter and there was the usual stew of viruses about. The antibiotics helped for a time, but he began to complain of soreness in his chest and back, shortness of breath, lightheadedness.

One night he spiked a fever of 102, and Julia drove him to the emergency room. "This sure is kicking my ass," he said. Talking made him cough, and Julia told him to just rest. When he leaned against her she felt the fever pulsing through his skin. She thought that someday they might have a child, and the child would get sick and they would both worry about it, and this would be what it would feel like.

He was admitted to the hospital with pneumonia and pulmonary edema and given oxygen, diuretics, IV antibiotics. It was alarming—they had surely thought he would be treated and sent home—but the ER doctor assured her that they had things under control. She decided to go home and get a few hours of sleep. First, she looked in on him to say good night. He was sleeping, or some exhausted, medically induced version of sleep, and his breathing had settled low in his chest. It sounded like underground snoring. She touched his face and thought it felt cooler.

When she came back the next morning, he was dead. A different doctor explained to her that there had been complications, perhaps an underlying heart condition. He talked about left and right ventricles, cardiomyopathy, the many and heroic interventions. Julia tried to argue with him, as if it was simply a matter of proving the doctor wrong. "He's only twenty-seven years old."

"I'm sorry for your loss," the doctor said.

It was as if the hospital had snatched him away and refused to give him back. Alone, she had no sense of what to do with herself, with the shock of it all, and walked up and down the hallways for a while. *Dead* was the shut door that kept blocking her way. She had not thought to call anyone the night before. She didn't know any of his family. They had only been together for four months. She didn't even have a key to his apartment. A nurse retrieved his cell phone, and Julia used it to call one of his friends.

After that, events were taken out of her hands. The funeral was in his hometown in Pennsylvania. She knew some of the people attending, his friends and the people he worked with, but none of them belonged to her. They had not had time to develop mutual friends. She met his parents, although they were at a loss for things to say to one another. One of his old girlfriends was there and she did a lot of breaking down and sobbing. Julia was too embarrassed by her own presence to be anything other than polite. She studied the easel board and the pictures of him in different incarnations: as a baby, a kid playing football, a high school graduate. Death had turned him into a stranger with an ordinary history. The coffin was closed and draped with a spray of red roses. It filled her with queasy horror, thinking of him shut inside, still struggling to breathe. Should she even have come? There was no place for her here, the accidental girlfriend.

Later, at his parents' house, one of his friends came up to Julia and said, "Nobody blames you. I'm sure you did everything you could have." It was a statement that seemed to mean exactly the opposite. It implied that she had been careless, had not valued him sufficiently, that they had entrusted their loved one to an unreliable stranger.

Perhaps if she had not gone home that night. If she had kept watch in a chair by the side of his bed, so that the moment his heart stopped fluttering, she could have raised the alarm. If she had been more vigilant, or smarter, or kinder, or someone else entirely, she might have kept him alive.

If they'd had more time together, she would have been more entitled to grieve. She'd loved him, at least she believed she had, but sorting through her memories made them feel shopworn and false, as if she was only building an affecting monument to herself, her devotion, her suffering. A kind of revulsion set in. In this way she lost everything.

Of course her friends tried to comfort her, but she could tell there were statutory limits in place for a short-term lover, and their sympathy was weighed out accordingly. The counselor she went to called it "incomplete mourning." That came closest to what she felt, but finding a label was no real consolation. The counselor's goal, as Julia understood it, was to allow her to "move on," which made all the sense in the world except she didn't want to. Why would you want to forget someone? Why would you want to be forgotten?

Two months passed. Half of the time they'd been together. This was the new calculus she used for measurements. By now it was March, and trying to be spring, but not trying very hard. In the city, seasons were perceptible mostly as configurations of sky. Julia was waiting for her bus home from work, wishing she had worn her heavier coat. The sun was out but a brisk wind took the warmth away. She closed her eyes and concentrated on the rush and racket of downtown traffic, the perfume of exhaust and chill air. She turned her face upward and let the sun fill it.

Someone touched her arm and her eyes flew open. The woman standing next to her said, "I'm sorry. I was afraid you might miss your bus."

Julia focused on the street before her and the bus she wanted pulling away from the curb. "Always another one," she said, then, "Was I standing here spaced out for, like, a really long time?"

"Pretty long," the woman allowed.

"I wonder," Julia said, "if people can tell when they're in the middle of a nervous breakdown, or if after a while it just seems like normal life? Sorry," she added. "I didn't mean to sound so melodramatic."

"You spoke from the heart," the woman said, "and therefore you are to be commended."

Julia turned to gaze at her. She looked like one of those

middle-aged women who manage to be both shabby and solidly respectable at the same time. Stern and thrifty householders, clippers of coupons, wielders of bleach bottles, believers in the medicinal properties of petroleum jelly. She had a broad, pleasant face and eyeglasses. A knit hat was clamped over a head of brown curls with gray corkscrewing through them. Her tweed coat suggested a bear newly emerged from hibernation. She said, "Most of the time we only say what other people expect to hear. Too many dead words smothered inside of us."

Julia nodded. She was reminded of all the reasons you did not strike up conversations with strangers on the street. She felt waves of heat coursing through her and wondered if she was unwell. The weak sun hurt her eyes and she closed them again, but this time she didn't drift away. She was too conscious of the woman's presence at her elbow. "'Speech after long silence, that is right,'" the woman said, just as if Julia had spoken and it was now her turn to reply. "It's a poem. By somebody or other. About heartfelt communication."

Julia glanced at her between her eyelashes, then looked down the street to see if her bus was approaching. There were a couple she could take if she wished to, with varying degrees of inconvenience, but none was in sight. "Yeah, that's important." Usually it was best to just agree with people.

"See," the woman said, "right there, you're just being polite, making some polite noise, instead of letting that great big sadness out."

"I don't know you, do I?"

"Anyone could see it in you." She opened her pursy handbag and began rummaging around in it.

"I'm sorry," Julia said. "I didn't mean to be rude. I'm just feeling out of sorts. Acting out of sorts. Sorry." She was behaving like a total crazy idiot, one of the city's population of crazy idiots. Next she'd probably take to walking the streets with a sandwich board draped over her: I Am So Screwed Up.

"There's a spirit around you," the woman said in the same conversational tone. "Or more like an aura. It's very disorganized. But he's a sad spirit, that's what's shadowing you."

Julia felt her face pulling in different directions, losing its shape.

"Yes, it's definitely a man. I'm not getting much else. Except the sadness. All around you, like a gray cloud."

"Stop it."

"I'm so sorry." Again, the hand on her arm. The woman's blue eyes behind her glasses were magnified to an alarming degree, like looking at insect life under a lens. "You must miss him terribly. You poor dear."

It would be so stupid to start crying, so maudlin and unworthy, just because a stranger pitied her. And what did she have to cry about anyway; she was young, healthy, she was unscathed. And yet she was crying, small, crabbed, ungenerous tears, as the sun shone and the traffic rolled and sighed, rolled and sighed around her.

It didn't last long, and she sniffled a bit, and looked up, glassy-eyed. The woman was no longer in the space beside her. Julia thought she saw her lumpy wool hat in the windows of a departing bus.

She didn't believe in ghosts, auras, or any other such New Age notion. She thought it was for the weak-minded, she thought it was sentimental. When people talked about guardian angels or spirit guides, she was embarrassed for them. And it was certainly true, as the woman had said, that anyone could have seen her sadness, even without her own helpful commentary. Who was she anyway, an unlikely gypsy or street person? Maybe it was a scam, a setup, something done to get money.

But her mind wouldn't let loose of it. A disorganized spirit! She would have loved to share the joke with him; he was the most disorganized person she knew, always losing track of the time, day of the week, keys, shoes, anything. If there were such things as ghosts, his would have managed to get confused and turned around by the whole death thing. He would be drifting around in the ether, much as he used to keep circling the same block, looking for a parking space. See? Julia would tell him. You're doing it again. Which was either communing with a spirit, or simply talking to herself, or maybe one began where the other left off, and she was an addled fool to give it any space in her mind.

Although Julia waited for the same bus at the same time of day, the Psychic Housewife, as Julia came to think of her, did not reappear. It was a little disappointing, but even more of a relief. Then one night she had a dream about her boyfriend, the first she'd had since his death, and in the dream he was lying next to her in bed, but dressed in a suit that she associated with funerals, and he was asking her, sadly, why she had given up on him.

It freaked her. That was what she said to her friend, who she phoned later that day. "I could feel him next to me, I woke up and I was panicking, groping around in the bed for him."

"That is so weird," her friend said, in a way that irritated Julia. *Weird* made it into a spectacle, a curiosity. "But you know, that's what the mind does. Plays gruesome tricks."

Julia said she guessed so. Of course it was what she'd told

herself. It wasn't, after all, a complicated dream. She said, "But say it was you who died. Wouldn't you want to come back and see people? Wouldn't he want to come back and see me?"

"Julia, honey."

"Especially if you didn't expect to die, if you died young like that, without any chance to say good-bye. Just allow for the possibility."

The silence on the other end of the phone indicated that her friend was considering how best to respond. Julia encountered many such silences these days. While people wanted to be supportive, and while they knew it had been a loss, nothing you'd wish on anybody, it wasn't some mega-tragedy. Julia hadn't discovered his lifeless body, or witnessed his shooting in a street robbery, or any other horror that happened on a daily basis, no, the man had died in a nice, sanitary hospital. The friend said, "I think it's one part of you talking to another part. You still miss him, you're still hung up on what happened, but here you are, living your life, going on with it, and you're all guilty and conflicted."

"You're probably right."

"We need to find you some fun dates. Beer and pizza. Bowling. Any old dumb thing to get your meter running again."

She didn't want to get her meter running. She didn't want a logical explanation. She had always thought of herself as practical, steady, reliable to the point of dullness. Different people she knew had launched themselves in odd directions, had a fling at Buddhism or Christian farming co-ops, embraced animal rights or Alcoholics Anonymous, or changed genders, adopted Chinese girl babies, any manner of dramatic transformations. All the while Julia went about her business, put money in her

401(k), changed her oil and antifreeze on schedule, remembered people's birthdays. She'd been unhappy at times, all the usual growing-up stuff: loneliness, self-hatred, the boys who hadn't loved her back, the drip drip drip of her mother's criticism. Then later, the disappointments of adulthood: doubt, fatigue, the realization that some struggles were the sort that lasted the rest of your life. She thought she'd faced her share of suffering, thought she'd acquired solid credentials. But nothing had upended her as this had, unraveled her nature to the point where she might believe anything of herself, and of the confounding world.

That night she tried to coax him to her, sat in unmoving silence while the evening drained out of the windows and shadows softened the rooms. Then she got up and lit a candle, stared into the small universe of flame, tried to will herself into a receptive state. There were different layers and levels of silence, of concentration; she felt herself falling through them one by one. Then a noise from the street dragged her back up to the surface, and she was embarrassed. It wasn't something she would have admitted to doing.

No more dreams came to her. People gradually ceased making solicitous inquiries. This was the much-desired moving on. Then one day at a bookstore, Julia saw an announcement of a talk by a man who had written a book about psychic phenomena. The author's photo showed him to be extravagantly bearded, with the in-the-know smile of a man who had unlocked a few of the universe's secrets. Julia decided to go listen to him, even though it seemed rather unworthy, almost like going to see pornography.

She got there early, visited the coffee bar, then browsed

through the magazines, keeping an eye on the ranks of folding chairs set up in a corner. When they began to fill, she took a seat near the back. There were more people than she would have expected, an actual crowd. The author's name was Rory McAllister, and he seemed to be famous in some way she'd never heard of. He was introduced by a bookstore employee as Dr. McAllister, although what it was he doctored was not specified. There was some light applause. He was older and puffier than his photo, more like an off-duty Santa than a portal to the metaphysical. Julia scolded herself for being so unpleasantly judgmental and dismissive. Lay off. She'd come in the first place, she might as well hear him out.

Rory McAllister thanked them for attending and made a few jokes about his previous books and his publisher's misgivings, remarks that sailed right past Julia, although the rest of the crowd chuckled comfortably. He said, "I thought tonight I'd spend some time talking about synchronicity, coincidence, and the probability studies that have tried to examine the phenomenon. To put it one way, is experience random? Or part of a field, in the way physics uses the term, a field of moving spirits, with its own set of variables, vectors, and velocities?"

In spite of her good intentions, Julia was already faintly bored. Her eyes wandered to the other people in the audience, who looked to be what you'd expect: serious, unchatty people, most of them older than herself. They were paying close attention, as if variables and fields and probabilities were what they had come to hear. Julia wasn't sure what she'd expected. A séance? She was wondering if she might get up and take herself quietly off when two rows up, the Psychic Housewife turned and looked directly at her. Julia's heart banged around in her chest.

Rory McAllister was saying, "Once we allow for the possibility of an order and a plan to the universe, a guiding intelligence, what some call God, it is as if we journey through a strange country where we've never been, yet keep encountering beloved faces."

Julia composed herself for the remainder of the speech, and when people applauded, and began to crowd around the table where Rory McAllister was installed to sign books, she got up and made her way over to where the woman stood, in conversation with a tall man who stooped a bit to hear her; her hand was on his arm. ". . . discouraging," Julia heard her saying. And, "Even the rock gives water when it is called upon."

The man murmured something Julia couldn't catch, and they parted. The woman turned toward Julia, smiling. "What a coincidence," she said, and laughed at her own joke.

"I want to know how you did it."

She was wearing a warm-weather version of her earlier dowdy costume: a bunchy cardigan, lavender in color, ornamented with fabric daisies, a white cotton turtleneck, and a long denim skirt. Through some oddity of the reflected light, her eyes behind the glasses looked almost transparent, like milk poured into a blue saucer. "How I did what?"

"What you said about the spirit . . ." Again she felt suddenly and horribly conspicuous, as if she might be wreathed in unseen energies.

The woman considered her for a moment, then held out her hand. "I'm Fay. Fay Kjellander."

Julia spoke her own name and shook Fay's hand, which was small but lingering. Fay was a couple of inches shorter than Julia was; she tilted her face upward, her eyeglasses catching the light and reflecting the room in miniature oblongs. Fay said, "Really, there's no need for you to be upset."

"Either something really bizarre is happening, or else I'm losing my mind."

"Surely," said Fay pleasantly, "those aren't the only possibilities."

"I have to know if it's real, what you saw, or if it's just some kind of party trick."

"'Real' is one of those unfortunate words, in my opinion."

"And what do you mean, help. It doesn't help anyone to tell them they're being *haunted*."

Fay looked at her, a little sadly. "It might make you feel better not to think of it as a haunting."

Julia didn't answer. She felt like a furious child after an outburst, backed into a corner of her own making. Fay sighed. "Come on, let's go see Rory."

She stepped to one side, an invitation, and Julia trudged forward, irritated and apprehensive. Other people greeted Fay as they approached Rory's table. So nice to see you again. You too. The psychic regulars, Julia guessed. Finally the crowd around Rory McAllister thinned, and Fay steered Julia to stand in front of him.

"Fay!" Rory McAllister rose out of his chair to greet her. Viewed from up close, he looked rather unwell, the skin beneath his eyes dark and sagging. There was a hint of palsy in his hands as he clasped Fay's. "I was hoping you'd be here."

"Now you know I wasn't about to miss it." To Julia she said, "It's Rory's eighth book. He's at the top of his form. This is Julia, I wanted you to meet her."

Julia, sulky now, murmured hello. She kept her eyes lowered; even so, she was aware of Rory McAllister looking her over, not unkindly.

Rory and Fay both began talking at the same time.

"I thought it would be nice—"

"Perhaps if you had time—"

"That would be lovely."

"And if your friend—"

Fay said, coaxingly, "Please come get a bite to eat with us. We'd be so pleased."

"I don't think I—"

"You have questions, don't you? And Rory's the best there is. He's been at this more than forty years. Now don't be shy. You're actually not a shy person, are you? Quite the contrary. Anyone could see it in you."

Rory was a vegetarian, and so they ended up at an Indian restaurant where the menu ran to cauliflower and lentils. They were joined by a man who was introduced as Saybrook, although it was unclear if this was his first or last name. He had a shaved head, like a biker or a convict, and he busied himself with a BlackBerry he worked away at, hunching his shoulders around it. "I'm the media escort," he explained to Julia, as they were standing at the entrance, waiting to get a table. "This is the fourth stop on a ten-city tour."

Julia said that ten cities sounded like a lot. She was unsure just how impressed she was meant to be. Saybrook was the kind of man she might have once found attractive, all self-consciousness, hipness, and energy. She wondered if she should flirt, pretend an interest, take him to bed. Just to get her meter running.

"Yeah, he's a pretty big deal among all the psychic friends. Sorry. Didn't mean to make fun."

"That's all right. I'm just tagging along."

"Yeah?" Saybrook kept an eye on Rory and Fay, standing a little distance away. The restaurant was noisy and he leaned over to direct his words into Julia's ear. "Most of the time I think, woo woo, too much, you know, etheric vision, indigo children, harmonic convergence, these guys are off in their own private Disneyland. Then sometimes they come up with something that really makes you wonder. In a creepy way, I mean—" His phone buzzed and he spoke into it. "Not yet. Give me twenty minutes. Yeah." Then to Julia, "Sorry. More media drama." He smiled to indicate that it was a date or an assignation, he was that kind of guy, and did she want to play? "So, are you into this psychic stuff at all?"

"Not exactly into it. More like, having it come after me."

"How's that?"

"I think my dead boyfriend's following me around."

Saybrook took himself off, and Julia, Rory, and Fay were seated at a table in an alcove, screened off by sagging curtains. Tea was brought to them. Julia kept silent except to order, as Fay and Rory talked lightly about people they knew. Piped music, some spidery Indian instrument, played overhead. Currents of food smells, hot and aromatic, curled almost visibly through the air. It wasn't the sort of place Julia or her friends frequented. They preferred their ethnic restaurants to be well, rather less ethnic.

Their food came, little plates of brown things, curried things. Rory ate very slowly, putting his fork down between bites. He said to Julia, "I understand you've had a recent loss."

"Yes. Well, recent . . ." She wasn't sure what qualified.

Fay said, "All sorts of time issues. They're coming up everywhere. She's so confused."

"Time," said Rory, echoing.

"Too soon too soon."

"And suddenly."

"He was so young."

"But not an accident. Nothing like that."

"No. The air went out of him."

Julia's hand was on the table top. Fay reached out and curled her fingers around it. "He was cheated. You both were. It was over just as it was beginning. You thought you had all the time in the world and so you were careless with it, but how could you have known? The last time you would speak, eat a meal together, make love. Oh, it's terrible to still want what the body wants, like phantom pain in an amputated limb, but so much worse . . ."

Julia jerked her hand away. The thick smells of the restaurant food filled her nose. She was afraid she might vomit. She closed her eyes and a roaring sound enveloped her, like the noise of a crowd heard from far away. Then a cold cloth touched her forehead. Fay said, "Can you hear me? Julia?"

She opened her eyes. Rory and Fay and one of the Indian waiters were hovering over her. She felt bleary, disoriented. "What . . ."

"Mint tea," said Fay, lifting a cup to her. "Try and drink a little."

Rory asked, "Do you have a history of seizures? Anything of that sort?" To the waiter he said, "Perhaps you could bring her some broth." The waiter withdrew. "How are you feeling? You went on quite the little holiday there. We're so sorry. We shouldn't have done that."

Julia took a sip of the tea. It steadied her. "What did you do?"

Fay said, "Both of us at once, reading you. It can be strenuous."

Rory said, "But we don't often come across someone of your resources."

"I don't have any . . . resources." She was gradually coming around, sorting herself out, although she still had a floating, disconnected feeling.

Fay and Rory both smiled. Fay said, "Usually, we wouldn't be able to connect so strongly. With the young man. But you're a wonderful receptor. That day on the street I could tell. Most people run on batteries. You're like nuclear power."

"Connect? What . . ."

"Loud and clear," said Rory.

"He doesn't care for Indian food," said Fay. "Some joke he's making about hamburgers."

"All right, let's not upset her again."

The waiter returned with the broth and set it in front of Julia. Then he left and the curtains closed behind him. Rory and Fay were watching her with concern. They looked like kindly grandparents, although perhaps grandparents who turned out to be burying bodies in their backyard. She swallowed a spoonful of broth, then set it aside. "You're saying he's here."

"Well, not the way you might imagine," said Fay. "Not like some of those silly movies where spirits are walking around, or sitting in chairs, or smashing things up. More like a radio or television signal with a lot of static."

Rory said, "Try to conceive of energy, emotions, thoughts, as taking up space. Existing in some other plane just beyond our senses. The way dogs hear sounds we can't. Or like ultraviolet or infrared light. Things you know are real, even if you can't perceive them."

Maybe they were just telling her what she wanted to hear.

There was a skeptical, critical part of her that wasn't going to budge, like a rock that would not be pried out of the ground. But there was a current of water that cut paths and channels around the rock, going where it needed to go, and that was the other part of her nature. "Hi," she said to the air around her, feeling foolish. "I miss you." Nothing came back to her. To Fay and Rory, she said, "I'm sorry, I don't think I have any gifts. Resources. No superpowers. I'm the most ordinary person in the world."

"Well that's because you haven't practiced using it," said Fay, picking up her fork and returning to her food. "Even Mozart had to sit down at a keyboard once in a while. You have the slightest little tendency toward laziness, don't you, dear? I'm sorry to be so blunt. I tend to speak my mind. You may have noticed. God gives us our talents. It's up to us to develop them."

Julia was somewhat surprised to hear both of them talk in religious terms, but she guessed she shouldn't be. After all, religion, at least the kind she was raised on, was all about visions, visits from angels, conversations with the deity, burning bushes, pillars of cloud by day, pillars of fire by night, weeping statues, miraculous wounds.

She said to Fay, "If you don't mind my asking, what is it you do, I mean, do you earn a living being, ah, psychic?"

Fay laughed. "Oh my, no. Rory can, in a manner of speaking, because of his writing. I'm a clerk at the Division of Motor Vehicles. Talk about ordinary."

That made perfect sense to Julia. She could well imagine Fay as one of those cheerful bureaucratic obstacles, telling people they'd failed their vision test or didn't have the right ID.

"Let's try something," said Rory. "Look at me. Just look. Concentrate. See what you get out of it."

She did so. His dark, tired eyes. The big beard that didn't seem to fit his face, its hollows at the cheeks and temples. "You're . . ."

"Say it."

"You're ill."

"Yes," said Rory. "Keep going."

"You're not going to get better."

"There now," said Rory, as if pleased, and Fay beamed at her.

"I'm so sorry."

"No need," said Rory, briskly. "It's simply a great and wondrous transformation. Now, didn't we tell you? You reached out with your mind and spoke the truth."

"But, I'm sorry, but you don't look very well, that's not hard to see, and . . . the rest of it, you were giving me hints, and anyway, it didn't feel like some big revelation or psychic earthquake, I didn't go into a trance or anything. I just said it."

Fay said, "And you could have said, 'You're going to have surgery,' or anything else in the world, but you didn't."

"As for trances," added Rory, "I consider them histrionic."

Julia got her feet underneath her and stood up. "I think I need to go home now. Good luck," she said to Rory. "I hope I'm wrong."

Fay rested a hand on her arm. "Don't be afraid. And do not deny your gift."

By the next day, she was uncertain. Because really, nothing had been said that could not have been fabricated, or a lucky guess, or a psych job. Nothing that could be proven or documented, nothing rare or astounding had really happened. Just as nothing mysterious had ever really come her way, nothing beyond normal, unremarkable premonitions or hunches. Every so often in the next few weeks, a little sheepishly, she tried to meditate, coax her stubborn mind into doing something exalted, but she always ended up bored, or distracted, or even asleep. It didn't seem to be anything she could squeeze out of herself. Something Fay had said, about the rock bringing forth water. She was a dry rock.

The summer's heat dragged on into September and then October. Leaves of trees didn't fall but hung on, coated with dust, like drooping tongues. Julia went out for a time with a man she met at a party, to the relief of her friends, who were afraid she was stuck in some morbid rut. It began promisingly, and she even slept with him a couple of times. He belonged to a softball league and Julia went to one of his games, sitting in the bleachers and cheering along with the other fans. Afterward the team and their assorted wives and girlfriends all went out to a tavern. The tavern was hot, although no one seemed to notice or mind except her, as the day itself had been hot and the day before that, and the people around her were red-faced from beer and sunburn, bawling happily at each other, whole conversations taking place at top volume.

Her date slid his arm around her waist. He could expect them to go home together and make love. Why wouldn't he? But she was so tired. And heat-addled, so that all her senses had an untrustworthy, miragelike cast. She was not meant to be here. It was all a mistake. This room of happy strangers— she seemed to see it from a great distance, a movie on a tiny screen—belonged to someone else's life. Then she thought about the man who had died, and the life they should have had together. There was an unfairness to that, since they might have just as easily grown bored or irritated with each other by now, or fought in ways that revealed some fault line between them. But it was just as fair to imagine happiness. This was how he would haunt her, the ghost of all her foreclosed possibilities.

There was nothing to object to with this man, the ball-player. He was pleasant and normal and full of uncomplicated virtues. But she had been cheering for a team that meant nothing to her.

Julia worked her way out of his circling arm. "I don't feel very well. I think I'll go on home."

"What's the matter?"

"Nothing, I'm just kind of worn out. I need to get to sleep." He frowned, concerned, perhaps, but also irritated that his evening was being disrupted. "No, you stay here. I can get home by myself."

"If you'll hang on a little while, I can—"

"Really. Don't bother." She could not wait another minute to be alone.

The next day he said to her, "You're pretty independent, aren't you?"

"I guess so," Julia said, watching him appraise her. "Thanks," she said, although she knew he had not meant it as a compliment.

So that was that.

A few weeks later she saw Rory's obituary in the paper. She hadn't been watching for it, and in most respects she had forgotten all about him. But here he was, the same photograph that had been on his book jacket, and a headline identifying him as "Author, Spiritualist." He was seventy years old and had died of pancreatic cancer at his home in California.

After twenty-five years teaching in the anthropology departments at Brown University and the University of New Mexico, Dr. McAllister embarked on a second career as a researcher, author, and popularizer of various paranormal phenomena, such as extrasensory perception and clairvoyance. Although his methods and conclusions drew criticism from those who viewed them as unscientific and speculative, his books, as well as his Foundation for the New Paradigm, were influential in . . .

Julia didn't read the rest of it. It filled her with unreasoning dread, as if she had pronounced sentence on him. Another death trailing her. That was shallow, idiotic thinking, if you could even call it thinking, not to mention narcissistic. The man had died; it had nothing to do with her. It was on par with believing there was some special providence in her choosing that day to buy a paper—which she seldom did—or turning to the obituaries.

It was coincidence pure and simple, there were such things as coincidences, and anything else was all mush-headedness and superstition. But you did not need to believe a thing in order to feel it. She was tired of arguing against herself. It took so much effort to be a fully functioning grown-up, so many self-admonishments for being anything other than sensible and resolute, that is, for being anxious, hopeful, or uncertain. It was not some psychic gift she had been in danger of denying, but her own fears.

Finding Fay in the phone book took some effort. Kjellander. It wasn't spelled the way it sounded. Julia dialed and got an answering machine, Fay's chiming voice instructing her to leave a message. She waited for the beep, but when it came, instead of the careful speech she'd rehearsed, she said, "Fay? You're there, aren't you?"

The line clicked and Fay said, "Julia? I was just this *second* thinking about you."

Her heart leapt up, and she half-remembered something Rory had said, something about encountering beloved faces, silly, this was not a face, but there was that same sense of welcoming comfort. "I read about Rory. I'm so sorry."

"Thank you. His spirit is at peace. But of course I miss him, as many will."

"I felt bad about what I said to him. That . . . it was going to happen."

"Now why should you? It wasn't any of your doing. Honestly, you are a worrywart. Would you like to get together for lunch sometime?"

They met a few days later, at a coffee shop not far from the Division of Motor Vehicles branch where Fay worked. It was November, and the weather had changed to blustering rain. Julia took off her damp coat and located Fay sitting in one of the booths. Julia sat down across from her. In spite of what Fay had said, there were times she felt shy, as she did now. "Hi again."

"Hello, so nice to see you." Fay looked grayer, heavier, or maybe that was the oversized black sweater she wore. "I have to be back at work by one, so I went ahead and ordered. There's nothing fancy here, but I like their grilled cheese and tomato."

Julia picked up the laminated menu, which featured full-color photographs of hamburgers. The waitress came and took her order. Fay said, "I'm glad you called. We were worried about you, Rory and I. We felt we rather overwhelmed you."

"Oh . . . well . . ." Fay's eyes were always unnerving, over-prominent to the point that you felt self-conscious about looking at them, the same way you might feel bad about staring at some-one's artificial leg. What did she need the glasses for anyway? "I've thought a lot about what you said since then, but . . ."

"You're not convinced. You'd like to be, but you can't quite bring yourself to it."

"I guess so." It felt peculiar to be talking about such things in the middle of a busy lunch hour, people passing ketchup bottles and getting refills on iced tea. But then, where would it not feel peculiar? "I don't feel anything. I mean, my boyfriend. I don't think he's here anymore. Maybe I shouldn't even want him to be, if he was sad." Did spirits dissipate like smoke? Did they move on to some gauzy heaven? "I don't know how this works."

"Tell me about him. Any old thing."

"He was a friendly person. People liked him." That sounded insipid, something you could say about anyone. "He was taking Italian lessons, he wanted to go to Italy. We were saving up for a trip. He had a motorcycle that he spent all kinds of time and money on. He said that once the weather got better, he'd take me out for rides."

"Keep going."

"He was always healthy. He was only sick for a little while and we didn't think it was anything that serious. I keep think-ing I should have nagged him, made him get to the doctor sooner."

She stopped talking because she didn't want to rehearse her own muddy feelings of guilt and longing. Fay's gaze focused on her, or rather, around, about, and through her. Fay's eyebrows drew together, faintly frowning. So he was gone. She supposed she should be glad, although it felt like a new kind of mourning.

Then Fay's hand brushed against hers. Fay said, "Softball."

"What?"

"He keeps saying, 'Softball.'"

The waitress arrived then, bringing them water glasses and silverware rolled up in paper napkins. When they were alone again Fay said, "That means something to you, I can tell. Never mind. None of my business."

Their food came and they ate without speaking. Rain blew against the window glass; cars in the parking lot switched their lights and wipers on. Julia said, "I need to ask you some questions. When you touch people—"

"Yes. That helps me read them. It's different for everyone. Some psychics work from photographs. Others use automatic writing, or sketches. Or they can read you right over the telephone."

"Have you always been psychic?"

Fay nodded. "Growing up, you don't think anything of it. You think everybody sees what you see, feels what you feel. Only later do you realize people think you're a freak. A witch. Oh yes, I've been called that."

Julia murmured that she was sorry. The check came, set face-down, slightly damp. Fay said, "It doesn't make for an easy life. People think it should be, that you can do tricks, like predict the stock market, make all kinds of money. But it's lonesome. No one else understands. That's why we seek one another out. It's another reason I miss Rory. I think you came along for a purpose. Let's exchange phone numbers, shall we? I think we're going to be great friends. I have to be getting back to work now.

You can just imagine the extraordinary sensibilities that people bring with them when they come in for a driver's license."

They paid the check and went out into the weather. A few raindrops spattered against Fay's glasses. "May I give you a hug? Good-bye, hurry on now, don't get wet."

Julia called her the next week and asked if they could meet again. "I have to know what I'm dealing with. You have to help me." She hadn't slept well. She felt the dead man watching her, carrying on his one-sided conversations, trying to get her attention with his bad jokes. Then doubt would shake her and she dismissed it all as stupid, a fantasy, only to waver, wondering if it might be true, if she even wanted it to be true, and the cycle began all over again.

Fay invited her to come over the next day after work. Julia thought about taking a bottle of wine as a hostess gift, but maybe Fay didn't drink. She settled instead on carnations from the grocery. Fay lived in a part of town that gave her pause, on a residential street just off one of the city's catastrophic thoroughfares. It was a place of hurtling traffic, car dealerships, down-and-out motels, dollar stores, liquor stores, small hutches where you could have keys made, buy lottery tickets, burritos, Polish sausages, a place for armed robberies, drug arrests, high-speed chases.

But Fay's block was quiet enough, rows of brick four flats sitting in their squares of lawn and thin, fenced-off trees. Julia wouldn't have lived in such a place, though she told herself not to be a snob. What did she think DMV clerks made for salaries? Fay must have been watching for her because she buzzed her inside and opened the door right away, exclaiming over the carnations—"So pretty!"

"What a cute apartment," said Julia, although she found it

small and rather fussy. All those smothering drapes, old-fashioned lamps, embroidered cushions. A row of decorative plates were displayed in special holders. It had a grandmotherlike feel to it, dingy and dated, although surely Fay was not all that old. Perhaps she had inherited it all from her own grandmother. Then, hastily, in case Fay was able to sense her thoughts, she said, "Your directions were great, I had no trouble at all getting here."

Fay had a plate of triangle sandwiches for them, and tea, and there was a tray of hard little chocolate cookies. "I didn't know if you had a chance to get your dinner." Julia said she'd already eaten, then added, for politeness' sake, that she hadn't eaten all that much. She selected a couple of the sandwiches, which were filled with over-moist ham salad, washed them down with the tea. She set her cup in the center of the saucer. Now that she was here, she was filled with prickly dread. She wished she hadn't eaten anything. Her stomach lurched.

Fay drew two chairs together, facing each other in the small living room. "Come on, let's get started."

Julia took her place and Fay sat opposite. "Nervous?" Fay asked. Her magnified eyes were so close, Julia could see the pink lining of her eyelids.

"I guess. A little."

"Of course you are. This is the first time you've given yourself over willingly. Taken a step forward on your own. Every other time, I'm afraid, it was something of an ambush. Try not to hold your breath."

Julia exhaled. Her stomach was still mutinous and there was a curdled, metallic taste in her mouth. "Why do I always feel sick? Every time. It's like being beat up."

"It takes a toll, doesn't it? Other people don't understand

that. They think we send out lightning bolts from our finger-tips, or some kind of mental gamma rays. But it can hollow you out. The body is just a vessel, after all. 'The sword outwears its sheath and the soul outwears its breast.' That's a poem, but I forget who wrote it. Go ahead and close your eyes."

Julia did so. She felt Fay's fingertips stroke the back of her hands, and resisted the impulse to shake her loose as she would a mouse or a spider. Fay said, "He means you no harm."

"He's here now?"

"I'm quite sure of it."

She searched behind her closed eyes. Nothing came to her. How were you meant to sense such a thing, how were you meant to know it? "Why is he here? Still here?"

"His spirit can't find its way to God."

What if God was just the biggest ghost of all? The thought popped into her head, unbidden.

"There's something he doesn't want to let go. Maybe there was unfinished business between the two of you. Things left undone and unsaid. Can you think what they might be?"

"Everything."

"Speak up, dear."

"Everything between us was unfinished."

Again, the stroking pressure of her hands. It was unbear-able. She would scream.

Fay said, "If there's anything you would like to say to him."

"Tell him I'm sorry. I should have known how sick he was. I should have been nicer." Should have should have. The list of her omissions and regrets. She waited, but the silence remained dumb and black. She opened her eyes, pulled her hands away. "Why can't I feel him?"

"Because you're still keeping up all the defenses of your rational mind."

"I'm not trying to. I don't mean to."

"You must get past the idea of *trying*. Even trying not to try."

Julia shook her head. She despaired of doing anything right.

"Now don't be sulky. Why would you expect this to be easy? And for heaven's sake, don't make such faces."

Julia's head hurt. There was a hot lump in her stomach, as if she had eaten something unwholesome. She would not try to not try. Not think about not thinking. How much of yourself did you have to give over? What would be left of you once you were hollowed out, a perfect vessel?

But she wanted this. She wanted to find him again. So much had been taken away, so much was unfair and would always be her fault.

Fay took her hand, as before, and this time Julia didn't flinch. "Eyes closed," Fay instructed. "Don't do anything but listen."

Julia imagined herself as an ear, as a seashell on an empty beach with the waves echoing through her. The sound of Fay's voice reached her from a great distance. She didn't attend to the meaning at first. There were only words floating on the surface of the water. Fay said you had to become nothing, like the dead themselves. Who were you anyway, what was so important about your little collection of opinions, likes and dislikes, this or that feeling, memory, sensation? Your soul was only part of the one great soul. Give up your questioning, your stubbornness. Believe in miracles. The dead were not dead. Dissolve into water. You were already halfway there. More than halfway. Just a little further.

But her stomach hurt. Don't, Julia told it. As if it was a

matter of will. Her stomach was having none of it. The lump of sickness pushed through her, inexorably down, the pain of it making her body shift this way and that. And this was what brought her round, so that her ordinary, commonsense self began to rouse itself, fight back. Why would you not want to be you, why would you want to be nothing? There was something soft, sly, dangerous at work here . . .

That was when she came to and looked around her at this peculiar room, this stage set of a grandmother's house. Fay was still talking, murmuring just under her breath, and when Julia made a convulsive movement to shake off Fay's arm, Fay looked up, and pure terror made Julia scream.

Why Grandmother, what big eyes you have.

Then she was out of her chair, bumping into furniture, dizzy and sick, desperate to find the door. Fay was following her, saying something, a blur of noise. Her purse strap snagged on the doorknob; Julia tugged at it and it broke. The latch stuck, then gave, and she was outside the shut and silent door.

Where was her car? The street was black and strange, and she was lost, shaking, cold, *what happened*? She had another panic, thinking that her car had been stolen, but she had walked past it without recognizing it. She drove in the wrong direction and had to turn around, renegotiate the nightmare thorough-fare with its blaring traffic and hard-edged shadows, and almost by accident found her way back to her own neighborhood.

The phone was ringing when Julia opened her apartment door. She didn't answer and whoever it was hung up without leaving a message. In the bathroom she sat on the toilet, her insides cramping. The phone rang again, then the answering machine, the hang-up. The third time it rang, she unplugged it.

Before Julia had her number disconnected and changed, Fay did leave messages. She asked how Julia was, she was worried about her. It was unfortunate that Julia was given to overreacting.

And: "Julia! I had the most wonderful dream! There as a ladder between heaven and earth, and angels were going up and down it. Just like Jacob in the Bible. I feel sure it means some special message from your departed friend."

And finally: "I know you've been thinking about me. I can feel it. We have such a strong connection. It goes in both directions, like the angels on the ladder. I can see you right now, as you're listening to—"

Julia hit the delete button. She kept the phone off from then on.

One day when she left work, Fay was waiting at the bus stop where they'd first met. It was winter now, with snow in the air, and Fay wore her same shaggy tweed coat and knit hat. An ordinary middle-aged lady. She could have been anybody. A retired piano teacher, perhaps.

"Don't touch me," Julia said, as Fay approached.

"All right, mercy sakes." Fay held up her hands. She was smiling, but her eyes blinked in rapid semaphore. "No need to get upset."

"I don't want to hear any more of your readings, or messages from the spirit world, or talk about angels. I'm through with that. I want you to leave me alone."

"'They flee from me that sometimes did me seek.'"

"What?"

"It's another poem. These things just show up in my head and stick there. It's embarrassing that I don't know the authors.

Someday I'm going to look them all up. What I mean is, you were the one who came to me, wanting my help, wanting to learn. And more than once."

Julia stayed silent. The light of the winter afternoon clicked down a notch. Their breath came out in frost clouds, rising into the white air. It had been almost a year since that death. The time that had passed felt like a dream. She said, in a quieter voice, "I can't do it anymore. It does me harm."

"Because you fight it."

Julia shook her head. She could have told Fay that she had tried to believe, to bend herself into a new shape, and it had nearly broken her. She was who she was, and always had been. Instead she said, "I'm sorry if it's lonely for you." And that was true. She had some notion of what it must be like for Fay, who also was who she was: the freak, the witch, the seer, her head full of other people's voices. "But I can't be any part of this."

"You have a gift."

"I give it back."

"Your friend is still sad," Fay called out, because Julia had already walked away.

She turned back again. "No. I'm still sad. I think it was me all along, that's who you were reading. He was always gone. Good-bye, Fay. Be well."

Not long after that, Julia's office transferred her to a new division in the suburbs, and there was no reason for her to commute downtown. It was a busy time, full of new people and new tasks. It crowded out the past so gradually that she didn't notice, except on those occasions when she looked back and marveled at its disappearance. Once, hurrying to beat a rainstorm, she thought she saw Fay across the street unfurling a sturdy plaid umbrella, testing it against the wind, then setting off with her purposeful walk. At the sight of her something kindled in Julia, the old glad recognition. She opened her mouth to call out, greet her. Then she stopped herself and let the moment pass.

Escape

Hurley eased the window up and tried the screen. The screen was inclined to stick. He was pleased to have remembered this. It was a gift from his brain, like a coupon for half-price dry cleaning. Even with the screen all the way up, it would be a tight squeeze. One side balked and he had to risk a quick blow with the bottom of his fist. It made the dull noise of a hammer landing on meat. Hurley held his breath and listened but heard only his own body's ticking. He tried the screen again and it slid open.

A beautiful square of black night and moving air and cricket noise.

Hurley bent down and grasped the bulky metal complications of that thing that thing that was used to get out of high windows. It had two big hooks you fastened over the window-sill, then you let the rest of it drop down, piece by piece by piece. It made a racket, a jangly noise. He hoped it couldn't be heard from inside. He peered out the window at it. That thing that thing ladder! The streetlight gilded each step, a path for him to follow.

He swung one leg over the windowsill, wiggled around until his foot found the first step. Then, supporting his weight with his good hand, he reached out with the other foot. Nothing to it. Practically his old self. Face to the wall, he lowered himself to the next step. The ladder swayed and knocked him against the wall. One side of him didn't work right, like the screen. No matter; he took it slow and steady, he wasn't about to make some foolish mistake. And anyway, there was this amazing *night* to pay attention to. He hadn't been out at night since since since . . .

Crickets and black perfume and here was a bird of some sort making its solitary, liquid noise. What kind of bird? He didn't know. He didn't think he'd ever known.

Then he slipped and scraped his good side and dangled there like a giant crippled spider. He remembered every swear word in creation and silently turned them all loose. He was still too high up to let himself go, unless he wanted to smash up what was left of his pudding head. Not that he hadn't thought about it. Go ahead and finish the job.

Just as the effort of hanging on was making his chest squeeze and the sweat slide under his clothes, he managed a new toehold. Inch by inch by inch, he brought himself around, got his legs underneath him again.

In this way he reached the end of the ladder. Just the smallest hop to the ground. He let go, fought for his balance, lost it and toppled over. When he managed to right himself, Claudine had come out of the back door and was watching him.

"Cute," she said. "One of your better stunts. What do you think you're doing?"

"Fire drill."

"What? Say it again."

"Fire drill." Hurley's head drooped. His eyes got teary. He couldn't do anything right.

"Real cute." Claudine led him back inside. She didn't even scold him. He was that pathetic.

But later, after she had deposited him in bed, the sheets tucked tight and hard around him, she scooped the ladder up in both arms. It made a bundle of metal sticks. "I guess if the house burns down some night with us in it, it'll be because I had to keep this under lock and key." She headed off down the hallway to the guest bedroom, where she slept these days.

Before all this, he had not known just how much she hated him. But then, he had not realized how much he hated her.

All day long he sat in his chair and listened to Claudine talking on the phone to different members of her fan club. Her voice was low, in keeping with the atmosphere of hushed crisis. But he could hear perfectly well, thank you! Sometimes the phone rang, sometimes it was Claudine who started up talking, meaning she'd called someone. "About the same," she said, or, "Well, I just do the best I can," or, his favorite, "In sickness and in health. That's what I signed on to."

Hurley had taken to laughing his horrible laugh whenever he heard that one. He could still unsettle her that way, get to her by making his noises.

Claudine had shut and locked the windows—did she think that would stop him, if he wanted to jump?—but she hadn't closed the blinds. Hurley stared at the black square as if it was a television screen. He could stay up and watch it all night if he wanted. She couldn't stop him.

But here was the window full of bright day, and Claudine

shaking him, and his head was all joggly, and always that muddy, waking-up panic, something gone horribly wrong. . . . "Come on, you can sleep anytime. I got other things to do besides haul you up and down."

Today was a Doctor Day, and so he had to be clean and presentable. He was finally allowed to manage in the bathroom by himself, thank God, though Claudine still shaved him. She didn't know crap about shaving and dragged the razor across his face like an old plow. Even now when he was alone in the bathroom she set a baby monitor on the sink to keep track of him.

With jerky effort, Hurley lifted the clothes hamper to the edge of the tub. He stood back and gave it a push. It landed with a solid thump. Then there was the sound of Claudine stampeding up the stairs. Hurley stood back and she banged the door open, wild-eyed.

Hurley laughed: "Haaorghhaghha."

Claudine put her hand on her heart and set her jaw. "One of these fine days you'll want me to do for you, feed you or tie your tie, and then we'll see what kinds of tricks I play on you."

"Hoorhgh," said Hurley, sulky now. He didn't doubt that she'd start right away, inventing some special meanness.

Hurley was made ready. The complications of his socks and shoes were mastered, his teeth scrubbed until his gums bled. Claudine had done something to his hair. It felt painted on. His body was made of wood, like a what what what puppet not puppet the other kind. With somebody else jerking the strings so he flopped and flapped. Claudine made him lean on her on the stairs outside. She was too short and he kept rolling into her. Claudine's neck was fat. Her hair had been hairsprayed. He got some of it in his mouth and spat furiously. Why couldn't she let him take the GODDAMN stairs by himself? He knew it was because somebody, neighbors, might be watching. They needed to see how devoted she was.

Then he had to watch Claudine drive, from the miserable passenger seat. He had become one of those men whose wives drove them around.

At the hospital they put him in a wheelchair, all the better for Claudine to ram him into walls and corners. They got on an elevator and everyone cleared a respectful space around him. Except for Claudine, who planted herself square behind him so that his head was trapped between her two enormous breasts in their pansy floral bunting. He could smell her. Baby powder and perfume stink.

She rolled him up to the doctor's window-thing. The woman behind the desk peered over at him. "Well, who do we have here? How's my favorite fella?"

"Sit on my face, you old trout," Hurley told her. Of course they couldn't understand a thing he said. Claudine and the woman got busy talking about him, his progress or lack of progress, his good and bad days. He had to hand it to Claudine. If anybody else was around, she did a great job of putting on that halo. Her voice fluttered. She practically cooed at him.

When it was his turn to see the doctor, Claudine came in with him so she could do some more showing off. The doctor was too young. Hurley didn't trust a doctor who didn't wear glasses.

In they went. "Mr. Hurley, how are you?" The kid doctor made a point of looking him in the eye and shaking his hand, and even though that was just something they told them to do, something they learned in med school, Hurley was so grateful, he felt himself weeping. He cried all the time now. It was mortifying, it was another mysterious broken part of him. He tried to say he was fine, fine, found that his mouth had gone unaccountably loose, and settled for nodding his head.

"He won't do his exercises," Claudine said. "I'm after him all the time, but he won't mind."

The doctor looked grave. "Now Mr. H., you know if you want to get better, you have to work on it. Balance, strength, and flexibility. We've talked about all that, remember?"

"Rather sit and feel sorry for himself," Claudine said, the spite leaking out from behind her what was it what was it sweet talk fake face.

Hurley squeezed every muscle in his throat, opened his mouth and got his tongue in position, put enough air in his lungs to force out a single intelligible word: "Lie-ey."

"Mrs. Hurley, why don't you give us a minute here?"

It took Claudine an extra beat to realize she was being asked to leave. She grabbed her handbag, gave Hurley a curdled look, and stomped out. Hurley showed her his teeth.

Now it was just the two of them. The doctor probed his bad hand bad arm bad leg. All his broken puppet parts were extended, examined, then returned to him. The doctor said, "I'd like to see a little more improvement. Are the exercises just too frustrating? Is that why you aren't keeping up with them?"

Hurley would have liked to tell him. In his head it came out perfect. How Claudine put his weights and ropes away in different places so he couldn't find them. How he did the best he could on his own, grasping and stretching and pushing his weak side against the wall to strengthen it, how he'd managed on the ladder, in spite of everything, but how he got tired from nothing these days, nothing at all, him, Hurley, who used to work like a lumberjack!

The doctor bent his head attentively to catch any sounds that Hurley made. But no sooner had Hurley shaped the words he needed then other words crowded in behind them, so much it was important for the doctor to understand, how he'd been his mother's youngest, her late-born child, how his father had always looked cross-eyed at him, accused the mother of spoiling him, how he'd gone out for baseball, played shortstop, his nickname Killer from the way he dove to make plays, ate his share of dirt, always hustling, never a slacker, never asked for a handout, served his country in wartime, in Korea, was honorable discharged, came home to build up his own trucking company and marry the pretty, button-eyed girl who had become the old hellcat in the waiting room and they'd never had children but maybe that was just as well since they might have turned out like Claudine. And how one perfectly normal night, reading the newspaper after a dinner of fried chicken and coleslaw, his brain had misfired, had flooded with white, paralyzing light that struck him down, robbed him of his peace of mind and body and left him in this miserable state, an overgrown baby making googly noises.

The doctor placed a hand on Hurley's arm, the good one. "I'm going to arrange for some intensive speech therapy for you. I think if we can get your communication skills to a higher level, it's going to make a big difference in your quality of life."

Hurley nodded. Fine. Great. He didn't think for a minute that anything they came up with was going to help, and even if it did, what then? Nobody was going to want to hear the kinds of things he'd stored up to say.

The doctor seemed pretty pleased with himself though, and he told Hurley he'd be right back. Hurley waited, boring himself with the charts on the wall. The Circulatory System, a freeway laid out in red and blue. The Endocrine System, a heap of rocks you had to carry around inside you.

The doctor was gone so long, he wondered if they'd forgotten about him. He opened to the door to the little room, peered out. Wheeled himself a ways down the corridor. Voices reached him from behind the closed doors he passed, though he couldn't be sure if it was the doctor. Took himself all the way up to the front desk, hoping his mere presence would serve as a reproach, a complaint.

But nobody was there. You had to wonder about hospitals these days. They didn't so much run them as run them into the ground. And when he pushed his way out into the waiting room, it was populated by all manner of waiting people, none of whom was Claudine.

Here was the levelevelevelator, now that was silly, he knew exactly what it was. He stabbed the button, down, and when he got on, here was a crowd of nice people anxious to help. Hurley held up one finger. "Lobby, sir?" And when they got there, didn't they let him off first, all smiles.

He could hardly believe his luck. He rolled soundlessly along the well-carpeted corridors. No one paid him any mind. The great thing about a wheelchair was that people expected you to be all kinds of crippled up, nothing they had to stare at trying to figure out. There was a side entrance with those automatic doors that whooshed open as you approached, and in this way Hurley shot through, a free man.

He decided to stick with the wheelchair, at least for now.

It was the closest he'd come to driving in a long time. Lord, he missed driving. He'd come out onto a cement courtyard, and beyond it a busy street, sunlight making him squint, and the only question how far he could get before Claudine turned the U.S. Marshalls loose on his trail.

Hurley chose a direction that looked promising—no hills, not too crowded—and set off at a pretty good clip, even with the obstacles posed by curbs and cracks, even though his weak arm couldn't push as hard as the other and he kept snailing to his left. The downtown buildings were largely uninteresting, banks and such. He couldn't remember one block from another, what might be up ahead. Hoping he might come across such a thing as a tavern, foolish hope, because he didn't have any money, hadn't seen his wallet in weeks—where had Claudine put it?—and anyway he'd want to walk in on his own two feet like he always had, order his drink as unremarkably as anyone else. Because that was what you missed more than the liquor—which Claudine had also put somewhere he couldn't find—the comfort of simple ritual, being a man standing among men, taking his ease.

But say he never got any better. It was still possible to imagine a place where they might come to know him, get used to his squawks and thumps, understand that his drink was Jim Beam with a little water, give him a peaceable corner where he could sit and watch a ball game . . .

Hurley was just beginning to think in terms of subterfuge, getting off this particular street, when his own car came screeching to the curb. Claudine was driving, and a young man in green hospital clothes stepped out of the passenger side. The jig was up.

"Mr. Hurley?" Approaching him cautiously, like he was some dangerous wild animal instead of his busted self. He was even younger than the doctor. The world was run by children. "Hi there. We've come to get you back home."

"Why don't you just shoot me in the head," Hurley told him, no good, it came out garbage.

Hurley allowed himself to be hoisted out of the wheelchair and placed in the car's front seat. Claudine was staring straight in front of her. The young man stuck his head inside to speak to her. "Don't worry about the wheelchair, Mrs. Hurley. I'll just run it right back." When Claudine didn't answer, he said, "You all have a nice day now," and closed the car door.

Claudine jerked the car into gear. She didn't speak while she bumped and braked her way through downtown traffic. She drove the way she did everything else, with a heavy hand. Once they were out on the parkway, she started in on him. "Whatever pleasure you take from humiliating me, go ahead and make the most of it. Where is it you think you're headed on these jaunts anyway? You take the cake, mister. I wish you'd took yourself off before, when you were a whole man. Would have spared me a lot of work and worry. You couldn't just up and die a natural death, could you? No, you had to do it halfway."

There was a slow-moving bus ahead of them and Claudine occupied herself with stomping on the brake before she took it up again. "All those years I spent picking up after you, setting your food on the table the exact moment you had to have it. You think I lived for that? You think I never wanted anything else in life? You always begrudged me any little bit of money I spent on myself. Oh how I got tired of that sour face you made over anything I took pleasure in. And don't think I don't know about that piece of trash from your office that you snuck around with. I've got your number, yes indeed, and it comes in at a big fat zero."

Right then and there Hurley changed his mind about speech therapy. What a pure pleasure it would have been to answer back.

He had to wonder just which girl from the office she meant. He only wished there'd been a few more.

Claudine put bells on all the doors and motion sensor bulbs in the outdoor lights. His car keys were long gone. There were people he might have called—some of the old birds, the old truckers, were still around—if he wouldn't have scared them off with his telephone voice. His notions of what he would do once he got away were hazy, a daydream he kept practicing and perfecting. Sometimes it was enough to think of himself out in the world again, enjoying the free air. Sometimes he went further, set himself up someplace quiet where people minded their own business. He could get a dog. Claudine had never had any use for a dog.

The one fight he won was over shaving. The next time Claudine came after him with the razor and the shaving cream and the towel, he rose up and shoved her arm away, hard. Claudine yelped. Hurley could tell from the shaken look in her eyes that she was genuinely afraid. Then she rallied.

"Have it your way, then. Go ahead and look like a complete bum. I'll just tell everybody you're too hateful for me to deal with. And if you start in abusing me, I will pack you off to the VA home. Nobody on earth would blame me."

Hurley wondered what everybody she was thinking of. It wasn't like they saw other people these days. He didn't think she'd put him in a home, for the same reason she never let him get away without tracking him down. He had to be there for her to complain about, and for the rest of the world to see how nobly she suffered and sacrificed.

But the thought made for a little yellow flame of fear that he couldn't quite extinguish.

Hurley had just about forgotten about speech the the the give up, until Claudine got off the phone one morning and said, "They're sending somebody over tomorrow to help you practice talking. Try not to act like a wild animal." Hurley figured the insurance was paying for it. He couldn't imagine Claudine handing out a penny for his thoughts.

The visit put Claudine into a fit of housecleaning. The vacuum revved up. The air smelled of bleach. Hurley himself was dusted off and made to put on a clean shirt. The doorbell rang and Claudine went to answer it. Hurley could tell from the tone of her voice that whoever was there, she didn't like them. It had to be a girl.

Claudine led her in to him. "This is Miss Lewis. Don't give her any trouble." Claudine left and went into the kitchen to throw dishes around.

Hurley and Miss Lewis stared at each other. She wasn't a looker. Skirt down to there, big black glasses. He couldn't help being disappointed. "Good morning," she said. "Let's hear you say it too."

"Groming," Hurley came out with. Hopeless.

"Good breath control. Not bad. Can you say my name? Lewis."

"Looo."

"And your name."

"Killer." It wasn't what he'd meant to say, but at least he'd said it right.

Miss Lewis probably thought it was just more gibberish. She had a big cloth bag with her and she set about unpacking it. "Music therapy," she said, hauling out one of those music-playing machines. "We use the music functions in the undamaged part of the brain to help rewire your language functions. I can explain more if you like."

Hurley shook his head. He could have told her that he wasn't big on music. Mostly whatever came out of the truck radio, back when they played songs you might actually sing along to. He hoped he wouldn't have to sing. That would be purely embarrassing.

She got the machine plugged in and a miniature orchestra started up, playing what used to be called longhair music, back before other types of longhairs had appeared on the scene. Music Hurley associated with the unlucky kids back in school who had to tote violin cases around, music that required seriousness and foreign words. But he had to admit it was tuneful enough. Long ripples of notes running up and down. Hurley found his foot, his good foot, tapping along.

"Mozart," said Miss Lewis. "I like to start with him. He seems to make the brain happy. Let's try some exercises now."

She put a red glove on her right hand and a blue glove on her left. Another pair for Hurley. Hurley was supposed to follow her, red blue right left, as the same little piece of music played again and again. It didn't make much sense to Hurley, but he didn't mind. He liked the music just fine. Red red blue blue. His brain needed new wires. That was something he could understand, like needing new sparkplugs. He had a short somewhere.

The music flew up and down. He reached and tapped, tapped and reached. Red red ready, bluebird blue. Claudine had stopped making her kitchen noise. Probably trying to spy on them. Let her. What color was Claudine? Black, like a black eye.

The music stopped. Miss Lewis put down her red blue hands. "Tell me your name."

"Henry." It just came out. He marveled.

Miss Lewis put her thin lips together into a smile. "That's very good. Let's try again tomorrow."

Miss Lewis came every day for two weeks. He learned the whole of the Mozart and now he was on Vivaldi. "Vi-val-di." He could say it. He thought he liked Moz-art better, though. He still sounded like a moose with a cold. Getting rewired took time. He hummed to himself in the shower. Lefty blue, righty red. He soaped his hair, ran his hands over his beard. It was coming in patchy and needed trimming.

Once he'd dressed, Hurley went in search of Claudine. She was watching one of her television shows, with her short little legs propped up on a footstool. He stood in the door and waited for her to say something. When she just kept staring at the screen, he shambled over and stood in front of it.

"Get out of the way, old man, or I'll call the loony house and have them come pick you up."

She said something like that every couple of days. It wasn't anything he paid attention to anymore. "Where?" Hurley demanded.

"Where what?" Claudine bounced around in her seat, trying to look past him. Hurley bounced too. "Oh, Jesus, Mary, and Joseph, if you want something, tell me. I notice you always manage to have something to say when your little friend comes over."

Only Claudine could have managed anything spiteful about Miss Lewis. Miss Lewis was very not interested in being anybody's little friend. She didn't have any more juice in her than a board fence. Hurley rubbed his chin with one hand. He tried to say "shave." It came out as "vashe." But Claudine knew what he meant.

"I threw all the razors out. You won't let me do it and you can't do it yourself. End of story. Grow hair up to your eyeballs, see if I care."

Hurley looked at the television and he looked at Claudine. Of the two, the television would be easier. He unplugged it and pushed it on its stand across the floor. Claudine was out of her chair and slapping at him. She grabbed the television and tried to push back. Hurley blew past her. He noted with pleasure how much stronger he was getting. Moz-art! Viv-al-di! He trundled the television cart into the kitchen and all the way to the back door. Opened it and with one hand held off Claudine, with the other rolled the cart to the teetering edge of the back stairs.

"Vashe!"

"Get back in here with that!"

"Hellcat!" It came out clear as a bell. They were both shocked.

Claudine made another swipe at him. "Don't. You. Dare."

Hurley regarded the television balancing on the brink of the concrete steps. He was holding it back by its cord, the way you might hold on to a dog's tail in a fight. He looked at Claudine's purpling face. He let the cord go. The television fell end over end, hit the steps three times, and landed, smash, facedown.

Now it was open war between them. There was no more of Miss Lewis. Two days after the death of the television, a new television was delivered. Claudine had it carried up to the guest bedroom. She installed a hasp on the door and kept a combination lock on it. Hurley crept down to the basement and threw the breakers in the fuse box in the middle of her shows. Claudine cooked only food that he hated, like oatmeal for breakfast. Hurley spit it out. He suspected Claudine of dosing him with sleeping pills. When she brought him his medicine, which she still did, iron-faced, mornings and bedtimes, there were more pills. If he took them all, he dragged himself through his days and fell into a black hole at night. Sometimes he slept in his chair and woke, dry-mouthed, to find Claudine in the kitchen rustling grocery bags.

Why didn't she just let him go? Spite, Hurley guessed, revenge for all those years she was forced to spend her days occupied with the television and the telephone, when she could have been the toast of two continents. And if the neighbors were to see him stumping along the sidewalk and Claudine lighting out behind him, trying to lasso him, they might draw conclusions.

Hurley thought it was the blue pills that made him sleep. The others were for all his different jumbled parts, his blood pressure and twitching muscles and fatty heart. He started holding them in his mouth instead of swallowing, and squirreled them away in a matchbox he kept under the bed. Then one morning he pretended to fall asleep in his chair. He heard Claudine swish into the room and stand watching him. Hurley let his mouth sag, sent a wet snore her way.

There was the churning sound of her legs as she left, then the snick of the back door lock, then, more distantly, the car starting up.

He had to hurry, and he wasn't very good at hurrying these days. First there was the screwdriver to be fetched from the kitchen drawer, then the stairs to climb, resting along the way, then the devilish little screws, his hands shaking, but finally he had the hasp off, the useless lock dangling from it.

The guest room, Claudine's room now, was scattered with her magazines and face creams and crumpled Kleenex. For all her fuss about housecleaning, the woman was a downright slob and always had been. The new television was set up like an altar. Where to look? Hurley braced himself to search through her underwear drawer, was instantly reminded of parachutes, but here was his reward, a wad of hidden bills, really, she had no imagination. Twenty forty two three four and one hundred and one phooey, counting still hard for him. He scooped up the money and galumphed downstairs.

Out on the street! He needed a a a slow down, a little stroll, nothing to get concerned about calling the police about. Taxi! Taxi! They didn't have any around here. The sidewalk was too hard. It sent jarring pains along his spine. His leg was lopsided, he was afraid of it giving out. But just when he was starting to feel hopeless, expecting Claudine to come around the corner any minute, a car pulled up next to him and a girl said, "Hey, do you know how to get to the mall from here?"

Girls! Three of them! High school girls with lipstick and pink ears! Hurley hitched his way over to them, trying not to look like something scary.

"Nice. Car." And it was, a sporty little red he used to know it Japanese thingy. The girls gaped at him. Foolishly, he pulled out the wad of money, peeled off a bill. "Ride?"

"You want a ride to the mall?" The driver had a twang in

her voice. She wasn't the prettiest one. The others were probably only friends with her because of the car.

Hurley waited while they conferred, heads together. Finally the driver held her hand out for the money, and the girl in the backseat got out.

None of them would sit with him; they all crowded into the front seat. It would have been nice if one of them sat on his lap. Hey! But this was all right because he could watch them all he wanted, the soft neck of the one with short hair, their earrings and thin shoulderblades, their faces, when they turned around to giggle at him, made up with pink and blue and glitter. Their perfume smelled like bubblegum. The radio played noisy, bang-boom music.

They were out on the highway, going fast. Wind from the open windows buffeted him. There had been an argument about how to get to the mall and now they'd settled it one way or the other, though not all of them seemed convinced. Hurley didn't care where they ended up. He could have stayed there forever, listening to the girl voices and the racketing music, while the wind tried to blow him all over the sky.

But the car slowed and began circling acres of parked cars. The mall, he guessed. The girls were arguing about what do with him. "We can't walk in with him, I mean, *God.*"

"Well, we can't just dump him out either, come on. They have, like, security cameras."

"I think he's got some kind of, like, condition."

In the end they pulled up to an entrance and one of the girls helped him out of the car and trotted him through the doors. "You okay, mister? Look, you probably ought to put your money away now."

Hurley realized he still had the wad of bills in one fist, and shoved his hand into his pants pocket. He watched the girl's tight little behind as she ran out the door. He guessed he was what they called a dirty old man. It didn't seem like such a bad line of work.

The mall wasn't any place Hurley got excited about. Claudine used to try and drag him here, turn him into one of those tame husbands loaded down with handbags and packages. But now he felt giddy with possibilities. It wasn't that crowded, but it was more people than he'd seen in one place in a long long how long and all the lights and all the things for sale and first he was going to get himself one of those scooter carts that people zipped around in. And then maybe sit in one of the massaging chairs and get a pretzel and a cup of coffee and a hamburger.

Once or twice he thought he saw, at a distance, the girls from the car, or maybe they were other girls. Even if he didn't find them, he figured he could pay somebody else for a ride home or just stay here until everything closed and then somebody else would have to figure out what to do with him. Meanwhile, he was having quite a time. He bought a number of small items, after judicious examinations and considerations. A roll of peppermint Life Savers. A new wallet for his money. A package of bandana handkerchiefs. A hamburger in a paper wrapper that could have been better but so what. And best of all, he scoot scooted into what at first he took for a ladies' place, a beauty whatsit, then, seeing men go in also, made so bold as to request (in a process lasting some little time, utilizing gesture as well as strangled words), a haircut and beard trim.

And though he would have preferred a proper barber

instead of a girl—ah, the universe of girls!—she was so deft and respectful of him, her butterfly hands so light and skilled, Hurley had to make an effort to avoid ignoble weeping.

She handed him a mirror to inspect his newly shorn and clipped self. Hurley held it in his good hand. His beard, trimmed and tamed, gave him the air of a sea captain. His skin was pink and fragrant. He looked, by God, like a whole man, no matter what kind of ruin he was inside. He gave her what he hoped was a big tip.

After that he bought a pretzel, a big soft one dripping with cheese, and negotiated, with difficulty, the public restroom. He found a spot by a giant potted palm to park the scooter. Struggling against sleep, and losing, he wished it would end right here for him, Hurley's Last Stand, without fuss or fretting or anyone telling him what he couldn't do for his own good.

No such luck. Someone was joggling his shoulder. "Sir? Sir?" Hurley swam up to the surface of waking, saw a man's face peering down at him, another man nearby, the police but not the police, the shopping mall kind, anyway, whoever was in charge of old men falling asleep after closing hours.

Hurley tried to tell them his name but he didn't try very hard, and then there was his brand-new wallet, which identified him as absolutely nobody. He sat in the guards' office, watching a boxing match on their little black-and-white television while they called around, trying to find somebody to take charge of him. Hurley gathered, from their conversation—nobody ever thought he could hear!—that they believed someone might have abandoned him, like a baby left on a doorstep. Maybe Claudine wouldn't report him missing. His picture in the newspaper, Do You Know This Man? A houseful of softhearted girls would adopt him, take him home with them to be their honorary grandfather.

No such luck. The real police arrived and gave him a ride home in a squad car. Marched him up to his own front door and rang the bell.

Hurley could tell that they had their suspicions of Claudine. "If you didn't take him there, ma'am, how do you think he ended up at the mall?"

Claudine said she had no idea, and that he was brain-affected, prone to wandering off, in spite of her vigilance. She tried to look all kinds of concerned and weepy, but the evil light was in her eyes. Hurley clung to the policeman's arm, gibbering. "Please," he tried to say. "Take me me me me." Name of God, couldn't they see her for who she was? "Hellelel." Hellcat.

They might have believed him, but they didn't know what to do about it. They told Claudine to call if she needed any further assistance, and they backed the squad car down the driveway and accelerated out of sight. Hurley's Last Hope.

Claudine faced him down. Her lipstick was smeared in one corner, as if she had been eating something bloody. "The police! Now you brought the police out here, to shame me in front of everybody! I will not live this way!"

Hurley leered at her. Or attempted to; he wasn't always sure what his face was doing, and anyway her vampire mouth unnerved him. He stomped out to the kitchen, opened the refrigerator door and stood there, bathed in its chilly light. He wasn't hungry. It just seemed like a good place to ignore Claudine.

She followed him. She started talking. Hurley opened the freezer compartment and stuck his head in. The motor kicked on, humming. Cold noise enveloped him. He thought, This is what it will be like to be dead. All the moving parts of you, frozen. No more thought than a package of corn. He was aware of Claudine behind him, beating on him, pulling at him. I Will Not. Live This Way. I Will Not. Not Live.

The next day phone calls were made. Hurley sensed them rather than heard them. A current of whispers. His breakfast and lunch were left, cold, on the kitchen table. In the basement, laundry machines thundered. Claudine was everywhere and nowhere, like a gas. She had done something to the windows and he couldn't get them open. Doors too. Maybe he'd already died without noticing it and this was hell. Locked in the house with Claudine's pissed-off ghost.

Then the suitcases came. Or rather, they came and went, since once Hurley spotted them (at the bottom of the stairs, in the pantry, nudging out of the coat closet), they disappeared again. He heard Claudine yanking drawers open and slamming them shut. He feared the worst. He tried to remember Mozart, but the notes got jumbled in his head and came out brassy. He couldn't find the new bandana handkerchiefs he'd bought. He dreamed about the blue pills, woke, and scrabbled around under the bed until he found the matchbox.

He caught a suitcase sneaking up on him outside his bedroom door. Hurley kicked and dragged it inside the room, heaved it up on the bed and wrestled it open. Shirtsleeves waved at him. His socks, rolled into balls, spilled out and bounced across the floor. Here was the bathrobe he'd missed. Layers and layers of his clothes. It turned him cold.

Hurley dumped out the suitcase and went looking for

Claudine. He heard her in the bathroom, flushing. He parked himself outside the door, leaning into it, and shuffled his feet. He heard her go still, then draw her breath in with a hiss.

"Get out the way, old man!" Her voice was shrill. The door lock snicked shut.

Hurley put his mouth up against the crack in the door. "Where I don't go."

"Oh yes you will. Tomorrow morning I am taking you to the VA Hospital in Danville. They can keep track of you from now on. They're going to put you in the demented ward so you can talk to the other crazy people."

Hurley shook the doorknob and heaved his shoulder against the wood. "Bitch whore!"

"Go right ahead, act as ugly as you want. I guess you can talk just fine when you got something nasty to say." Claudine's voice gained altitude and assurance. "I can have the police here in two seconds. I can have the crazy people ambulance haul you off. Don't think I won't."

"———!" There was some word word word he wanted to call her, the worst and most poisonous word ever, but he couldn't think of it or maybe it hadn't been invented yet.

"So you might as well come along with me peaceable. Because what is there left of you? You used to have some pride. I'll give you that much. Now you drag yourself around like an old dog. What difference does it make if you rot away here or someplace else? At least at the hospital you'll be among your own kind. They won't take as much notice of you. Now get out of my way. Somebody around here has to do a day's work."

Hurley stepped aside. After a little while the door opened and Claudine came out. She looked at Hurley as if trying to decide on one more thing to say, but then, seeing that she had already defeated him, she sniffed and headed downstairs.

There was no more escape, unless it was from his old dog's body. Show some spunk, Hurley. He thought he'd had a pretty good life, except for the Claudine part, and he'd worked around that as best he could. There were things he'd miss and things he wouldn't. That seemed fair. All divvied up. He wished he could make a speech, put everything together like the last scene of a movie. Hurley, The End. Dead Dog.

There were a lot of blue pills. He decided to wait until morning so he would at least have the ride to enjoy. Get out of the house for a last sniff of fresh air, as well as stick Claudine with the embarrassment of arriving with his dead self. He took apart the blue capsules, emptied out their chalky insides, scraped them together into a corner of his handkerchief. His hands shook worse than usual. It was hard to believe something so small, some little bit of powder, was enough to kill you. But then, the clot that made his brain bleed and his body seize up was small too. The world was full of things that made no sense. Maybe that could be his exit line.

The next morning, even as Claudine was fussing with the car, smacking his suitcases around, he panicked, thinking the blue pills might not be enough to get the job done, or maybe because it was really going to happen. In the bathroom he rummaged through any other pills he could find, pills for forgotten maladies, pills for all the ailments he and Claudine had between them, hoping that something in the mix would bubble up inside of him like a cartoon chemistry experiment.

He thought about writing a note, or maybe a will, except of course his writing was as bad as his speech, nothing landing on the page right. I, Hurley, being of sound mind and unsound body, do give and bequeath my wife of too many years, my brand-new corpse, may it stink up the place.

Claudine had his breakfast set out. Coffee, orange juice, cereal, bacon, toast. The condemned man eats a hearty last meal. The phone rang and Claudine went to answer it. Hurley braced himself against the wall, took out the handkerchief and dumped the mess of powder into his orange juice. It made a little heap in the bottom of the glass. He poked at it, stirred it up with a spoon, trying to be quiet, but his idiot hands made a bad job of it, the very last thing he ever had to do and he couldn't do it right, his chickenshit body betraying him one more time. The glass clanked and rattled like something caught in an earthquake, and here was Claudine charging back into the room.

"If you're just going to play with that food, I'll throw it out." She snatched the glass from his hand and set it on the counter.

"Back!"

"No, sir. You can have a plastic cup, like a baby." She reached into the refrigerator for the juice. "There now. Drink that and try not to make a dribbling mess of yourself."

"Back me!" Hurley lunged forward in his chair, took a wild swipe at her. Claudine sidestepped him, picked up the juice glass from the counter, and, with a slick little smile, drank it down.

"Now then," she said. "You decide you don't want that bacon, I'll take it off your hands."

Hurley ate the bacon. He was trying to work out what he might say. I. You. Juice.

J's were especially hard for him. They always came out

sounding like he had a mouth full of glue. He put extra sugar on his cereal, spooned it up and chewed thoughtfully. "Hurry *up*," Claudine told him, shoving the last of his suitcases out the back door. "I haven't got all day."

No, she probably didn't. He got up from the table and set his dishes in the sink. There was the rolling noise of the garage door and then the car's engine, VOOM. Claudine always hit the accelerator starting up and fed it too much gas. He figured he'd finally get his chance at driving. It was time to go. He took a last sip of coffee. Killer Hurley, ready for the world.

The Woman at the Well

Of course they had Bible Study in prison. It was important that you take to heart the notions of sin and redemption. They made you sing, and not just church hymns, but "Rock-A My Soul" and "In the Sweet Bye and Bye," songs you could move around to, clap and sway. You sang, "Jesus Met The Woman At the Well."

Jesus met the woman at the we–ell
Jesus met the woman at the we–ell
Jesus met the woman at the we–eh–eh–ll
And He told her everything she ever done

It was a small group today, only six of them in the Activity Room. Five inmates and Janice, the volunteer minister. Janice was with the Disciples of Christ. She was nice, though once you figured out she was nice to everybody all the time, it took some of the shine off it. Janice was fifty or maybe sixty. She was homely, she had a face built for that word, *homely,* and so it was hard to tell age. A long, bony face. Glasses on a chain, a little frizz of gray-blond hair. Janice wore turtlenecks even now, in the middle of summer, baggy cotton pants, and Hush Puppies. She never seemed to feel the heat, while the rest of them choked on it night and day. Even the air in prison was locked up. Maybe Janice didn't have enough juice in her to sweat. She was married to a Disciples of Christ minister. Homely didn't seem to matter much to a minister.

That was not a Christian thought. It was the sign of a hardened heart. Anyway, you knew that nobody young or pretty or dressed or made-up nicely would ever come into this place. And, the sly, secret part of you whispered, even if they did you would hate and envy them like poison. Still, you would have liked to rest your eyes on something stylish for a change.

> He said, Wo-man, wo-man
> Where is your husband?

Most weeks the Bible Study meeting was bigger, because after all it was something to do, and the Activity Room was better than the Dayroom any way you looked at it. But then people found out it was too much like Group, where you had to talk about how worthless and pitiful you were, except here it went by different names, *For all had sinned and fallen short of the glory of God.* And you actually had to read the Bible. So many of them couldn't read, just flat-out couldn't, it was amazing. If they'd ever spent a day in school, it was impossible to tell. It was sad, really, to hear them struggle over Bible words like *salvation* or *humble*.

It was un-Christian to look down on them, but you couldn't help it, they were stupid. Stupid, and black, most of them, and poor, and crack-addled, and while you knew that none of it was really their fault, well maybe the drugs, knew that they had been treated viciously, beaten and raped and whored and kicked in the head again and again, still, it did not seem possible to love them in a Christian way.

Christ was perfect love and perfect forgiveness. Of course it was discouraging when you fell short of that. You prayed for God's help in becoming more Christlike, although it was understood that you would always fall short. That was where *humble* came in. You were supposed to make a real point of not measuring up. The whispering part of you said, Why bother if you'd never get it right, and religion was just another prison sentence, a lifetime sentence, and only a fool would love everybody or want to. Love skinny, dried-up Janice, who smiled so hard her gums showed, smiled and smiled when nothing was funny so she could get you to believe in God? Love big fat mouth-breathing Bunny with her permanent yellow crescents of underarm sweat? Or mean-mouthed Jameelah, or scary, epileptic Crystal, or any of the warthog guards who by accidents of fate or circumstance had been granted absolute power over you . . .

"Teresa?"

Janice was smiling at you, that big, crucified smile. Bible Study was about the only place you were ever called by your given name. It was your turn to read and you hadn't been paying attention. You smoothed your Bible and pretended to hunt for the verse.

"Matthew 5:45," said Janice helpfully, as you hoped she would. You cleared your throat and read:

That you may be the children of your Father in heaven.
He causes his sun to rise on the evil and on the good,
and sends rain on the righteous and the unrighteous.

"Thank you, Teresa," said Janice. You were a good reader and you knew Janice called on you more often because of it. You had always done well at school things.

"Let's talk about this," said Janice, folding her hands in her lap and leaning forward to include them all in the beam of her attention. "First, let's break it down, see what it's saying. Who has questions? Questions are what we're here for, so don't be shy."

Nobody wanted to say the wrong thing, so there was silence. And you had just finished reading, so speaking up right away would have been showing off. It wasn't good for a white girl to be seen as showing off. Janice measured the silence, and when it went on for too long she said, "I like the part about the rain. I think about a big crowd of people walking along under umbrellas, and nobody looking at them would have any idea which ones were good or bad."

You had to wonder what would happen if Janice ever allowed a silence to die a natural death. Or maybe she knew what she was doing, because Bunny spoke up:

"There's people who take one look at you and right away they're acting like they're way better than you are."

Everybody nodded. They all knew what she meant. Even if it was true, in your own case, that you'd been pretty and had done your share of looking down on others. It took prison to let everybody think they were better than you.

Janice said, "But that's not how God sees us. I know it's hard for us to imagine. Somebody who doesn't care about our outsides, only what's in our hearts. God is beyond our imaginings. That's where faith comes in."

While Janice was talking, Jameelah and Keisha were nudging and rolling their eyes. It was very disrespectful. The worst part of prison wasn't being locked up, it was who they locked you up *with*. Jameelah and Keisha were just kids. Screwed-up, ruined kids. They were always acting low and obnoxious and trashy. It was their first time at Bible Study, and probably their last. Here was Keisha, singing under her breath and chair-dancing, here was Jameelah mouthing a little wah-wah chorus with shoulder shimmies. You'd think that prison would be the one place you could get people to behave . . .

"Jameelah?"

Janice blinked and smiled, blinked and smiled. Janice could report you, get you kicked right into segregation, even if she did it nicely. So Jameelah quit her showing off, quieted, and stuck her bottom lip out in the ugliest possible fashion. Which was her way of demonstrating she wasn't really giving in and nobody could make her do anything, and you understood that, you did, but you got tired of seeing it.

"Maybe you could tell us what faith means to you."

Jameelah turned to Keisha with a look that clearly said, *Who this bitch think she is?* But Keisha was staring down at her Bible with a pious, cow-eyed expression. Keisha was always pretending to be even dumber than she really was. Jameelah took another long, narrowing look around the room, found no help there. Cornered, she muttered, "Means my grandma and her church talk."

"Your grandmother went to church?" Janice's helpful echo.

"She wore us out prayin. Prayed for things to get better and nothing ever did."

"We can't always see how God is making things better. That's where faith comes in."

But Jameelah and Keisha were trading secret, amused looks again. Jameelah liked to sneak up behind you, jab two stiff fingers into your kidney. Or walk past and flick her wrist your way, snag just enough hair to yank it out of your scalp. Then make a big production of showing it to you from across the room, smirking and rubbing your hair between her fingers, putting it in her mouth and sucking and tonguing it and any other disgusting thing she could invent. Jameelah bragged about everybody she'd ever beat up or cut up. There was always a different story and you figured some of them were lies but you didn't know which ones. *Cut old girl right through her top and bottom lips. Down to her teeths. Old girl won't be talking her shit no more.*

Someday, and you hoped it came soon, Jameelah was going to run out of luck, get her ass kicked by a guard who would know how to hurt her without it showing, or an inmate who wouldn't care, turn her black face lumpy and purple with bruises.

Here you sat in Bible Study, Amen-ing along with everybody, and all the while you were thinking such thoughts. No matter how quiet and *humble* you looked, inside of you was a monster, and the monster talked to you in that sly, secret voice. But the monster had done a lot worse than talk.

She said, Je-sus, Je-sus
Ain't got no husband

This was why you had to believe in Jesus Our Lord, because who else could forgive you and lift you up from hell? Or maybe hell was just like prison and you could get used to it too. Get used to the toilet stink and the lights that went on and off, on and off, always by somebody else's choosing. Who would have thought that you'd miss that, turning a light on when you wanted it? Get used to prison underwear and generic sanitary pads and your skin growing coarse and thick because there was no such thing as decent soap or lotion. Get used to the sight of your own face reflected in a stainless steel mirror, a little older every day.

You were twenty-six when you came here and you were thirty-four now and one of the things your sentence, *twenty-five years to life*, meant was that you would never have a child.

Which was worse, never to have a child or never see it, have it grow up a stranger to you? Almost everybody here had children. The children had been parceled out by the state, or given over to relatives, and sometimes they came for visits and sometimes not. Sometimes there were pictures and crayon drawings and baby dolls, and sometimes not. Almost all the children were black, even the children of the white women, and that probably signified something but you kept such thoughts to yourself.

The children were what was left over once the men were gone. Nobody had a man waiting for them on the outside, even though men were the reason they were in prison to begin with. That was true of nearly everyone, in some fashion, whether they had fought over the men or the men had to be impressed or gotten back at, or maybe the men had made them do things. Like Bunny, who'd driven her boyfriend and some other jerk all over Decatur, from the 7-Eleven to the Clark Station to the Bigfoot, filling a gym bag with cash register money, a regular taxi service. At the Clark station, the boy behind the register had been shot in the face. The boyfriend's name was Reno. Bunny talked about him like she'd just seen him this morning, like they were a normal couple and did normal things like go to the laundromat or out to the movies: *Oh, Reno hates it when you give him a hamburger and it's not cooked through. Reno has him a big laugh every time that Taco Bell commercial comes on, the one with the little dog. He says we should get a little dog like that, name him Junior.*

Maybe you could still have fond thoughts about a man if the worst thing he'd talked you into doing was drive a car.

Janice said, "Faith is what helps us through the times when everything else seems bleakest."

Except that was every day. Every day of twenty-five years to life, and there wasn't enough faith in the world for that. They advised you not to count the time you had left, months or years, it would drive you crazy. Besides, there was always the possibility of early release, good behavior credit, if those possibilities didn't drive you, et cetera, the way they tossed the numbers around: *You might get as many as seven or eight years off. Definitely three to five.* The lawyer who'd never liked you much anyway, serving this up for a consolation prize as he cut you loose. Like there wasn't any difference between *three* and *eight.*

Janice said, "Who can think of another Bible verse about faith?"

You knew what she was fishing for, they'd talked about it just last week, but you still didn't feel like volunteering. Epileptic Crystal spoke up, surprising everyone: "You mean the one about the mountains."

"Yes, that's one. Do you remember all of it?"

But Crystal wasn't saying anything more. She was a jack-in-the-box, with her frozen, medicated stare, her habit of popping up with unexpected speech, or, if the electrical storms in her brain broke through, with unearthly squeals and snores and gargling. Once they took Crystal in to the Beauty School, gave her a permanent that made her red hair stand up like a rooster's comb, painted her face pink and blue. She didn't seem to notice any of it, which made her even scarier. Like she'd forgotten she had an outside. Crystal had been here as long as anyone could remember, ten twelve fifteen years. They said she'd strangled her own mother, but other people said no, it was only a neighbor she'd killed, and the mother was thrown in there just to make a more interesting story. Crystal had hands like shovels.

"Matthew 17:20," said Janice. "Because you have so little faith, I will tell you the truth, if you have faith as small as a mustard seed, you can say to this mountain, Move from here to there, and it will move."

"Ain't no seeds in no mustard."

"Shut up, fool."

Bunny said, "I wouldn't waste time on mountains. I'd say, 'Open up that big front gate, let me out of here.'"

There was general hilarity and agreement at this. Janice let it run its course, smiling, before she got back to business. "I wonder if Jesus meant real, actual mountains. Maybe he was thinking of the way our troubles can feel like mountains. Mountains in our heads."

Jameelah said, "That exactly what it feel like. Big ole lonesome mountain in my head."

You figured she was mocking, but she had an intense expression, an expression you only saw when she'd singled you out for some special meanness: what had you ever done to her? Jameelah had blackberry eyes and a round face, the face of a furious child. Now, who would have believed such a thing, maybe Jameelah would get herself saved along with everybody else, and then you and your monster thoughts would be the only one left out.

"The real miracle," Janice said, "is when we ask Jesus to move the mountain, come into our hearts. We know he is only waiting for us to call on him, confess our wrongdoing, invite him to dwell within us."

He said
Wo-man, wo-man
Where is your husband?
I know everything you ever done

The mountain was everything you'd ever done. The miracle would be to roll it all back so it never was.

Say Jesus fixed it so you'd never gotten married. That would be your mountain. Make it unhappen. It didn't seem like a lot to ask, and it wouldn't hurt anybody. That long-ago time had been freedom, but you hadn't recognized it then and so it didn't count. If Jesus or anyone else was to hear you now, they'd think you'd been dragged kicking and screaming into marriage, but of you course you hadn't. You'd called your freedom *lonesome,* and you'd traded it in for Howell Wolfe, a man with a joke for a name, mostly because he'd asked you to. And because he'd been so sure of himself. Howell Wolfe was a big man with a big man's booming voice, and he knew what he wanted, and besides he was older than you were, he had knowledge of the world that you'd never have. He knew about money and politics and heavy machinery and electricity and football and the stock market and a whole list of other things that you didn't really care about, but it was nice to know that the knowledge was right there if you ever needed it.

And so the two of you got married, and since Howell Wolfe had been married before he wasn't inclined to make a big deal out of it, but you still had your dress and a cake and flowers and the wedding favors in lavender and silver, like you'd always planned. And then there was a whole house that needed to be furnished and stocked and decorated. Howell Wolfe wasn't one to care about things like curtains or china, but he understood, from his previous effort at marriage, that it was natural for women to fuss with a house. Over time, his ideas and opinions and likes and dislikes had just naturally taken up space in your head, the same way that Howell Wolfe took up the space on a bed or a couch. You learned to keep a mug in the freezer so he'd have a frosted glass for his beer, and to buy a certain brand of beef gravy he had a taste for over mashed potatoes, and to wipe the bathroom mirror clean of steam after a shower, and any number of other things necessary to maintain the comfort of Howell Wolfe.

In many ways you'd been a good wife to him.

Jameelah said, "Why he got to be invisible? I mean God. And why he got to be some *man*?"

Then you'd been married awhile, settled into it, and it wasn't that you were unhappy, not really. Unhappy made it sound like something had happened, and it was more as if things stopped happening. The wedding was over and the pictures placed into an album and that was that. The house was finished, that is, all the interesting things had been purchased and the house required only inconvenient repairs and maintenance. As did Howell Wolfe himself. Not terribly often, after the first few weeks and months. But you knew what it meant on nights you came in from the bathroom to find him propped up in bed, his pajamas folded on a chair and an impish expression on his face, as if he was playing a particularly naughty joke. And all you could do was try to reflect some portion of that naughty enthusiasm back in your own face, although you were also supposed to act as if the whole idea took you by surprise, and you hadn't considered any such thing until Howell Wolfe's intention brought it irresistibly to mind.

Then it was a matter of positioning yourself and letting him wad your nightgown up around your neck, because he liked that part, like making you bare and all the looking and touching it allowed him. Although you wished he'd turn the bedside light off, because there was a particular view of Howell Wolfe, inflamed and engorged, his mighty stomach atop it all, which you found discouraging.

It seemed natural enough to think about having a baby. And really, everything might have turned out differently if you had. But Howell Wolfe was not in a hurry for a baby; he said he wanted you all to himself for a little while longer. Besides, he already had children, big, grown-up children who were only a few years younger than you were, although it was not considered polite for people to point this out. The children hated you even before they met you. You hoped this would change over time, but of course, that was not what happened.

Janice said, "God is everywhere. Even in prison. And because he is invisible, because he is a spirit, he is mostly in our hearts."

No one looked very convinced by this. Their hearts were not hospitable places. Their hearts were furnished with unmade beds and dirty sinks. Jameelah and Keisha were getting restless again, shifting and whispering. Janice said, "What is it, Keisha?"

"I say, the devil made me do it." A joke.

"Made you do what?"

"You know. My troubles."

You were unclear on what, exactly, Keisha's troubles were. Something with crack, more than likely, the thievery and low-life business that went along with crack. You had to wonder what all that was about, drugs, because you never even smoked cigarettes or drank more than a glass of wine at parties, and here you were, biding your time with girls who put who knows what into their skins, and in the most disgusting ways possible. Crack: even the name was nasty.

"The devil doesn't make us do anything. And you know what? Neither does God. God gives us free will. He wants us to choose to love Him. To make our own decision to turn over our lives and hearts to Him."

Nobody had anything to say to that. There was one of those lulls when attention drifted and shifted, and the women moved their haunches stealthily beneath them on the molded plastic chairs, and examined without really seeing the posters on the walls that exhorted them to seek prenatal care, get job training, achieve self-respect. The overhead fan stirred the heavy air. From somewhere outside the Activity Room, down an echoing corridor, came the sound of a shout, abruptly cut off. There would be another fifteen or twenty minutes of Bible Study, that was all, and then they would rejoin what was known as the general inmate population.

How could you choose what you loved? God or anything else? It wasn't a decision thing. If it was, you could have decided to love Howell Wolfe, and that would have been that. Serviceable, married, everyday love. The other kind, the crazy, boy-mad, broken-heart kind of love, was something you figured you'd outgrown, and revisited only when you went to the movies. Lovelovelovelovelove. Say it often enough and it was just a noise. What good was love to you now? For similar reasons, there was a man who you no longer thought of by name. He was just He. Like God. The monster in you sniggered.

Jameelah said, "I know for a fack there's a devil. And they peoples follow the devil too."

At work, at the hardware store, you wore a uniform smock over your clothes, designed to protect you from all the hardware grime. It had the fortunate result of preventing men from being able to look down your shirt. But since your name was embroidered on the pocket, that meant everybody had the use of it. *Teresa, huh. What's the other one's name?*

You were accustomed to men who said such things, even at the strangest times. Nine in the morning while you were ringing up their tubes of caulking or washers or staple guns. Invitations. Jokes you pretended not to get. One or two of the worst cases made a habit of asking you about merchandise that was always either on the bottom shelf so they could make you bend over, or up high enough so that they had to hold a ladder for you to climb, maybe brush up against you while you tried to hold yourself aloof, tried not to see their faces reflecting the pictures in their heads.

You'd thought that once you were married you could quit your job, or at least cut back on the hours, since your new husband made a good living. But Howell Wolfe was thrifty. No, outright cheap. In fairness, it was the only thing you could really say against him. He fussed importantly over grocery bills and phone bills. Ordinarily, cheapness wasn't a thing that ended up killing a man.

Not that the job was all bad. Sometimes it was nice to have something that was yours, a place to go to. And there were always nice people who came in, people you looked forward to seeing. He was one of those. A face you came to recognize. He was always stopping in for one thing or another, though later he admitted that he'd made extra trips on your account. He was polite. Never in a big important hurry. He waited his turn, and even once he got up to the register he didn't go in for small talk. You appreciated that. So many people were convinced of the urgency and importance of hearing themselves make noise. He kept his eyes to himself, although you noticed him watching your hands. Later, after a great many other things had happened, you realized it was a kind of flirting. How slow you could make your hands move. Slow dance of wrists and fingertips, coins and receipts. His knuckle slid across your palm. And then one night when you got off work, he was outside waiting for you.

And the woman said, the serpent beguiled me, and I did eat. He didn't have a name you used now, but back then you'd covered yourself with his name as if it were perfume. Saying it over and over in your head. Lovelovelovelove. Here was the part where the memories got confused, or maybe over time, from overuse they'd simply worn out, and you couldn't remember the order of things. Or because they were shameful things that would grieve Our Lord Jesus, you tried not to dwell on them. You couldn't remember touching. Or you could, but you couldn't feel it anymore, the greedy ache of it. You weren't fool-

ing Jesus or anybody else. You were a monster. You hadn't said
no to anything he'd told you to do.

If you want us to be together, it's the only way. Because surely
Howell Wolfe would never give you a divorce, was likely to
act in violent and unpredictable ways if you asked. And they
couldn't just run off, since Howell Wolfe would have ways to
find you, would come after you, would lay in wait to exact his
vengeance. You had long since come to appreciate the absolute dumbness and evil of such arguments. At the trial there
had been a lot of testimony about Howell Wolfe's insurance
money and how you stood to benefit from it, and that was reason enough for most people.

*I can't stand the thought of him touching you. It makes me
crazy.*

You remembered the weight of secrets. And once or twice,
when going about your chores at work or at home, when you'd
stopped absolutely still, transfixed with wanting. And in the
fever and hurry of wanting and secrets, it had come to seem
that kissing touching *fucking*—might as well say the word—
a man who was not your husband was the same as any other
betrayal.

All you have to do is leave the side door to the garage open. And
then go to spend the evening at your sister's. The house backed
on a forest preserve and it was possible to get in and out without
people noticing. It was possible to enter and wait in the garage
until Howell Wolfe came out to watch the portable television
he kept on his workbench, something he did every night. There
were two full-sized televisions in the house but he liked sitting
in the garage. It was a big garage and he had it fixed up with a
lawn chair and an electric heater for cold weather.

Janice said, "Maybe you're right. Maybe the devil is just the absence of God's love."

Janice looked tired. Well of course you'd get tired, trying to beat the Bible into heads like these. Janice craned her neck delicately within her turtleneck. The faintest sign that she might be feeling the heat. In a little while she would pack up her Bible and go home to her minister husband and fix dinner and pray some more over it. What did Janice pray for? She was already full of charitable deeds and holy thoughts. *Oh Lord we thank thee.* For her harmless, holy life. Because Janice had never let anyone talk her into anything. Had never wished to be talked into anything, or maybe she had, but nobody was interested, and so she was not going to hell. Like you were. And while you were waiting around for hell to happen, you lived in an obscene barnyard where the animals were made to line up, count off, squat during strip searches so their labia could be inspected, eat with plastic spoons, answer to their last names only, even if that name belonged to a dead man.

All this time, you had been what they called a model prisoner.

If I do what I mean to do, I'll leave the front door standing open. Then when you come back, don't go inside. Go to the neighbor's and call the police.

He had not wanted you to see the body. But the police, who had not been fooled for a minute, showed you the photographs of Howell Wolfe's liquid, flattened face. They asked you about the state of your marriage. It seemed there had been some gossip already.

I know everything you ever done.

"Let us pray," sighed Janice.

That was the signal that the session was over, and you stood up and held hands in a prayer circle. Oh no. You'd been careless. Usually you arranged things so you held hands with Janice and maybe Bunny, but today you reached out and here was Jameelah on your left and Crystal on your right. Jameelah's hand was curled over, ready to fist, and you looked at each other sideways, because even though your eyes were supposed to be closed in prayer, it would be bad judgment to be that unwary. Jameelah's face was full of thunder, and her black eyes moved back and forth beneath her lashes, some kind of skitter Morse code: *Hurt/Don'thurt/me/you/me/you.* Janice had closed her eyes. So had Crystal, on your right—you made sure of this with a glance—and Crystal had your hand locked in her strangler's grip, and maybe that was what sent the electricity in Crystal's brain right through you.

One minute you were pretending to follow along with the prayer, even as the monster inside you hooted and sneered. Then there was something just below the threshold of sound. A vibration. Bees in a hive. A wind gathering itself.

Your right hand sizzled. Crystal jerked and flopped and pulled you over on top of her. Crystal's mouth was inventing new obscene words, a whole new alphabet of spit. Her eyes were hard-boiled eggs. She squealed, a purely mechanical sound. Her heels drummed the floor and there was a smell, metallic and urinous both, as if all of Crystal's fluids had been superheated. A commotion of voices, but it only reached you dimly, because Crystal's electricity was surging and snapping through you, blue and yellow brain fireworks. She had you so tight that your eyelashes tangled together, and when one of Crystal's eyes opened—opened normally, that is, as if there might be seeing involved—it was like looking straight through a telescope at the universe in miniature, otherwise known as *heaven*.

And you saw in that instant how all the mathematics in the world might be erased, so that *three* might indeed become the same as *eight,* and how one particular, burning day would stop lasting twenty-five years or forever.

And then Crystal's grip loosened and you were raised to your feet. Incredibly, your left hand was still in Jameelah's and had been all the while. Guards were running in and talking importantly on their radios, and Crystal moaned at the center of a circle, people telling her to do this or that, calm down, sit up, speak or don't speak.

No one seemed to notice Jameelah, crying and crying, bawling really, butting her inky head against your breasts, soaking your shirt with her tears.

Oh sweet baby girl, don't cry, don't cry. But you were crying too. Who would have believed such a thing? That here was your child, arrived at last, and it was true what they'd said all along. Love was the only way back into heaven.

Treehouse

Garrison lived in one Chicago suburb and worked in another, so that the freeway between the two was as familiar to him as his own face in the mirror. He knew its moods, its good days and bad, its haggard mornings and tired nights. In summer, veils of heat haze and pollution draped across the sky. Sunlight reflected in blinding metal smears. In winter, the windshield wipers dragged through layers of churned-up brown slush, and taillights lit the early dusk. If Garrison was lucky the drive took forty-five minutes. If luck was against him it was an hour or more. On the drive to work the skyline of downtown Chicago was fastened to his windshield, its impossibly massive towers rendered light and floating by distance. Of course there were occasions when he went into the city for one reason or another, but it was hard to connect the pretty mirage he saw while driving with the actual place.

He drove a ten-year-old Lexus, built back before they began loading them up with too many overcomplicated features. He maintained it immaculately, changed the oil himself and took the car into the dealer at the first sign of vibration or imbalance. The Lexus had an excellent sound system. He carried with him a variety of music, jazz and classic rock and, for days when he had to muscle through fast-moving traffic, opera. He had all manner of equipment designed for his comfort and safety: a compass mounted on the dashboard, a cupholder for his coffee, and a hi-tech insulated mug his daughter gave him for Christmas. There was a special stand for charging his cell phone and a sheepskin seat cover to ease his back. The trip could be measured out in miles, minutes, landmarks, other people's bad driving, fatigue. He was used to it and didn't complain overmuch, since complaining never got you anywhere.

One evening in early spring, Garrison drove home aware of a dangerous lack of concentration, an extra effort required to keep his eyes and hands and reflexes focused. It had been a bad and numbing day at work. He was a division head for one of the large health insurance companies, or, in the preferred terminology, a health care provider. The first two floors of the building were taken up by the call center, at least what was left of it after much of the work had been routed to a group of Indian subcontractors specially trained in colloquial American speech. The rooms contained dozens of computer screens, each of them glowing with the blue of aquariums, another mirage that momentarily distracted him.

An elevator took him past the actuarial and payment processing departments and up through the corporate layers, auditing and human resources and support staff, until he arrived at his own precincts. Garrison's division oversaw the financials from three different regions. Garrison reported to a vice president for national revenues, and the vice president to the CEO. In this way money traveled upward, against gravity, like water forced through pipes.

Garrison was good at his job, which was different than enjoying it. At one time he would have said he enjoyed it, found it challenging, relished the problem solving he had to do and his small and large successes. But in the last year or so, the minor annoyances, things he had previously ignored or shrugged off, had begun to catch at all his worn-down spots. He found it an effort to maintain the jokiness and small civilities the office required. More often than not he would have preferred to be left alone.

The corporation, like all corporations, was relentless in its need for more and more of everything: income, productivity, growth, happy stockbrokers. More and constant pressure on the money-carrying pipes. Aside from the ritual congratulations to those who had met this or that benchmark (designed to make those who had not done so anxious), there was seldom any sense of a job well done, or even completed. This was the nature of the beast, it was what it was, and any staleness or exasperation Garrison willed away through sustained and diligent bouts of work. He was a believer in the virtue of work itself, of activity and honest effort, which would pull you through a bad patch when nothing else could.

This day's routine had been disrupted by a meeting involving two of the assistant managers who were at war with each other. One of them was a woman who had worked there longer than Garrison but had never advanced beyond this first managerial rung. Garrison knew she believed this to be due to sex, and now age, discrimination. Garrison couldn't honestly say she was wrong, even though she had been told by Human Resources, and presumably by other people, that her complaints were not actionable. There was a certain type of female personality, *fussbudget,* Garrison labeled it, which overreacted and over-personalized, took offense too easily, nursed grudges. She would have been fine running an antique shop or bookstore, somewhere she could bully a couple of employees and wallow in gossip. Here she undermined herself at every turn. There had never been any reason to promote her, nor any real reason to let her go, except for her own unhappiness. She'd hung on all this time and seemed determined to end her days here, mostly out of spite.

She was already seated alone in the conference room when Garrison came in. He felt a familiar fatigue, measuring out the effort it would take him to handle her. "Good morning Loretta, how are you?"

"Fine. Thanks." She spoke as if she had dipped a bucket into some vast reservoir of hurt feelings, meaning to convey that she wasn't at all fine, and this was in some way Garrison's fault, but she hardly expected him to care. In this, at least, she was right.

Garrison said, "Let's see, we still need Rob, Mindy, Chris, and Derek." Loretta made a particular face at Derek's name. She should try not to do such things. Garrison couldn't recall why or how she and Derek had started feuding. Probably one of them had broken the other's crayons.

He asked her a question about one of the report sections, to draw her attention to the matter at hand. She bent over her files, and Garrison saw that she had a bald spot the size of a fifty-cent piece at the top of her head, and that the hair along her part was thinning.

She found the section Garrison needed and looked up. "What?"

"Nothing."

Loretta opened her purse and extracted a tin of mints, shaking it at Garrison to offer him one. He said no thank you. She popped a couple in her mouth and crunched them. "Got to have something. I still get the cravings. Smoking," she explained, since Garrison wasn't getting it.

"Ah." He was pretty sure she'd told him before about quitting smoking, and he hadn't remembered it. He wished the others would get here.

Loretta said, "Look, maybe I shouldn't say anything . . ."

You shouldn't, Garrison thought. Don't.

". . . but I'm having problems getting Derek to respond to my emails. He just ignores them. Then I find out that when he sends his updates, he copies everyone but me. It means that some things just aren't getting done right."

"What does Rob say?" Rob was their immediate supervisor. It was not a happy job.

Loretta's mouth had deep, hinged lines on both sides, like a marionette's. "Oh, he thinks Derek can do no wrong. Believe me, I've tried."

"I'm sure that Rob wants everyone to do their best work." She didn't really expect him to say anything different, did she?

The marionette jaw worked up and down, then quivered. "I know everybody around here thinks I'm old and whiny and don't have to be taken seriously. But every day I come into this office, I give it a hundred and ten percent. I bust my poor old whiny ass." She tried to offer this last in a humorous, self-mocking tone, which made it even worse.

"Of course you do, Loretta. People respect your effort."

"Oh do they? It's hard to tell, what with all the eye rolling."

The others came in then, milling around with coffee mugs

and making their cheery noise. "I brought doughnuts for everyone," said Derek, holding the box aloft. It was such a Derek thing
to do. Garrison didn't like Derek any better than he did Loretta.
He just found Derek easier to deal with. Derek was sleek and
well-barbered, all transparency and ambition. Derek was the one
you could count on to salute the flag once it was run up the flag-
pole, laugh at jokes when laughing was required, fetch the stick
when it was thrown. Garrison could never decide if he was a
smart person playing dumb or if dumb came naturally to him.
Derek would go far, but never as far as he'd think he deserved.

Loretta had retreated into abrupt, curdled silence. Derek
stopped presiding over the doughnuts and gave her a searching
look. "Hey, did you do something different to your hair?"

The day wore on. An irritated sensibility grew in him and
he couldn't settle into his usual working pace. He was losing
some capacity for simple human response. It wasn't just Loretta.
Other people too launched themselves at him, demanding his
attention, sympathy, response, active interest, and it all dropped
away from him as if he were a wall. He wished he could fall
asleep where he sat.

A little before five he gave up on accomplishing anything
of substance and headed home, tired from doing nothing. The
freeway was already moving slowly and he resigned himself
to a long trip. He'd only managed a couple of miles when his
wife called, asking if he'd run into the bad weather yet. He said,
"What weather?" just as he looked up at the looming sky.

This was March and early for tornadoes, but that was his
first thought when he saw the strange banded clouds extend-
ing the length of the western horizon. He told his wife he had
to go, and hung up to attend to his driving. The sky was still

bright above him but that wouldn't last. A front was moving through, visibly demarcated with strips of clear and dark sky. Garrison calculated that they were moving toward each other on a direct heading, although it was hard to tell just where they would intersect. The cars coming at him on the other side of the highway had their headlights on but no windshield wipers. He switched on the all-news radio station and waited through a restaurant review and an advertisement for used photocopiers. There was a severe thunderstorm warning, a storm moving in from the northwest. Cautions about floods and damaging winds, nothing about tornadoes, at least not yet.

He'd never seen such a sky. He kept resting his eyes on it, then jerking them back to the roadway, the kind of driving he cursed in other people. The leading edge of the front was the color of soot, and the layer behind that was steel, and the body of the storm a bulging purple. As he and the front drew closer together, he saw whorls of clouds embedded throughout it, places where some upper-level vortex swirled. They looked exactly like the clouds in science fiction movies that billowed and boiled and disgorged alien spacecraft.

By the time he reached his exit he was entirely beneath the purple canopy. Buildings glowed, luridly backlit. The rain itself held off until he was a few blocks from home, then it came hammering down. In a few moments the gutters turned to shallow lakes and the wind pushed waves across their surfaces. The same wind strove against him head-on. He slowed to keep control of the steering and to avoid the worst of the standing water. He didn't want to wash out his brakes. At the same time he had to keep up enough momentum, without hydroplaning, so he wouldn't stall out.

Garrison made the turn into his own driveway and the automatic garage door opened to receive him. He'd never doubted that he'd make it home safely, so it wasn't nerves, the aftermath of nerves, that caused him to sit in his car for a long minute once he turned the engine off. He was trying to remember the exact way the sky had looked, fix it in his mind's eye.

Garrison's wife was waiting for him in the kitchen. She reached up to give him a quick, hard hug and asked him if he'd had the rain all the way and he said he hadn't. She said there were power lines down in scattered places, she was worried he might run into a downed line, and he said she shouldn't worry about things like that. She got a beer from the refrigerator for him and told him it would be just a little while longer until dinner, and would he go check the battery on the backup sump pump?

Garrison stood in the den, drinking his beer and looking out the patio doors to the backyard. The rain was still sheeting, driving sideways, but already the worst had passed and the wind had slackened. The yard was deep and extended beyond the patio and his wife's dormant flowerbeds to a clear space raggedly edged with shrubs and then to some full-sized trees along the lot line. If he'd been there alone, he would have gone outside and let the rain soak him to the skin. He put his fingers to the glass and they hummed with the small vibration. His wife called him for dinner and he turned away, feeling heavy-headed.

His daughter was away at her expensive college but his son still lived at home, and so it was the three of them who sat down at the table. There was a casserole of ground beef and rice and a salad with bottled dressing and the frozen potatoes that his son ate at almost every meal. His wife said that the television news was all about the storm, flooded streets and power outages and planes at O'Hare dodging lightning strikes, mass transit delays and people stranded. She said that they'd been lucky here so far but tomorrow she was going out and stocking up on batteries, lanterns, bottled water, all the things you were meant to have on hand in an emergency.

"That's probably a good idea," Garrison said. He finished his portion of casserole and put a few of the frozen potatoes on his plate. He cut into one and steam rose from its white, overprocessed interior. He put his fork down. "How can you eat these things?" he asked his son, and the boy, that incurious consumer of so many suspect commodities, shrugged and said that french fries were french fries.

The next day after work, Garrison slid open the patio doors and stood at the edge of the paved border. New grass was only beginning to come up and the bare spots in the yard were still muddy from the drenching rain. Garrison walked carefully out into the yard. The trees at the back were a mix of things he'd planted years ago when they were new to the house and had been ambitious about landscaping, along with some older, preexisting hardwoods. There were flowering crab, redbuds, an apricot that had never fruited, as well as a hackberry, a couple of silver maples, and one big oak that made the other trees grow in lopsided ways around its borders.

Garrison walked up to the oak, tripped over one of its above-ground roots spread out in knotty ridges. You could never mow around the things. He tilted his head back and looked along the trunk to the central canopy where the main branches began to spread, about fifteen feet up, he calculated. The tree had not yet leafed and some of last year's leather-brown leaves still hung on in patches. He wondered how old the tree was, how old oak trees lived to be. He felt stupid not knowing.

When he came back inside his wife asked him what he'd been doing out there and Garrison said he was checking for wind damage.

That weekend he went to the big home improvement store near his house. In the lumberyard section he picked out the oldest employee, a gray-haired man with heavy shoulders, and waited until he turned his way. "Help you?"

"I hope so. I want to build a treehouse."

"Ah. For the kids?"

"Grandkids." Garrison paused. "Not that I have any yet."

He waited to see if the man would turn stony or uncomprehending, but he laughed. "An investment for the future."

"You might say that."

"Ever build a treehouse before?" Garrison shook his head. "Why don't you start with telling me about your tree."

Garrison spent forty minutes talking to Dave, that was his name, about the different strategies of treehouse structures. Supports could be built from the ground up, or the foundation could be anchored to the tree itself. There were such things as fixed and flexible joints, and you needed flexible, since trees moved and treehouses moved along with them. Was he going to put in windows? Garrison thought so. Sure. He could get them prehung, all you had to do was install the frames.

When he left, Garrison had a sheaf of sketches, a list of supplies, and some helpful booklets. He stopped in the hardware department and bought a twenty-foot extension ladder, and, at Dave's suggestion, a ladder leveler so he could set it up on uneven ground. He arranged for it to be delivered and spent another few minutes browsing the saws, planes, nail guns, and drills, calculating what he already had at home, what he'd need to add or replace.

The ladder arrived two days later. Garrison had them bring it inside the back gate, then he loaded it on a yard cart to get it to the far end of the lot. He bought a lawn chair from the patio so he could sit and read all the safety instructions. It pleased him that even a ladder had so much in the way of information attached to it, things he would have to learn.

His wife and son weren't home, so he managed the ladder by himself. That was just as well. He wasn't yet ready to answer a lot of pestering questions. Once he had the ladder up and resting against the tree, he worked the rope and pulley until the extension locked into place, pulled the base away from the tree at a thirty-degree angle, and began to climb.

He was cautious at first, testing the footing, but then he allowed himself to trust it. When he was a good twelve feet up, his head reached the level of the first branch. He looked around, trying to imagine it. The day was chilly and a sharp spring wind rattled the old leaves. In every direction a tracery of bare, overlapping branches enclosed the space. It was fine. It was more than fine.

He made several more trips to see Dave and together they came up with a set of working plans. The foundation would be bolted to the tree, but would extend out past the trunk and there it would be supported by a couple of cement-anchored ground posts and struts. They would edge the platform with sections of rubber tire to protect the bark from rubbing. "Where would you be without the tree," Dave said.

Garrison said he had that right and apologized for taking up so much of his time. Dave said that somebody was sure as hell going to take it up, and it might as well be him. Dave said that if Garrison wanted, he and his boy could by some Sunday and give him a hand with setting up scaffolding and getting the biggest pieces in place.

Garrison, a little surprised, said he'd appreciate it, thanks. He could manage the basic carpentry himself, if only barely; he didn't mind if the finished product turned out more shack than house. He already had a house, a place to keep all the equipment of his life, and the lives of his family. This would be something else.

The day he and Dave agreed on was the last Sunday in April, warm enough to work up a sweat, but still cool enough that sweating felt good. "Real nice place you got," said Dave politely. "Thanks," Garrison said. He knew the house didn't really interest either of them. Garrison allowed himself to envy Dave's panel van, which was all business: the loops of power cord fastened to hooks in the side, the heavy-duty toolboxes with their array of saw blades, drill bits, wrenches, fittings, bolts, and fasteners, the row of ten-gallon buckets, splashed and stained with paint and primer, holding work gloves, shop rags, files, switches, coiled wire. They unloaded what they needed and got to work. Right away Garrison saw how out of his depth he was, how impossible it would have been to proceed on his own. He sucked it up and made himself useful.

Dave's grown son turned out to be an ace at tree climbing, balancing in unlikely perches. (Garrison's own son sulked in the house, refusing to come outside.) Bracing the ground posts was what gave them the most trouble. Garrison had set the cement for the bases a few days ago, and in spite of his cautions the forms had shifted one side off plumb. He felt like an idiot. "Ah, we'll git her done," said Dave, and so they did.

By noon the first long boards of the platform were in place, making it possible to stand upright in the tree's leafy center. Garrison climbed up and took his first cautious step. It was the damnedest feeling, this untethering from the ground, even if it was only by a dozen feet or so. Dave stood on the scaffold below him and levered a board over the platform's edge. Garrison bent to receive it. It would be easy to lose your balance. Or give in to the perverse impulse, take a step off the leading board. He understood why someone might do that, just for the sensation, that instant of green flight.

Dave and his son worked stolidly away, and Garrison put his head down and tried to match their pace. He found the rhythm of swinging a hammer, and little by little it steadied him. These days he felt strange to himself, as he knew he must seem strange to others. It quieted him to guide his muscles, hit his mark, move on to the next one. Mindless work, people called it, and that was exactly right. Mindlessness was what he wanted. But you couldn't go after it straight on. You couldn't even really want it. You had to sneak up on it, forget all about it, and if you were lucky it showed itself, like a rare bird. He drove another nail home and then another and another.

At the end of the day they sat in the lawn chairs, drinking beer and contemplating the neat, 8'-by-12' platform, braced and level, ready to receive walls, windows, door, and roof. Dave said, "Another thing about a treehouse, you can keep adding on. Go into the next tree if you wanted, say, a rope bridge leading up to a whattyacallit. Crow's nest." Garrison agreed that this was something to think about. He knew he'd have to do the rest of the work himself, just to keep it his.

Garrison's wife tried to make sense of the treehouse in different ways, once she was convinced he was "serious" about it, meaning, she was unable to talk him out of it. "But why?" she kept asking, reasonably enough, and when he couldn't provide much of an answer beyond he felt like doing it, she grew silent, injured, as if he were withholding some part of himself from her. Which he guessed he was, although not in any way he could have helped. He knew she had discussions with her women friends, as she did about all other aspects of their life together, a committee of females evaluating him at every step. She turned ironic and tolerant toward him. He was, after all, a man of a certain age, and all sorts of blundering misbehaviors might be expected of him. No doubt the friends had told her that a treehouse was harmless, such a transparently juvenile thing. Much better than an affair, or even a sports car. After all, he was right there in the backyard where she could keep an eye on him.

For a time she brought lemonade and sandwiches out to him as he worked, and asked questions to show she was interested. "Why did you leave all those cracks between the boards? I can see right through them."

"So that rainwater can drain." He was using a power sander to shave the top edge of a wall panel, and he had to turn it off in order to talk to her. When she looked like she was done, he started it up again.

His wife covered her ears and once he paused to take another measurement, she said, "I'm surprised the zoning laws let you do this. I mean, what if everybody on the block went around putting little houses in their backyards?"

"As long as it's not rental property, they're fine with it." He gripped the panel and laid it flat on the hoist he'd rigged to get the heavier lumber up to the platform. He was pleased with the hoist. A sling of canvas with grommets was threaded through with nylon rope and attached to a donkey, a Y-shaped branch he'd pruned out and carefully cut to size. The donkey was fastened to a higher branch and when he'd winched the donkey, turn by turn, to take up the slack rope, he tied the sling off to the platform.

"What color are you going to paint it when it's done?" his wife asked.

"I haven't decided." He hadn't thought about painting it. It hadn't occurred to him.

"You could do it white and green trim to match the house. So there'd be the real house and the miniature version."

"Yeah, that would be nice." He finished securing the panel in the canvas and was ready to climb.

"I wish you'd wear a safety harness when you're working up there. What if you slipped? Or had a dizzy spell or, God forbid, a heart attack?"

"I'll get one if it would make you feel better."

"You mean, you'll promise anything if it will make me go away."

"I didn't say that, Janine."

"You don't even see me anymore. I'm just this object you have to avoid running into."

"I'm sorry you're unhappy." And he was. He was sorry for all the unhappy people in the world. "Maybe you could start playing tennis again, you used to play a lot of tennis when the kids were growing up. You were really good at it."

"Do you know how long it's been since we made love? Huh? Do you even remember the last time?"

"We can do that too, if you want."

"If I want? If *I* want?" His wife's shoulders shook, although the shaking had begun somewhere else, in her clenching hands, perhaps. She turned and ran across the yard to the house. Garrison waited until she'd gone inside, then he climbed the scaffold and maneuvered the wall panel upward, taking care not to let it swing wide and hit the trunk.

By now he had four walls and the trusses for the roof in place. He lay on his back on the floorboards and looked through the open spaces to the interlacing leaves, still new and unfurling, red-veined on their undersides. The sky between them was the blue of a watercolor. The trick was to forget what you were looking at, forget that those things had names, leaf or sky, green or blue. Forget that there was such a thing as a name. You had to try not to try. His breathing slowed. He was not asleep; his eyes were open. A space of time passed, or rather it did not pass, since he was not aware of it. Something roused him, a noise in the street, and brought him back to himself. "Wow," he said out loud, what a silly word, and so he laughed and said it again, "Wow."

He wondered if he could figure out how to put a skylight in the roof, decided regretfully against it.

At work he managed well enough, turning on his business self as if with a switch. It was like driving, a set of reflexes he could rely on. Once in a while, in conversation, he was aware of leaving a gap where words should have gone, or of people giving him measuring sorts of looks. But on the whole, it was remarkable how little of his attention and energy it took to keep his work life in motion. The smallest push from him sent it wobbling about the track.

Loretta was out sick for two weeks, then the word came that she had lung cancer and wouldn't be coming back. A card made the rounds for everyone to sign. Even for people no one much liked, there was always a card. Garrison lingered over it for a long time, looking at the messages his coworkers had already inscribed, their expressions of sympathy and encouragement—Hang in there!—the festoons of exclamation points and hearts. Finally he wrote, "I hope you have peaceful days." He drew in a breath and let it slip out again, all sweet air.

One evening his wife said to him, "Your car is dirty."

"Yeah?" He looked out to the driveway. The Lexus's windshield showed a clear half-moon where the wipers had cut through the dirt. "I better take care of that." He felt bad about the car. It deserved better from him.

"What are you going to build next?" his wife asked. Her newest approach to him was to remain very calm, as if she were dealing, professionally, with someone of diminished capacity.

"Next?"

"When you finish your treehouse. I thought you'd probably start a new project."

"I hadn't planned on it."

"I thought you liked building things. The hands-on part of it."

"Sure." She'd followed him into the kitchen, where he'd gone to make a sandwich. She was always doing that now, tracking him through the house. "But that doesn't mean I have to keep on doing it."

"I am trying very hard to understand this, Brian."

"I know." She was waiting for him to say something else.

He put the top on his sandwich and cut it in half. He said, "I saw one of those announcement boards in front of a church. You know the kind I mean? It said, 'Life Handed Us Our Paycheck and We Said, We Worked Harder Than This.'"

His wife nodded. "You've always been a hard worker. I can see why it spoke to you."

"I thought it was more about, just, life. What life's supposed to be."

"Would you be happier in a different job? We could manage. Get by on less. There are these people, career coaches. They're supposed to help you figure out what you really want to do."

Garrison knew he was explaining things badly. "I don't mind my job. It just doesn't seem as important as it used to be."

His wife looked past him, as if some aspect of the cabinet behind him arrested her attention, the way she might if its surface had arranged itself to resemble the face of Christ. "Am I still important?"

"Of course you are," Garrison said, but he didn't say it fast enough, and she turned and walked from the room.

The roof was a struggle. Even though his carpentry skills had improved over the course of the project—they almost couldn't help but improve—he gave himself about a C+ for the roof. He tar papered and shingled over the center seam and hoped for the best. Then he thought, so what if the roof leaked? He could lay himself down where the rain came through, let his skin fill up with it.

He made one more trip to see Dave and get the lumber for the permanent, anchored ladder. It would consist of half-round pine logs, sanded down to show the grain of the wood, like an extension of the trunk. He and Dave shook hands. "How's life in the trees?" Dave asked, and Garrison said it was coming along pretty good. "You should stop by and see the finished production sometime," he said, meaning it, but knowing Dave wouldn't do so without a fixed and specific invitation.

"Sometime," Dave agreed, and they talked awhile longer about the best way to fit the ladder treads, and what kind of stain or varnish he could use to protect any wood that wasn't pressure-treated. They shook hands again when Garrison left, and he thanked Dave once more for his time and help. "Happy to oblige," Dave said, then turned to assist the next waiting customer. Garrison, walking away, thought that he could do worse than to be like Dave, mild, knowledgeable, patient. But it would be too easy to let himself be lured in by that universe of equipment, all the sharp and shining busy-making things.

His daughter came home for a few weeks between her summer adventures. Her little red car pulled into the driveway one Sunday afternoon. She opened the car door and stretched out her thin, tan legs. Then her mother appeared on the front walk and the girl waved and squealed and ran to embrace her. Garrison, watching from an upstairs window, felt his heart tear like paper.

Dinner that night was made into an occasion, with a cloth laid on the table and drinks served in stemware. His daughter was a vegetarian now, like many other daughters, and so there was a mushroom sauce for the pasta, and a more elaborate salad than was usual, and an attempt at an eggplant dish. His son fixed himself a hamburger, ostentatiously rare, which he ate with considerable smacking and chomping. "That is so not cool," his daughter said. "Why don't you just feed him from a dish on the floor?"

"Wow, sophisticated college humor."

"It's his way of saying he's missed you," said Garrison's wife.

"Oh yeah, like a dog misses fleas."

"How's his housebreaking going?" asked his daughter, with such a serious, concerned expression that they all started laughing. The boy made a comic face, like a dog begging at the table.

When they'd settled down and were once more working on their food, his daughter said, "So Dad, tell me about your treehouse."

Garrison took the time to chew his bite of salad and swallow it. He saw that their earlier light and silly talk had been a kind of script, performed in the shadow of the central problem of himself. He took a sip of water. "What do you want to know?"

"Why didn't you build us a treehouse when we were little, huh? That would have been awesome."

"We would have had to worry about you falling."

"That's just a big fat excuse. You didn't want us to have any fun."

"That's right," said Garrison, with a heavy attempt at playfulness. "Fun, bad."

"So why are you doing it? I mean, why now?"

His wife refilled her iced tea glass. "Anyone else?" she asked, holding the pitcher aloft. Garrison imagined the kind of information and complaints that she'd passed on to their daughter. He didn't like to think of it. He said, blandly, "I guess I wanted a hobby. I thought it would be a challenge."

His daughter pouted. "That's not a very good answer."

"You want a different answer, ask a different guy."

"Will you give me a tour?"

Garrison was mildly surprised to realize that neither his son nor his wife had ever asked to see the treehouse. He wondered if they went up there while he was at work, if they stood in his spot on the bare boards, looking for clues to himself he might have left behind. "Sure. How about tomorrow, after I get home?"

The next day Garrison changed out of his office clothes and told his daughter to put on some shoes she could climb in. The extension ladder and scaffolding was still the only way up. "Careful," he told her, standing on the ground, bracing the ladder. She worked her way up faster than he could have. "Hey," he heard her say from up above him. He followed her to find her standing at the window of the small room, her face lit with the green, reflected sunshine of the canopy of leaves. The air was summer-warm. Cicadas buzzed around them. "This is great, Dad."

"Glad you like it." He unfolded the camp stool and deck chair he'd brought up. "Have a seat."

She chose the stool, hugging her knees up to her chest. She'd been growing her hair out. The ends of her ponytail were sun bleached gold. "So what's the deal here, is this your secret clubhouse, no girls allowed?"

"Except for you."

"You'll teach me the password and the secret handshake, huh?"

"Sure." In spite of his best intentions, he felt fatigue creeping over him. He rallied against it. "You look like a surfer girl. Like a Beach Boys song." She made a face; geezer music. "It was a compliment, honey."

"Mom thinks you don't love her anymore."

Garrison considered this. "I don't *not* love her."

"That's not so good, Dad."

"No, I guess it's not."

"What's wrong? Don't say 'nothing.'"

Garrison shook his head. There were words inside him somewhere, too heavy to dredge up.

"Dad."

"I'm all right. I guess this is"—he made a sweeping hand gesture, meant to indicate the treehouse, and everything that had led up to it—"I just wanted a place where I could be . . . quiet."

His daughter looked around the small space again. "You did a good job. It smells nice. All woodsy."

"Thanks." He thought, yes, he had done a good job. The corners were square, the door frame tight, the wall boards straight. Now he could rest.

"This would be a great place to read. That's what I'd do. Bring a book and an apple and hang out."

Garrison considered. "Maybe the apple."

"Or music. You could bring your music up here."

"Ah." He shrugged. "I haven't spent much time on music lately."

She pursed her lips softly, as if to whistle. She had always been the talker in the family, the one who needed the sound of answers. "Are you doing meditation?"

"Meditation always makes me think of incense and naked guys sitting around cross-legged, chanting."

"Then could you just tell me what's going on with you, instead of making me ask all these stupid questions? Are you sick? Are you mad about something? Jeez."

"I'm not mad. Not sick either. Maybe just tired." She wanted the secret password, the explanation that would unlock him. "You wake up one day and you realize, you just keep putting one foot in front of the other, like you're going someplace. But you're not."

She was visibly trying to understand, wrinkling her forehead. She said, "Where is it you want to go?"

"Nowhere. I want to stop right where I am. Right here and now."

"Stop?" she said, doubtfully.

"Stop pushing so hard. Get rid of all my tired, worried, mean, sad parts."

"You're not mean, Dad."

"I can be. I have been."

"Then don't be. Cut it out."

"I want to be . . . more like a tree. I don't want so much baggage. Opinions. Judgments. Moods, good or bad."

"But you're not a tree! That's all human being stuff! Dad! You're freaking me out!"

"I'm sorry. I don't mean to."

"If you're depressed," she began, determined to argue him out of what he was saying.

"I think maybe I was depressed. Before. Now I'm better."

"Because you don't care about anything anymore? Because you totally shut yourself down?"

"I like to think of it as opening myself up."

"This isn't normal. It's not healthy. It's *stupid* and horrible, it's like you're telling me I don't even have a father anymore!"

If he was honest about it, he had always loved her more, and more purely. More than his difficult son, more than the wife who had worn him down over time. She would be the hardest to let go. She was waiting for him to deny it, reassure her, enclose her in the circle of himself, that empty circle. "I'm sorry," he said again.

Then she was gone, a brief, blurred moment in his sight, the sound of her feet receding on the ladder, rung by rung.

The first night he spent in the tree was by accident. He had taken an old quilt and a cushion up there, a resting place for his head. He closed his eyes in the long summer twilight and opened them to darkness. The air was alive with all manner of night-speech: leaf and branch, breath of wind, and whatever small creatures hummed or whirred or called out to one another. There was no moon, but gradually the blackness resolved itself into the finest gradations of pale and dark. He wrapped himself in the quilt and slept again until the first birds woke him.

He thought he could get a small foam mattress up there, and, when necessary, some kind of heater, kerosene, maybe, as long as you were careful to vent it. There was always the bathroom in the house, and the occasional discreet pee off the edge of the platform.

The permanent ladder was finished, anchored and bolted into place, its beautiful grains and whorls standing out like sculpture. He disassembled the scaffolding and cleaned up his work space, stored the tools away in an orderly fashion. He liked the look of them now that they were at rest. The Bible verse came to him: Well done, good and faithful servant.

Well done, eyes and ears, mouth that tasted, pliant skin and steadfast, beating heart. How remarkable that his body had gone about its business all along, in spite of his inattention. He'd walked around inside it as if it was only another car that needed driving. Brake, steer, accelerate.

The world had grown too large, he could have told them, too cluttered with bewilderment and pain. Now he had made it small enough to fit inside himself. Through the open window of the treehouse he saw leaves showing their gray undersides, flattening out in an uneasy warm wind. The birds had gone still. A storm was setting up to the west. The sky was as green as a glass bottle. In the distance a siren started up. Somewhere in its warning hoon he thought he heard voices, his name turned into a shriek, a lament. He closed his eyes and waited.

How We Brought the Good News

Sophie said it would be possible to be an eco-terrorist right there in New York City and that holding out for Idaho or Oregon was just an indication he wasn't serious. It was all very well to talk about blowing up dams and freeing the salmon to migrate. It was easy to get excited about salmon. They were one of the glamour stocks, the headliners. But there were so many practical and logistical barriers, so much preparation involved, and in the meantime they could do something about taxis. All the fuel-chomping, space-clogging taxis. Or watersheds! There were watersheds in trouble right under their noses.

Jer was doing his martial arts exercises. It annoyed her when he did that, went into his mind-body trance thing for the purpose of not listening to her. She said, "Anyway, they probably have all the eco-terrorists they need out west. New York is underserved."

Jer balanced on one foot and raised his opposite leg into attack position. His arms swam in slow motion, making elegant, killing shapes.

"Furthermore," Sophie went on, although *furthermore* was one of those top-heavy words that meant you'd already lost an argument and were just trying to prop things up. "You suck at anything that requires precision. Like dynamite. Duh. You majorly suck."

Jer pivoted, did a flick kick with his outstretched leg, let the momentum carry him around. He ended up in a half-crouch, arms overhead, fingers spread like daggers. "Oh, I am so scared," Sophie said. "I feel menaced."

She went into the bedroom and closed the door. The bedroom was built up as a loft so that you had to climb a ladder to get to the bed. When one of them was angry with the other, they pulled the ladder up after them, and that's what Sophie did now. She had the dismal thought that she should start looking for a new place, or call a few of her friends, sound them out about couch crashing. She was tired of Jer's big talk that went nowhere, his posing that was presumably for her benefit but from which she was so pointedly excluded. And here the eco-terrorist thing had been his idea in the first place. He'd gotten her all excited about it, but when she'd taken it up, started reading the books he read, firing up with the same righteous enthusiasm, it was clear she'd ruined it for him. She had only been meant to listen and admire as all those brave and scornful things came out of his mouth like a cartoon balloon.

Sophie fell asleep, and when she woke it was late afternoon and the apartment was quiet. Jer had gone out somewhere, perfecting the process of ignoring her. Sophie packed a few shirts, her other jeans, underwear, shampoo and stuff, some CDs he'd notice were gone even if he didn't notice anything else. It all fit into her ordinary canvas bag. Nothing full scale or spiteful, no broken dishes or nasty note. After all, she wanted to preserve her options. She wished she was braver, more determined, better at feeling indignant, fatally insulted, no turning back. Those were always the ones the boys came running after. Well, that wasn't her. She guessed she was still hoping they'd make up, be the people they used to be, all goofy with sex and fondness. She was so totally mushy. She'd make a terrible eco-terrorist.

She dawdled on the stairs but Jer didn't appear, nor was he on the street outside. No big gorgeous scene of the kind she'd been rehearsing. It was hot, she'd forgotten how it was outside, airless and malevolent. It was as if the concrete itself, and every other bit of man-made dreck—wires cross-hatching the sky, delivery trucks fatly blocking traffic, pissed-off honking, mechanical sweat of rubber and exhaust—had amalgamated into some sci-fi monster, bawling and staggering around, out to get you.

Sophie decided she'd go hang out at the coffee shop/art gallery/video game emporium where she sometimes worked. It was at least air-conditioned, and also Jer would think of looking for her there, or would be careful to avoid looking for her there, depending on how things stood. More stupid wishy-washy on her part. What did she think, Jer was going to show up with flowers? Ha! Did guys do that anymore? Had they ever?

She trudged the six overheated blocks. She wondered how many toxins she was breathing in per square inch. It had only been a few hundred years ago, the blink of an eye in geological time, when all of Manhattan had been wild and free. Forest? Swampland? She should look it up. Say somebody bombed the whole place, not that she had any active wish for that to happen. She wouldn't go that far, except maybe on a really bad day. How long would it take for the ruins to grind down into dust and sift away? For brambles and tough little weed trees, rabbits and deer and even more outrageous things—wolves! panthers!—to reassert themselves? Or maybe New York was incurable, a sinkhole of sludge and heavy metals and petroleum. An industrial whatchamacallit. Chernobyl.

These were diverting thoughts, or at least she meant them to be, but Sophie was aware that this was just another way of thinking about Jer, her and Jer, and whether they could be reconstituted into their former pristine state, or whether they were a doomed biohazard and should be sealed off for all time. She thought that was kind of a neat way to put it, she wished she could tell Jer, except it was likely he wouldn't appreciate it.

At the coffee shop she said hello to Danny and Rose, who said hey, didn't think you were working, and Sophie said I'm not, I'm just hanging out. She stowed her canvas bag behind the counter and fixed herself a chai latte. She sat in a corner booth where she could see the front door. Behind her a few of the gamers, the regulars, the total losers, hunched before their glowing computer monitors. She wondered if they thought they were pathetic, like everybody else did, or if their protective fantasy worlds extended to shield them from real-life opinions. Sophie didn't know which games were worse, the war/crime ones, bulging with muscles and danger and sleek, disposable bad guys, or the alternate universe ones. The big pasty kid in the corner, the one who wore the same sweatpants and *South Park* T-shirt every day he came in? Sophie happened to know that his avatar was a Lord of Fire demon with special powers of invincibility and mind control.

Jer was only her third real boyfriend. She had a private calculus which determined real; it had less to do with sex and more to do with expectations. So far none of her expectations had been met. They had not even been approximated. She honestly didn't think it had been her fault, but she guessed nobody ever did. Still, she had entered into each arrangement in good faith. She had been anxious, maybe too anxious, to please. Hence, eco-terrorism. But how did you stop caring about a thing, a cause or a boy, once your caring was no longer wanted?

Her phone buzzed, making her heart leap, but it was only her mother. Sophie decided to answer it, as not answering would require the extra effort of calling back later. "Hi, Mom."

"Oh good, there you are." Sophie's mother always began conversations that way, although "there" was anywhere covered by the satellite network, and like everybody else, Sophie had often taken advantage of this to report that she was somewhere she was supposed to be, instead of the questionable or forbidden place she actually was. "I've been so worried."

"Don't be," said Sophie, with some rudeness, because her mother was always worrying, a generic, nonspecific cloud of worry. Emotional pollution.

"It's so hot there," her mother said, from her home base in Michigan. "I saw it in the papers. I hope you're staying hydrated."

Sophie said that she was, and there was a little pause. The weather was one thing, but the untidy circumstances of Sophie's life made for trickier conversation. "How's Jerry?" her mother asked brightly.

"Fine. He's starting a new band." A piece of information she could offer up without revealing much of anything.

"Oh, that's nice. What's the name of it?"

"Polite Sleeper."

"What? Never mind. What fun would it be if people actually understood it? I had a dream about you last night. You were getting married, but not to Jerry. Don't ask me how I knew it was somebody else, I just did. In the dream you and whoever it was were driving away from the ceremony and you had a golden halo around your head, like one of the saints."

"Well that's weird. Was I wearing the big white dress? Saint Bride?"

"I suppose you were, but that's not the important part. Everybody there seemed to think it was perfectly natural that you were a saint."

"How about the lucky guy? Was he a saint too?"

"Now dear, you know the wedding is really the bride's big day."

"Yeah, fine," Sophie murmured. She mistrusted this dream business, the oracular quality people invested them with. She mistrusted her mother's dreams in particular.

"I think it means you're destined for something wonderful. Not sainthood, exactly. There's already a Saint Sophia, she's the patron saint of widows. But some other kind of shining, special life. No matter what things might look like now. I have to run, honey. Daddy says hi."

Thanks, Mom.

She was waiting for a chance to talk to Rose, a little girl-talk with the hopes of soliciting an offer of couch space. Just in case. But before she could do so Danny came over to sit with her, and this was not so good, since Danny had a major crush on her. There were some offers she didn't need.

"Sucks when it's slow," he said, dumping his weight onto the bench in a way that irritated Sophie.

She asked him how long he'd been there and Danny said practically all day. Since one. No, closer to noon. He was one of those people who always tried to make things sound more interesting and remarkable than they really were. "It has been sooo boring. Look up 'boring' in the dictionary, and there's a picture of—"

"You?"

"Hahaha. We should just shut the place down. There's better things I could be doing."

"Like what. What do you have to do that's better?"

Danny looked at her with his face a little slack, uncertain if she was making some kind of joke. "Chill out. Watch a movie, I guess."

"I get so tired of doing the same dumb stuff."

"Oh, well, we could do . . . something else . . . whatever you wanted . . ."

"No, I meant, in general. The stuff we all do." It made her impatient that he was thinking she meant the two of them doing something together, like a date. She didn't want to be confronted with somebody else's hopeless, unhappy love. The one thing you'd expect she'd be sympathetic about, but instead it hugely pissed her off. "I mean, TV shows and magazines and people in stupid bands and . . . *those* guys." Sophie made a shooing gesture in the direction of the gamers. She didn't trust herself to start in on them. "All the small, selfish, trivial stuff, when we ought to be thinking about the real deal. Real life."

"The meaning of life," suggested Danny. As always, half a step behind in any conversation, and anxious to catch up.

"That's not what I meant," said Sophie, although it probably was; she just didn't like the simpleminded way it sounded out loud. "More like, issues, problems—"

"You mean, like Jer's always talking, his environmental deal."

"It's not like it's just his planet. It's not like everybody has to give him all this credit." Sophie had to stop herself, she was being a total witch and Danny was looking at her like whoa, he might have to rethink this crush business, which was annoying on several levels. "Sorry. Heat makes me cranky."

"How about I get you some more chai?"

Danny grabbed her mug and double-timed it over to the counter. Sophie figured this was less about doing her bidding, more that he didn't want to stick around and see what she'd unload on him next.

So, scratch "dream girl" from her list of possible splendid destinies.

Instead of waiting for Danny to come back, Sophie followed him to the counter, paid for her drink, and went to examine the artwork on the back wall. This was the gallery space, so-called, although it had the dinky proportions of an afterthought. This batch of art was new, she hadn't seen it before, and so it was easy to pretend rapt attention. Then, as she let her eyes take it in, she forgot to pretend.

There were half a dozen vivid, frameless oil paintings, small, about the dimensions of a phone book. Each of them was intricately painted with scenes of a recognizable but distorted world. There were skies of dark violet or greenish brass, buildings that seemed to have lost any sort of right angles, trees that were as uniform as factory cookies. In one painting a small, fat-looking airplane climbed unsteadily toward a whirligig sun, like a bumblebee seeking a plastic flower. Anything mechanical or inanimate—cars, houses, roadways—had the soft contours of living creatures. And any natural element looked sharp-edged and unconvincing. There were no human figures in evidence.

Moving down the line of paintings gave her a sense of disorientation, almost of vertigo. Most of them had sparse, unhelpful titles—*Landscape 1*, or *Untitled, Study*, that sort of thing. But the last in the series was called *How We Brought the Good News*. Here a long road lay in flattened curves, like a dropped string. It cut through a countryside, if you could call it that, of odd, thickened orange grass, grass dredged in wet cement, perhaps, then sprayed with industrial paint.

By now Sophie was familiar with such reversals, could read the painting's code, as it were. What was different about this one, in addition to its evocative (but still unhelpful) title, was the presence of what she at first took to be a small cemetery in the near corner. There was a delicate white fretwork fence and archway— metal? painted wood? It had an eroded quality, as if nibbled away by something caustic, or maybe it was ancient, abandoned. What Sophie had taken for mausoleums and fields dotted with gravestones might just as easily be elements of an amusement park or carnival. Instead of a monument, this might be a festive pavilion. These rows of crosses might be tracks for a roller coaster or a small-gauge railroad. It all depended on how you looked at it.

Sophie went to the counter and asked who the guy was, the guy who did the pictures? Rose and Danny said they didn't know, they just went up the other day and neither of them had been here. Rose said, "I think there's a name," and fetched a card from within the cash register: Paintings by M. Najarijand.

"That's a big help," said Sophie crossly. It was too much like a trick or joke, intended to make you feel stupid because you couldn't figure it out. "Who is he, some friend of Pete's?" Pete owned the coffee shop and liked to refer to himself as a supporter of the arts community.

"I guess," said Rose. "I don't know where he finds these people. Do they all hang out at some artists' club, with secret handshakes? You like these? I think they're kind of depressing."

"I don't know if I'd say *like*. They're different." Sophie hadn't yet arrived at words that might say exactly what about the paintings had set off such a commotion in her. She only felt that the world she inhabited had turned out wrong, flawed in unexpected ways, and the paintings knew it too. Now she said, "Hey," in another tone, conspiratorial, urgent.

Rose moved a little ways down the bar, away from Danny. "What?"

"He's such a jerk."

"Well, duh." Sophie's mother, who had never met Jer, had the same opinion of him as Rose, who had met him, and furthermore was in possession of all Sophie's worst stories. "He's such a poop-head."

"Like we say in Michigan, he's so full of shit, his eyes are brown."

"Like we say in Baltimore, told you so." One reason they were friends had to do with them both arriving in New York at about the same time, from similarly benighted places. "What'd he do now?"

Sophie launched into her catalogue of grievances. He had done this and failed to do that. Had flaunted his insensitivity, indifference, even contempt. Nothing that she said was untrue, strictly speaking; facts were not in dispute, only motives and intent. Yet hearing herself berate him, and with Rose there, loyally chiming in at the chorus, she began to feel false, even unfair, and abruptly stopped talking.

"Well that sucks," said Rose, after a moment. "Look, you

feel like getting away, come stay at my place for a few days. We can do our hair the same color. Red or black, you pick."

"Thanks," Sophie said. "I might take you up on it." Or she might not. Now that she had the opportunity to follow through on her complaints, leave Jer on his own to miss her, worry about her (or not miss her, not worry—asshole) she hesitated. "How about I check in with you later? I'm going to go get some hummus or something." She hadn't eaten since breakfast, and although it would have been more satisfactory to languish lonely and neglected and unfed, she was starving. Besides, she bet that Jer wasn't skipping any meals. "I'll leave my bag here, okay?"

Outside in the wretched heat again. Somewhere beyond the swollen cityscape the sun must have been setting. Shadows were toppling sideways. People hurried home from work or out to important places. The usual yellow contagion of taxis thickened the streets, but tonight at least Sophie had no wish to do them harm.

Because after all, if you got rid of the taxis, what would all the men from Ghana and Senegal and Russia and Turkey and even worse places do, and indeed, what would happen to the families of those men, both here and abroad, without those little pieces of money passed from hand to hand, transformed into wired bank orders, into drachma, euros, rupees, pesos, and then into bread, bacon, shoes, roofing material, feed for chickens, milk for children, an entire economy fueled by traffic jams and bad driving. It depressed her to think how complicated it might be to unravel what seemed like obvious wrongs. Even dynamiting a dam to let the salmon run free probably had unexpected consequences, would drown or parch some other unsuspecting creature.

Having worked herself into an entirely black mood, Sophie arrived at the little sandwich shop and, instead of ordering the virtuous hummus and pita, got a hot dog with everything and fries. After all, she was an American. No point in pretending she was anything better than she really was.

As she stood at one corner of the ledge set aside for customer enjoyment, extracting her food from its paper wrappings, Sophie sensed the hair on her back of her neck prickling. It had nothing to do with chewing and swallowing; there would be later physiological alerts involving the food. Rather, she was looking straight at another of the unmistakable oil paintings, hanging just above the hatch for the cashier.

This painting seemed to break the pattern of the others by featuring an actual blue sky, but as Sophie craned to stare up at it, she became aware that the blue represented water, the viewer looked into water as if into an aquarium. Or the ocean, a section of ocean without a floor. Indeterminate shapes, white and ribbony, like elongated jellyfish, or perhaps giant squid, descended from the upper left-hand corner. Or no, they were smaller than she'd first perceived, because here was a collection of incongruous items to give everything scale: an empty picture frame, a single glove, what looked like the coils of old-fashioned bedsprings, glass bottles, lightbulbs, flowerpots. Debris from a shipwreck? Remnants of a flood? What she had taken to be tentacled sea creatures now appeared to be fragments of paper, newspaper, perhaps, with bits of smudged words on them. It was hard to make out with the picture so far overhead.

She was in the way of other customers placing their orders. "Excuse me," she kept saying, sidestepping, jostling. Once there was a lull in the traffic, she approached the window again. "Hi, could I ask you about your painting?"

He didn't know what she meant at first. He was a foreigner, like almost everyone in New York—which made for its own kind of puzzle—and he was too used to hearing "Coke," or "ketchup," words like that, too attuned to the cash register to fathom anything else. A slight, olive-skinned man, like so many others. Sophie had always assumed the proprietors were Lebanese, something about the pitas, but now as she searched his tired, tired face, she thought he might have come from anywhere in the world, and that she herself was perfectly ignorant.

He stood on a chair to lift the painting from its hook. It was obscured with a sheen of cooking grease and another layer of adhered grit. Sophie dabbed at it with a paper napkin and was relieved when the colors brightened. It seemed clear from the composition that you were meant to read the painting like a book, top to bottom, left to right. So that you began with the paper fragments and ended with the floating trash heap. The words on the newspaper scraps were just as jumbled as the objects. "Fantastic opportunity help expensive," she read. "Total convenience amazing sleep."

"Where did you get this?" she asked the proprietor. "You know him? The painter?"

The man spoke in his own language to someone behind the counter. "Friend of," he said to Sophie. "Trading for food."

"Do you know where he is now? Where I can find him?"

Another conversation. In Urdu? Farsi? The man went back to the kitchen and returned a moment later with a receipt torn from a pad. Sophie read the penciled address, West Twenty-sixth, somewhere in Chelsea, she calculated. "Is this, like, a studio? Is there a telephone?"

But there were new customers lining up and the man was done with her.

Jer still hadn't called. What was he doing right now? Hanging out with his friends in the band, probably, making their angry music. Or maybe just sulking around on someone's couch, waiting until later to go home so he wouldn't look overeager to see her. Of course, she was doing the same thing. But he was the man, after all, and men were supposed to try harder, want you more. It had been another disappointment to realize this was not necessarily so.

In fact she was pretty sure that if she went home, acted as if nothing was wrong, nothing had happened, Jer would go along with it in silent relief. He would be his same old noncommittal self. They would paper over the quarrel, go back to the way they were before, or maybe a little worse. But she wasn't ready to do that yet, out of either pride or spite, or a sense that the day—now the night—had not yet given full service. She didn't want to quit on it yet. To do so would make her feel dull, quiescent, unexceptional. She didn't want or expect to be a saint—the idea was so purely Mom. And yet she had her secret hopes, something along the lines of being the star of a great TV show, only real.

She calculated bus routes, boarded an evil-smelling local, and set off. In the latest edition of her trashy fantasy life, M. Najarijand saw her gazing attractively through his studio windows and invited her inside. "The moment I saw you, I knew I had to paint you."

By now it was dark and the city was a scaffolding of lights, near, far, or at middle distance. If Sophie closed her eyes to a slit and looked through her eyelashes, she saw streaks and smears of light, almost beautiful, in a disordered way. And her fellow passengers, crowding in on her, holding their faces aloof even as their bodies collided—if you could step back from them, take the long view, see them as a design or pattern, if you could rearrange their murmurs and squawks into an accidental symphony . . . Sophie shook her head to clear it. "Woolgathering," her mother used to call it. "Sophie's woolgathering again."

The bus made its pokey way up Tenth Avenue. Every so often it seemed to lose energy and stopped to lean against a curb. At Twenty-sixth, Sophie got off and walked two quick blocks, squinting energetically at the addresses. Without the sun, the heat crept up stealthily from below, from the still-baking sidewalk. It was a district of anonymous, blocky buildings, warehouses, maybe, or small offices. None of it looked very artistlike, but she had to remind herself that this was an artist who traded paintings for food, and not very distinguished food at that.

The address was another nondescript building with a loading dock and double glass doors. She tried the doors and found them unlocked. Inside, her feet tapped and echoed on the spooky tile floor.

A skinny young security guard poked his head out of the door marked Manager, eyed her, decided she was harmless. "Sup," he said, by way of inquiry.

"Oh, hi, I'm looking for . . . this artist guy . . ." It was beginning to feel like an entirely foolish errand.

"We got lots of artists. Artists R Us." He was a Puerto Rican kid with a narrow, fake-looking moustache. "Friend of yours?"

"Sort of," she said, unwilling to tell him much.

"Hey, I'm an artist. I draw real good. Horses. Race cars. Skulls. My cousin does tattoos, I drew this one skull and he put it on this dude's right arm. Full color."

When Sophie failed to be impressed by this, he turned businesslike. "Who you want to see? Almost everyone gone home already."

"Najarijand," pronounced Sophie, reading it carefully from the printed card.

"Oh yeah, they always here." (*They?*) "Go on up, I call and say you're coming. Fif' floor, last one on the right. Watch your step on the elevator."

It was a creepy elevator, a cage with an open wire grating on top, so that the passenger had an unreassuring view of the cables as they unspooled and grabbed. It ascended, shrieking, and ground to a halt at the fifth floor. She stepped into a bare, wide corridor, rather dusty, lined with solid doors. Most of them were unlabeled, although every so often one announced itself as "East-West Novelties" or "Back Seat Productions." A porn film studio? Those odd little businesses that advertised in the back of cheap magazines? Lifelike Glamour Wigs. Miracle Wart Cure. Send check or money order to PO Box Whatever, New York, New York.

At the last door on the right, which had nothing written on it, Sophie hesitated, listened, and knocked. The door was opened right away by an Indian lady, gray hair pulled back in a braid. "Ah, here is our little visitor."

"Hi, I'm sorry to bother you, I'm looking for ..."

The lady shooed her inside. She was short and plump and except for her sari and the red dot on her forehead, she might have been Sophie's Italian grandmother. "Avyark, here is company," she called.

On the other side of a folding screen, a gray cricket of a man sat on a low couch, reading a newspaper. "A girl," he said, peering over his spectacles. "Where did you get her from?"

"Don't mind him, sweetie. He is always being clever. He is a very educated man. Sit, I will get you an iced drink."

"I'm sorry," Sophie said again. "I think I have the wrong address." There was a little kitchen in the space beyond the couch, a table, lamp, piles of books, and a zebra-patterned rug on the floor. But no sight or smell of painting. "I was looking for a painter."

"Inside or outside of house?" the little man said, and this time Sophie could tell he was being funny.

"Oh be quiet, Avyark, you will scare her away. Sweetie, what is your name? So-fee. So pretty. Here, sit. Mango tea and ginger cookies."

Sophie sat and drank some of the tea, mostly so she wouldn't have to speak again just yet. The lady said, "My husband knows very well you mean painting-painting. Always comedy. Are you married yet, So-fee? Good. You must be very, very particular."

"Let her drink, Padmi. Always such a noise."

"Always never listening."

"What would Manoj think, that you misbehave so in front of his friend? I am afraid the young lady will be forming a bad impression."

"Manoj will have told her all about your foolishness."

"Your lack of sensible talk."

"Your very bad humor."

"Excuse me," said Sophie. "I don't know anyone named Manoj."

This caused enough consternation to silence them for a moment. "Ahh," Avyark hummed, sucking his teeth. "Ahh, ah."

"I saw the paintings at the Java Station. I work there." She was anxious to explain herself, anchor the conversation. "Are they yours?" She looked from one to the other.

"Oh, she is a friend to Manoj's paintings," said Padmi. "Well, that is nice too."

"Manoj is always sending us people."

"All kinds. Not only girls."

"Oh, surely not."

This conversation seemed to reassure them, and they smiled on Sophie with new tenderness.

"The paintings are for sale," said Avyark. "You can buy them, very reasonable. Proceeds to benefit Golden Age Society."

"Really," said Sophie, nodding as if she understood. She thought it must be some sort of retirement fund.

"Avyark, show her the new picture," Padmi commanded. Avyark got up and went behind the folding screen. "Avyark is president and founder of Golden Age Society, American Chapter." From a side table she handed Sophie a pamphlet, slightly filmed with dust.

VISHNU, PRESERVER OF ORDER

At the end of the Fourth, or Iron Age, Lord Vishnu will appear in the form of Kalki, the tenth avatar, a man riding on a white horse and wielding a flaming sword.

Within three days he will destroy the wicked among mankind, and the earth will be cleansed. The Krita Yuga, or Golden Age, will then begin, when humanity abandons all worldly desires. Signs of the final days of the Iron Age, or Kali Yuga: Greed and dishonesty will prevail. Cheating will be the order of the day in business relations. Wealth alone will be the deciding factor of nobility. Brigands and armies will overrun the nations of the world. People will eat voraciously and indiscriminately. They will live in cities filled with thieves. Men will become dull-witted and unholy, women, wanton and unchaste.

Sophie looked up. "Wow," she said politely. She'd thought that Christians were the only ones who got goofy about the Last Days. She'd been handed similar pamphlets on street corners, TEOTWAWKI, The End of the World As We Know It. "That sounds really, really . . ." She couldn't come up with an adequate word.

"Very exciting," said Padmi, complacently.

Avyark returned, lugging an oversized canvas much larger than any she'd seen.

"Our son Manoj," he explained. "Currently in India. President of Golden Age Society, Mumbai Chapter. His latest."

Now that Sophie knew the paintings were all about the apocalypse, it was easy to appreciate this new one, its denseness and detail, its lack of human beings, presumably already purged. In this picture a glowing wave the color of stainless steel rose up in an ornate curl, poised to crash down on a landscape of intricate patterns, like a fancy bedspread draped over a lumpy bed. There were groves of little sprouting trees, mountains, ponds with lily pads, orchards, tilled fields; also highways, villages, towns, cities, and within the houses, even smaller, chairs, pianos, bookshelves, dinner plates, clocks, wineglasses, all of it assembled in order to be swept away. She was momentarily reminded of the video games.

"Your son is a wonderful artist," Sophie told them. "You must be very proud."

"He is, like ourselves, an evangelist," said Avyark. "From the Greek, as you may know, meaning, 'Bringer of Good News.'"

"Greek," said Padmi, "is, as you may know, mostly used for showing off."

Sophie smiled and replaced her cup of tea carefully on its saucer.

It was another twenty minutes before she was able to leave, because they felt it necessary to instruct her about the maha yugas, the great cycles that lasted 4,320,000 human years, about the universal wheel of destruction and rebirth, first up, then down, about the future in which the minds of men would become as pure as crystal, and the growing evidence from innumerable prophesies that the world (As We Know It), would end in the year 2012. Sophie thanked them for their hospitality, and for the quantity of informative literature they pressed into her hands. "Such a pretty girl," Padmi was saying as the door closed behind her, and Avyark answered, "Yes, but she needs more clothes."

The security guard was not in evidence as she escaped the elevator and made her way out to the street. She crossed Tenth, then Eleventh, and continued west until she stood at the edge of a viaduct, looking out across the current traffic on the West

Side Highway, to the dark ribbon of the Hudson and the lights of New Jersey beyond it.

Was the river even a river anymore? So loaded up it was with human history and human effluvia. Were people still people when they swelled and clumped together in such a steady stream? The paintings had her all confused, her head was a muddle of holy talk, and she felt very small. Was anyone ever shining? Special?

Later, later, very late, Sophie climbed the ladder to the loft bed. It was too dark to see anything, but she thought it was a good sign that the ladder was down, like a drawbridge. She paused at every step, heard nothing. What if he wasn't there? Well, it was only natural that things came to an end. Everything did. It was only a part of the great cycle. To mourn overmuch, indeed, to mourn at all, was to row against the tide, to overstir the pot of the soul's misery.

Was she imagining the sound of his breathing? Was it a good or a bad thing that the world was coming to an end? It all depended on how you looked at it. Why was so much of religion about giving things up? All the sober wisdom of the ages. Why did you have to abandon your earthly desires, as long as there still was an earth?

He spoke her name, and she knew from his voice that he had been awake all along, waiting for her. She was on the top step of the ladder. There was nowhere to go but down. She let herself fall into him.

Her Untold Story

The television show aimed to find the most miserable and deserving people in America and shower them with consumer goods: clothing, appliances, real estate. This week they had selected a woman with fourteen children. Four were her own and ten of them were her sister's. The sister had died of cancer and there had been a deathbed promise. Husbands and fathers notable by their absence. Hah! Lynn raised her wineglass to the television. All those missing men. They probably had a secret clubhouse somewhere.

The family had been living in a dismal hotel. Things had gone badly for them and then had gotten worse. The kids seemed nice enough. The television hosts did their hopped-up best to yank at the heartstrings. How did it feel to be homeless, impoverished, exhausted, desperate? Huh? Huh? "Like holding on with one hand and about to let go," said the mother, wiping tears. "Like bein' at the bottom of the bottom."

She switched the channel. It depressed her to think that in order to get any public sympathy she would need to have twelve more children.

Her younger son walked past the room and stopped to look in at the door. "What are you watching?"

"I don't know, I just switched." She knew he didn't like it when she drank and so she said brightly, "Oh, it's the History Channel." Smudgy gray footage showed fighter pilots bombing a carrier. She patted the side of the bed. "Come sit for a minute."

He picked a spot at the end of the bed. "Here," she said, tossing him the remote. "Find something you like."

It was just the two of them now. His older brother was away at college. His father had decamped. The empty house spoke of failure. Lynn knew her son felt sorry for her, in a way that embarrassed both of them. One more year of high school and he could leave also, breathe air that she had not breathed first.

She said, for the sake of saying something, "Did you get your track clothes washed?" He was on the cross-country team and spent all his free time training.

"Uh huh."

"I wish I was fleet of foot. I'd bust out of here. I'd just keep running."

"Like Forrest Gump, huh?"

"What?"

"The movie. The guy runs and runs and people all over the country start following him."

"I don't remember that part." She didn't trust herself to say more. The wine was making her bleary. One picture slid into the next as he changed channels, settling on a basketball game. She watched with him in silence, but it was hard for her to focus on the different teams, the back and forth. It was like the History Channel footage, another war she didn't care about.

She must have fallen asleep. When she opened her eyes, the television was off and her son had gone. She had to get up for work in the morning. Piece of cake. One stupid foot in front of the other.

She was always nice to people at work. That part wasn't difficult. Nice was her default setting. She was agreeable, sympathetic, interested. It had been her habit, but, Lynn was beginning to suspect, it was not her nature.

After work she called Christine. They were divorce friends. They were allowed to complain until the cows came home. "Last night was bad," Christine said. "I baked a pan of brownies and ate them all."

"Did it at least taste good?"

"Up to a point. Then it was just mindless, terrifying self-abuse."

"Did you throw up or anything?" Lynn asked. It depressed her to think that this sort of thing was the worst they were guilty of these days.

"No, I passed out with the pan in my lap. Crumbs all over the sheets. It'll probably draw roaches. How are you?"

"Okay." She thought she'd skip the part about passing out herself. She hoped she hadn't drooled or snored in front of her son. "Do you anybody who has ten children? Or twelve, or fourteen?" She explained about the television program.

"Were they polygamists?" Christine asked.

"I'm thinking no."

"If one of us finds a man, we should both marry him. Sorry. What about the show?"

"I disliked those people. Even the kids. I really did. I disliked them for being poor and wretched and I couldn't believe that woman kept popping out children. I mean, hello, birth control?"

"It is sort of like the old woman who lived in a shoe."

"Yeah, but that's not the point. What's wrong with me? The whole idea of the show is, you feel sorry for them. You're supposed to laugh and cry with them and be all happy when they get their new house. And here I am thinking rotten thoughts." She did not say rotten racial thoughts, although there had been some of that; the family was black.

"Oh, it's just television," Christine said. "You shouldn't take any of it personally. Want to do something this weekend? Go see a goopy movie or something?"

Lynn said sure. Sometimes they actually went to the movie. Or else one of them said they were too tired, or too busy, and they stayed home. They were supposed to be moving forward with their lives. That was the message of all the self-help books and television therapists. As if all anybody ever needed was good advice.

Christine said, "I've started buying a lot of magazines. Interior decorating and Southern cooking and travel and crafts and country living. It's something about the pictures. All those beautiful rooms and fancy cakes. I can't get enough of them."

"It's better for you than the brownies," Lynn said. She didn't buy magazines now because the divorce had exploded everyone's finances and magazines were frivolous purchases. But she looked at them when she went through the grocery checkout line. She was drawn to the ones that showed movie stars and teen princesses on the covers, like giant, pouting paper dolls. *Her Untold Story!* one of the headlines blared, because interesting and tragic things were always happening to famous people in terms of their fertility, their sweethearts, their drugs. You weren't meant to confuse such things with real life, and she didn't. Didn't expect or want to end up on any magazine cover herself. But what if her life was already used up, and she didn't even have a story anymore?

She said good-bye to Christine, hung up the phone and went out to the patio. The long spring twilight gathered on the lawn and beneath the trees. The sky was opal, the air was scented with blossom and mown grass. She was going to have to buy more birdseed for her complex of bird feeders. Once you started, you were supposed to keep feeding them. There was no end to their exhausting needs. Across the back fence, her neighbors' kitchen lights were on, and her heart hurt at the welcoming yellow light against the clear sky. Anything lovely made her feel excluded, envious, melancholy.

Her son was spending the night at friends'. This was what the house would be like once he'd gone away to school. She sat down at the computer, checked email, then logged into the Men Looking for Women portion of the singles' website. She was too chickenshit to post anything herself, but she liked to check out the men and assure herself she wasn't missing anything. There was something wrong with all of them; too old, too young, too arrogant, liked country music, smoker, grammar errors. It made instant rejection easy. She clicked on one post she hadn't seen before. The dim picture showed a smallish man with a moustache, his face blurred from the light of the window. *Hello, my name is Allejandro and I am 58 years old. In the day I am a mechanic and in the night I am lonely. I speak some English but Spanish is better.*

If only he spoke no English at all. That would be perfect. She could make a gift of herself, show up at his door wrapped in ribbon and bows. Here you go, Allejandro. Congratulations. You've been selected. It would be like the television show, except without the home remodeling part. She would transform his life. They would be happy. At least, until he decided he preferred someone younger and more kittenish, as her ex-husband had.

His new wife was pregnant. Did she really wish some gruesome tragedy on them, a dead or deformed child? Was she that far gone, the wicked fairy at the christening? No, not yet. She did allow herself to hope that the new wife would get fat.

She had been divorced for more than a year now. But there had been a couple of years before that when she had not been entirely married either. Her husband's skulking affair had gone on for some time before Lynn discovered it, and then there had been the hanging-on, the long process of trying to convince Jay that he didn't really want what he wanted. Then, by the end, when Lynn had been worn down, defeated, willing to bargain, when she'd said, fine, keep her, do whatever makes you happy, but let's stay married, it turned out that what he really wanted was Not Her.

The other day she'd seen a man wearing a T-shirt that said, CHOOSE ONE: A. I DON'T KNOW. B. I DON'T CARE. Maybe the universe was sending her messages. She could cultivate a posture of hostile indifference. She could get some therapy. She could file her teeth into spikes, roll around on the ground until her hair trailed leaves and twigs. She was not moving forward. She was at the bottom of the bottom.

The phone rang. She saw from the handset that it was Jay's number. There were occasions, all of them unpleasant, when they had to speak to each other. She thought about not answering, decided it was better to get it over with. "What do you want?"

A space of flat silence. Then he said, "That's a nice way to start a conversation."

She didn't respond. Petty rudeness was the only weapon she still had against him. After a moment he said, "How are the boys?"

"Why should I know more about them than you do?"

He didn't answer that. How could he? He'd divorced his sons too. He was Dad 2.0 now. Corrects flaws in earlier versions. He said, "We need to talk about Tim's tuition next year."

The hair on the back of her neck prickled. "Mm," she said.

"I'm not going to be able to cover the whole thing. I'm just stretched too thin."

"Wow, Jay. I completely understand and sympathize."

"I don't think that tone is very helpful."

It hadn't taken long for his own tone to acquire that edge of surly grievance. He was crushed and dragged down by her unreasonableness.

"You know, Jay, between the two boys, there's eight years of college to finance. We've just gotten through the first one."

"Yeah." She heard the faint clink of ice cubes in a glass. She wasn't the only one drinking in the evenings. "That's why I thought we ought to come up with some kind of plan now."

"The plan was you'd pay for the boys' education."

"I am. I will. But I have other responsibilities now. I need a little flexibility."

"Say, how flexible is Margot? I mean, when she's not great with child. Can she really put her ankles all the way behind her ears?"

"Something very sad has happened to you, Lynn."

"If you're not going to pay for Tim's college, you tell him that. Explain to him how your new family's so much more absorbing than your old one. You tell him, hot shot. I'm through being your translator and mediator. It's not worth the effort to try and understand you anymore."

Jay started to say something, but she slammed the phone down. College expenses were in the divorce agreement. She'd sic the lawyer on him. She'd take off his skin piece by piece. She started crying, a noisy, open-mouthed crying, then stopped abruptly. Nothing she did made any difference. Cry or not cry. Who cared.

When her son came home the next morning, she said, "Tell me how I'd start training to run. What's the first thing?"

"You're kidding, right?"

"No editorial comments. What do I have to do, stretch?"

"What's this all for?" He didn't like it when she got excited about something. "You mean, show you right now?"

Yes, she said, right now. And so he led her through a basic warm-up. Side stretches, overheads, hamstrings, calves, quads. "Can you do sit-ups?"

She could, a few at least. Then she fell back on the floor, muscles wincing, out of breath. Her son loomed over her. "You're sure this is a good idea, Mom?"

She wasn't, but she went to the mall and bought a pair of serious shoes, some running shorts, and a sports bra. She was pretty sure that spending money would make her actually see it through. Back home she found some T-shirts that were big enough to cover most of the shorts. She wasn't fat or saggy. She was just shy about her body because no one else had any use for it now.

The next day after work she dutifully stretched, then drove to a nearby park where it was acceptable to do this sort of thing. There was a trail that circled around some tennis courts, then looped away into a hillier, forested area. There were already a few serious-looking runners moving along the track, men with nearly anatomical thighs and sports water bottles.

Lynn parked, got out, stretched again. A couple of kids were playing tennis, making crisp, ponging sounds as the ball hit. No one was paying any attention to her. She launched herself forward.

It felt unnatural, peg-legged. Her hip joints hurt. Each step jostled her breathing so she couldn't get air all the way into her lungs. She got around the track twice, then limped over to a bench.

She'd never see forty again. What was she thinking, she was going to turn into some Kenyan marathoner? Her muscles shrieked. So maybe it was a stupid idea, but it was the only idea she'd had in a long time. She sat for awhile and watched the tennis players. They were horsing around now, hitting smash shots into the net, chasing down balls they had no hope of returning. Sunsets were getting later each day, minute by minute. The topmost leaves caught the last horizontal rays and blazed gold. She was able to observe, without feeling tragic, that it was a nice evening.

The next day at work Lynn listened as Mike and Rigo went through their usual morning routine of scorn and putdowns. Rigo was a Cubs fan. Mike, the Cardinals. Or maybe it was the other way around. She so often lost track.

"Some weak-shit pitching. He got the arm of a little cheild."

"Says you. You guys are gonna have your usual season. El-foldo. Saving the worst for last."

"Yeah, yeah, big talk. Little bitty bats."

"Ah, you characters wear rubbers for hats."

"Guys?" said Lynn, and they looked up, surprised, having forgotten she was there. "Explain to me why it's so important. This team, that team. What difference does it make? A hundred years from now, will it matter to anybody?"

Now they looked at each other. Rigo, all biceps and nostrils. Mike and his flaccid blond good looks. "Seriously?" Mike asked.

"I'm trying to understand the man thing. After all these years, it's still a foreign language."

Rigo said, "When you're a fan, you have a passion in your life. I know everything my team does, every player, coach, manager. I know all their stats. I know what they did last year and the year before that and the year before that. When my team wins, I win."

"The players are the last warriors. Used to be, men would go out and do battle, do hard and bloody things, stand or fall by their actions. It was that simple. These days, life is way too complicated."

"Your team, man, it makes you feel alive, when everything else in your world beats you down."

Mike said, "My team is like me, but better. They live large. People know their names, care about them. They're on television. They are cool."

"Yeah, but my guys are cooler than your guys."

"Oh right, like your guys aren't crying their way straight to the bottom of the league."

"It's gonna be a long season for you, isn't it?"

"Oh, what a putdown. I'm dyin'."

Lynn said, "Okay, thanks, this is very helpful. But why does somebody always have to win or lose?"

Again they looked at each other. They were both on the same team now, and she was only the lady who smiled and sometimes brought cookies in to the office. She was nice but totally out of it. Rigo said, "I guess it's an evolution thing. Like sperm have to beat out all the other sperm."

"Ick."

"Hey, you asked."

That night on the way home she saw a bumper sticker: IT'S BETTER TO HAVE LOVED AND LOST THAN TO LIVE WITH A PSYCHO THE REST OF YOUR LIFE. Another message from the universe. Not that Jay was a psycho. Just a pig. Then there was the loved and lost part, which also required some thought, since, if she was honest, there had been more loss than love. She hadn't liked losing. Maybe she was more like the sports fans than she cared to admit, except that no one else was on her team.

Still, she liked the bumper sticker's spunky attitude. Maybe she was the psycho it was better to live without. Psycho wives, unite! At home she changed into her running clothes and drove to the park. She managed to go four times around the track, then walked two more laps to cool out.

Christine said, "Tony called. He sounded lonesome." Tony was her ex. "He kept me on the phone a long time, for no real reason."

"Oh, I bet there was a reason," Lynn said. "A reason will rear its ugly head."

"Don't be so negative. Maybe he just wanted to talk to me."

"Sure he did."

"You suck," Christine said. "Why can't you even pretend that this might be a good sign?"

"I am pretending. Honest."

"Is there any fried rice left? Gimme."

Lynn passed her the take-out carton. They were in Christine's kitchen, eating Chinese food and ice cream. Christine, like Lynn, was a house widow. Both of them still inhabited the homes of their marriages, overlarge and expensive suburban money pits. Christine's lawn, Lynn had noticed, was looking feathery and untended, even this early in the season. It was possible to mourn, in the abstract, the loss of those suburban men who marched behind lawnmowers and spent their weekends spraying and clipping and wielding power tools.

Christine poked at the empty carton. A tidal residue of grease and rice grains coated the sides. "I'm going to get control of the food thing. I'm serious. I can't stand my naked body. I bet nobody else could either." She had gained a lot of divorce weight. All her pants had elastic waistbands now.

"Any fish bites if you got good bait."

"This isn't about Tony. I'm thinking, all those fish in the sea."

"Sure," Lynn said. Of course it was about Tony. Christine still had those hopes. Tony had not remarried. He had wanted a divorce so that he could be his own person. Lynn could see how it would all turn out. Christine would diet, turn sleek and catlike, take Tony back again. Christine would become a happy person and would listen with cheerful remoteness to Lynn's sad-sack complaints. "Here," Lynn said, pushing another carton across the table. "Kung pao chicken. All yours."

"No thanks. Where are the fortune cookies? I can eat one of those. They have about zero calories."

"I'm not going to even read mine. I don't want to know my fortune."

"Then I'll read yours for you." Christine got up to get the fortune cookies from the counter. She was wearing sweatpants with the drawstring untied and she used one hand to hold them up. "All right, here, this one's mine: *Every man is a volume if you know how to read him.*"

"Hmm."

"Yeah, like, comic books. Here's yours: *You will soon be more aware of your growing awareness.* That's a little tricky."

"Would you really want Tony back again? After everything he put you through?"

"You don't like him. You never did."

"So you're saying, yes."

Christine flicked some rice off her sweater. "Look at that. I should just pour a bottle of Crisco oil over my head. So Tony's not perfect. I don't think anybody perfect is going to come my way. I don't think anybody else is going to come my way, period. What am I supposed to do for the rest of my stupid life?"

"I know, hon."

"Do you? I mean, of course you do, but you're pretty, you don't have to be alone if you don't want to. You'll find somebody sooner or later. Me, it's either Tony or somebody who'll murder me for a life insurance policy."

Once, at a dinner party, Tony had spent some time instructing Lynn on the basics of the stock market, using salad plates and dinner plates as props. "See, this little plate here is an individual stock, and the big one is your mutual fund portfolio. See how all the little guys fit into the big one?"

It was hard not to have an opinion. It was hard to remember what a nice person would do. Lynn said, "I could definitely see you and Tony together again."

"You think?"

"See what happens. Be brave."

"Do me a favor, take the ice cream home with you. Oh come on, a shrimp like you? I could eat Weight Watchers ten times a day and never be that skinny."

On her way home Lynn detoured to drive past Jay's new house. She guessed that if she kept doing this, there would eventually be some kind of restraining order. Jay and Margot had purchased a woodsy, faux chalet in a desirable district. The house had architecturally significant features and a stained glass oriole window. Maybe she could nibble off a chunk of it, like a gingerbread house, and use it for the boys' college expenses. She rolled slowly past, noting the dim light in the no doubt spacious kitchen, and the illuminated upstairs window where Jay massaged his pregnant bride's swollen feet. Or consulted with her over the hipster version of *What to Name the Baby*. (Elijah? Paola?) Or any of the other things he'd never done with her. By now she had imagined and catalogued all manner of painful scenarios, sexual and otherwise.

She turned a corner and veered around the block to make a second pass. Stupid and degrading behavior. How long did she intend to keep it up? The child would be born, learn to walk, head off for school, develop questionable friendships. The saplings in the yard would grow to mighty shade trees. The neighbors would wave at her as she made her rounds. Jay would be balding and fiercely deaf. She would have long ago forgotten the different layers of their life together: love, married struggle, boredom, acrimony, but still her curses would gather round him like crows on a wire.

Lynn changed directions and headed home. What could you tell from the outside of a house anyway? Wouldn't her own look just as peaceful and welcoming, no matter how forlorn the life inside it was? She was tired of chewing on her own black heart.

Back home, she sat down at the computer and went to the singles website. She needed a *nom de guerre*, an email handle with which to conduct naughty transactions. AngerMom. SweetnSassy. ExurbPrincess. She settled for the tamer Ladybird400 (ladybirds 1 through 399 presumably spoken for), and after some effort, composed her post:

> Hi, I'm a DWF, 43, 5'3" and slim, looking for a friend/
> soul mate to share quiet evenings in or dinners out,
> conversation, laughs, daytrips, etc. Please be employed,
> available, grown-up, sane. Shall we dance?

Lynn lingered a long moment over the Send button. On the margin of the site, a red banner flashed: FIND YOUR FUN AND ONLY! Fun and only? Who wrote this stuff? What further indignities would be required of her? Oh love, love, why do you choose a fool's disguise? She hit Send.

Within twelve hours, she had multiple responses. A couple seemed, well, nuts, from men who claimed they felt an instant and deep connection with her, or provided detailed accounts of the character flaws of previous girlfriends. Another asked, broodingly, why she thought dancing was so important. Did she have something against people who didn't dance?

Some sent pictures. These were disappointing. Life, or maybe genetics, had been unkind. There was a reason, Lynn decided, that people paired off when they were young, before they began molting and shedding. There was a gentleman who described himself as a "sprightly seventy" and who hinted at his financial generosity. Discouraged, Lynn clicked the screen away. There might be a lot of fish in the sea, but the waters were fraught and murky.

The next time she checked, there were a couple of more promising answers. A pharmaceutical salesman, a man who described himself as "part-time poet, part-time airline pilot." Both had hopeful, presentable faces. Lynn wrote back to each of them, enclosing her own picture and a few words of attempted goodwill.

The poet-pilot wrote back: Hey, I'm new at this too. Awkward, isn't it? If you're free for lunch on Saturday, we can share a meal and some mutual embarrassment.

She was free. She screwed her courage to the sticking point, made the date. It felt like arranging a drug deal or embarrassing surgery.

The pharmaceutical salesman never wrote again. Were you allowed to feel spurned? Was any of this real? Were people even who they said they were? Was she? She examined her photograph, which portrayed her smiling, with apparent delight, at nothing at all. It was the face she always made for cameras, a dazzling grimace. Age showed in the corners of her eyes and the corners of her mouth. This was her avatar, her image, the face that attracted some and, it seemed, repelled others. Somewhere behind it her flesh-and-blood self lurked, ready to shriek, attack, devour.

She went running at the park. Her wind was better by now, and she could manage twenty minutes' worth of laps, even if she was the slowest one out there. She took it as a good sign. Her great leap forward and upward!

Saturday came. What to wear for her big-deal date? Something that wouldn't make her son suspect what she was doing. Something you wouldn't mind getting stood up in. It was possible that the poet-pilot would lose his nerve or change his mind, or, observing her from the safety of the parking lot, put his car into gear and drive away. It was possible that she would do the same. Lynn chose some nice pants and a sweater, her raciest peep-toe shoes, some of her boring jewelry. Perhaps she should update and reinvent herself. She was the very model of a Michigan matron, as a careless ex-friend told her once. She would grow her hair out, wear leopard print and gypsy hoops.

At the restaurant she spotted him right away. He both did and did not look like his online picture, just as she guessed she did and did not resemble hers. His name was Scott. He was tall, stoop-shouldered, with a narrow, eager face and a bit of shining scalp poking up through his sandy hair. They shook hands. He laughed. "See," he said, "that wasn't so hard." Lynn agreed. He had a jerky, tootling laugh. She was already keeping score, adding up and subtracting points.

The restaurant was busy, noisy. It was one of those places where you stood in line to order your food, but they sat down first, feeling the need to get some conversation out of the way. Scott hitched his chair closer to let a woman with a laden tray pass behind him. He said, "Is this place okay? It's not fancy or anything."

"It's fine." The last thing she wanted was fancy.

"You're sure? I mean, we can go somewhere else if you want."

"No, this is great. Really." He seemed to need reassurance. "They have good sandwiches."

"Yeah, they do." Scott. She had to remember his name. His hands had big, arthritic-looking knuckles. She tried not to look at them, or any other part of him. She hadn't been on a date in more than twenty-five years. She had forgotten everything about it. "I like their soups too," Scott added. "Or maybe it's a little warm for soup."

"No, soup's good anytime." Oh, let's be awkward. She tried another conversational lurch. "You're a commercial pilot?"

He laughed his jerky laugh again. Something funny? No, just a kind of tic. "That's right. I was with Northwest for fifteen years, then I was furloughed, then I got on with ATA. Then they went under. The whole industry's consolidating."

"Yes, it is," Lynn said. Had he just told her he was unemployed? So much for conversation about the exciting life of a pilot. "I can't remember the last time I flew," she offered.

"Yeah, so it goes." He let his gaze make a circuit of the room, then turned back to Lynn with another antic face. "Kind of puts the 'real' in real life."

Was it time for her to offer up a personal failure of her own? Was he waiting for her to start? She opened her mouth, reconsidered, closed it again. Scott watched her losing fight with her tongue, then said, "If you know what you want to get, I'll go order it."

"Chicken pesto sandwich, side of chips, lemonade. Thanks."
She watched as he made his way up to the counter. He didn't
look like a pilot, or a laid-off pilot, but presumably the uniforms
did a lot for them. Of course there was the poetry component
too, but she wasn't anxious to talk poetry with him. He was
okay. Just that. She couldn't pretend excitement, but maybe you
weren't supposed to be excited. That was for younger people.
Graying, discouraged moms and pops were meant to match
up their mutual interests and personality profiles, shrug off the
inevitable disappointment. Did Scott have any children? Had
he ever been married? It seemed like something she should
have remembered from the ad. His stooped, angular figure
moved patiently through the line. He wore a shrunken-looking
blue polo shirt with yellow stripes. It wasn't the sort of thing
a skinny guy should wear. It was awful to think of him picking out this shirt, regarding himself in the mirror, deciding he
looked all right.

Then he was back, carrying her lemonade and a Coke for
himself. "Look what they give you," he said, showing her something that resembled a television remote control. "It buzzes
when your order's ready."

"Amazing, all the trouble they've gone to so they could
replace waitresses. I'm sorry, I really can't remember if your ad
mentioned this, but were you married, ever?"

"A long time ago. Just out of college. I guess I should have
put it in the ad, but honestly, sometimes I have to remind myself
of it. Like it happened to some different person. So you . . ."

"I was married for more than twenty years. Divorced about
one. I have two boys. How about you, any kids?"

"Not that I know of." Oh, funny. Lynn had an ever-expanding

collection of things she told her sons never to say, and that crack was one of them. The remote control thing began buzzing in an angry, peremptory way. "Excuse me." He got up.

She looked out the window, scanning the parking lot, thinking vaguely of escape. The car pulled up just outside had a license plate that read GONOGO 7. The universe wasn't giving her much direction today.

"Here you are." He set the plates down and they got busy with the mechanics of napkins and forks. He asked her how her sandwich was and she said it was good, and then he said his was good also. She would be nice to him, which was not the same as being a genuinely benevolent human being.

"So, who did you end up marrying?"

Lynn finished her bite of sandwich, swallowed it down. "Excuse me?"

"I was just wondering, what was your husband like?"

He was smiling again. Lynn decided not to. "He isn't dead or anything."

"Sorry. Just doing the cut-to-the-chase thing. Diagnostics. You know, learning from the errors of the past so as to start afresh."

He ducked his head, a little self-deprecating movement. What to make of him? She wasn't sure. There was that laugh. The unfortunate shirt, the fake smiling. A cloud was forming over his head and the cloud said, Loser. Lynn said, "For now, let's just say there was plenty of blame to go around." She didn't really believe that. Jay was a slime devil.

"Takes two to tango, huh." He worked a couple bites of his sandwich and swallowed them down. He was watching her with some private amusement, as if she had food stuck in her teeth. He was on the creepy side of awkward, Lynn decided. If he was a pilot, she wouldn't want to be on his plane.

Fifteen minutes. Twenty, tops. Then she could say how nice it was to meet him and scuttle back to her burrow. She would ask him about his interesting hobbies. No doubt he had some. She was formulating a remark when he said, "You don't remember me, do you?"

Her insides curdled. She stared at him. His face meant nothing to her. "No," she said, waiting to be ambushed.

"Scott Hallberg." Lynn shook her head. "We were in French III and IV at NIU. You used to read the books in English first so you wouldn't have to translate everything. *The Red and the Black. The Charterhouse of Parma. Madame Bovary.*"

She didn't remember reading them in either language. She didn't remember anybody who might have turned into this guy. She said, "I'm sorry, were we, what, study pals?"

"No, we just like, knew each other from class." Lynn could tell that he had counted on her remembering him. His smirking edge was gone. "I saw your picture and right away I figured out it was you."

Lynn murmured that it really was a long time ago. Now she was trying to recollect some scrap of French, which also seemed to have fled her brain. *Ou est la biblioteque? Je me demande.*

"I was just wondering if you married your boyfriend from back then. You know, the hockey player."

"Richard?" Him she did remember. He had been a famous alcoholic. "No, it was somebody I met later." At least it wasn't Richard sitting across from her and claiming acquaintance. That thought made her more cheerful. "Were you a French major? You weren't a pilot or anything in school, were you?"

"God, I was so crazy about you. I mean nuts."

Some kind of nervous, unlovely giggle made her throat spasm. "Huh huh," she said.

"You never even had a clue. I mean, why would you, who was I? Some jerk in French class."

"I honestly don't remember—"

"No, of course you don't. Girls like you don't have to pay attention to anybody you don't want to."

"What do you mean, girls like me?" She was getting over some of her first creeped-out shock, and she didn't much like his tone, whiny and aggrieved, as if he'd been carrying a grudge against her all this time, and what exactly was it she'd done to deserve him turning up now, the blind date from hell? "French class? Who remembers stuff like that?"

"Okay, okay, sorry." Now he was backpedaling, less sure of himself. "But hey, don't you think it's weird, that we both end up in the same place?"

"Yes, weird." Her memory was spotty, vague, like a movie seen underwater. He might have been the kid with the beard. It had been a scrawny, reddish beard that looked like he should have been wearing underpants over his face.

"I don't just mean, the same location. I mean the same place in life, single and starting over. Sort of, a level playing field."

"There isn't any playing field." Lynn shifted in her seat. Around them, people cruised for tables, cut sandwiches into child-sized portions, chatted about normal things. She could write HELP on a paper napkin, show it to the roving bus boy. Some hideous fascination kept her from getting up and leaving.

Scott pulled something out of his back pocket. "Here. Go ahead, read them."

A rectangle of folded papers, flattened and curling. Lynn shook her head. "What is it?"

"Poems I wrote you." He uncreased the paper and smoothed the creases. The typeface was dark blue, furred with age. She read:

MY CRUCIFIXION

She smiles and the nails of lust pierce my hands and feet.
In both her words and her silence, I am forsaken
Here is my bleeding testament, my soul sucked dry
The quick sharp rush of holy sperm

There was more. She pushed it aside. "I can't handle this."

"Some of them are in French, but I can't read them anymore. Look, here's one of your quizzes. You left it in class and I picked it up and saved it."

"That's a little pathetic, don't you think?"

He shrugged. His slumping posture made one of his shoulders seemed higher, crooked. "I did some other stuff too."

"What stuff?"

"Oh . . ." He hesitated, then plunged in. "I used to call your place and pretend I was a wrong number, or I was doing a survey. I stole some of your mail once, but I put it back. It was just bills, honest."

"Go on."

"I hired a guy to take pictures of you. Remember, he said he was doing a calendar, College Co-eds? On the auditorium steps? You were going to be Miss July? I got a dog, a beagle, because once in class you told somebody you liked beagles. I was going to invite you over to see him, that was my big plan, you'd come over to see the dog and the magic would happen. But the damned dog ate a chicken bone and got an intestinal obstruction and cost me three hundred dollars for emergency surgery. Then he ran away. Oh, I keyed your boyfriend's car. I really, really didn't like that guy. I'm so glad you didn't marry him."

She felt a kind of vertigo, as if the chair beneath her had disappeared and she was suspended in air. "So you're saying, you were my stalker?"

"They didn't call it that back then."

"Why are you telling me all this?"

"That Christmas package you never got from your Aunt June? The sweater? That was a mistake on my part and I apologize. I unwrapped it and couldn't figure out how to put it back together. But I don't think you would have liked it anyway, it was kind of ugly. I guess I went a little crazy. It's nothing I'm proud of. I just wanted you to know how far I've come from those days. Like I said, learning from the errors of the past. So that we can have a fresh start."

He was smiling a happy smile. "Jesus Christ," Lynn said.

"I've done a lot of work on myself since then. I'm a practicing Buddhist now. I've had several of my poems published. I'm very hopeful about the applications I have in at a couple of the commuter airlines. It's true I had a sort of a breakdown after I lost my job, but that turned out to be a blessing in disguise, because it forced me to reexamine a lot of my assumptions. I've always led a lonely life. Even when I was married, boy, let's not get into that story, but I'm convinced she was the reincarnation of some very ancient and evil soul. Anyway, I realized that flying, my love of flying, was a metaphor for my spiritual aspirations, my desire to rise above my lower nature. I've freed myself from all the old conflicts, the debased, primitive need to pick sides, compete, assign blame. People should be kind to each other and joyful in their beings. I honestly feel I have a lot to offer you."

Half of Lynn's sandwich remained on her plate. She wrapped it carefully in a paper napkin and stood up. "Scott? Thanks for lunch. I think the good news for you here is that after today, I will never forget you."

A week later Lynn picked up Christine and they drove to the park with the running track. Christine said, "I can't believe I was such a moron. I can't believe I let him get away with it." Tony had called again, and Christine had invited him over for dinner. He'd spent the night, then the next morning told her he didn't think the two of them had the right chemistry anymore. "Do I have to tell you how much food I cooked? I poached a whole salmon. Asparagus, duchess potatoes, pear cake with chocolate sauce."

"You forgot the Drano espresso."

"Prick."

"At least he didn't move back in, then tell you the same thing three months later."

"Once I get some weight off, I decided I'm going to take up pistol shooting. Do trick shots, hit targets from horseback, like Annie Oakley."

They parked and stood to the side of the track, stretching. Christine wore a pink sweatsuit with DREAM GIRL spelled out in sequins across the front of the shirt. "I can't touch my toes. I can't even see my stupid toes."

"My god. No toes."

The trees were leafing out and the track was spattered with cool shade. They took off at an easy jog. Lynn said, "I think it's possible to get bored with being unhappy. Some kind of natural defense mechanism kicks in, like antibodies."

"How can you . . . huh . . . talk."

"Just do a couple laps, then walk, okay?"

Lynn went on ahead. Joyful in our beings! She ran and ran, waiting for her second wind.